"Aren't you worried?"

Greyson picked up the half-full glass he'd left on the little table beside his chair and drank it off. "Why?"

"Someone tried to kill us, Greyson." Megan grabbed one of Greyson's T-shirts from his drawer and yanked it over her head. Exhaustion started sinking into her bones, and the bed had never looked more inviting—almost never, anyway. But though the memory of the car chase was fading, thinking about it didn't do her nerves any good.

"They weren't trying to kill us, darling. Don't be so dramatic."

"They did a pretty good imitation."

"No." Greyson poured himself another drink, and a shadow crossed his face. "That was just a warning."

"How do you know?"

"Because they were witches. If they'd wanted us dead, we'd *be* dead."

DEMON INSIDE

STACIA KANE

Pocket Books

New York London Toronto Sydney

Pocket Books
A Division of Simon & Schuster, Inc.
1230 Avenue of the Americas
New York, NY 10020

Copyright © 2009 by Stacey Fackler

All rights reserved, including the right to reproduce this book or portions thereof in any form whatsoever. For information address Pocket Books Subsidiary Rights Department, 1230 Avenue of the Americas, New York, NY 10020

First Juno Books/Pocket Books paperback edition August 2009

JUNO BOOKS and colophon are trademarks of Wildside Press LLC used under license by Simon & Schuster, Inc., the publisher of this work.

POCKET and colophon are registered trademarks of Simon & Schuster, Inc.

For information about special discounts for bulk purchases, please contact Simon & Schuster Special Sales at 1-866-506-1949 or business@simonandschuster.com

The Simon & Schuster Speakers Bureau can bring authors to your live event. For more information or to book an event contact the Simon & Schuster Speakers Bureau at 1-866-248-3049 or visit our website at www.simonspeakers.com.

Designed by Jill Putorti

Cover design by Dave Stevenson

Manufactured in the United States of America

10 9 8 7 6 5 4 3 2 1

ISBN 978-1-4391-5507-3
ISBN 978-1-4391-6453-3 (ebook)

*To my parents, and to my brother,
who are nothing at all like Megan's family*

Acknowledgments

The problem with writing lists of people to thank is that I'm always convinced I'll leave someone out, someone obvious and important, simply because I do things like that. So if I do somehow manage to not mention you here, you're probably the one who occupies so much room in my mental "I'm Grateful for These People" list that somehow my eyes convince me your name is here, even when it isn't.

That being said, I'm going to do the best I can. This book would not exist without my husband and his generous willingness to do his own laundry and go to bed alone so I can stay up late working. It couldn't have been written without the patience of my two little girls, who don't mind letting Mommy finish her paragraph before getting them juice or cookies or whatever else it is they want. I have to thank my best friend Cori Knell, who proves what a great friend she is by spending hours on the phone with me discussing what she read; and my other best friend Anna J. Evans who spends hours emailing me about what she's read. Then there's the whole Team Seattle crew, especially Caitlin Kittredge and Mark Henry, for always being there to boost me up when I'm down, and Jackie Kessler, my fellow Satellite Seattle-r. The League of Reluctant Adults, of course, who make everything more fun. Thanks also to Carole Nelson Douglas—you know why—and Maria Lima, Jill Myles, Karen Mahoney, Sherrill Quinn, Christine D'Abo, Kelly Maher, Sierra Dafoe, Red Garnier, Fae Sutherland, Kirsten Saell, Seeley DeBorn, Jane Smith, Bernard DeLeo, Justin Coker, Michele Lee, Bernita Harris, Miss Snark and the Snarklings, Evil Editor and the Minions, the ladies at Bitten by Books, the ladies at Urban Fantasy Land, and all of my blog readers; I will never stop being amazed and grateful that you take the time to visit me and comment.

Special thanks of course to my agent Chris Lotts, my editor Paula Guran, and Jennifer Heddle (and all the folks at Pocket); and to Todd Thomas, Esq., for reading the scenes involving legal matters, fixing my wording, and advising me that while the scenario may be a bit unusual, it's not impossible. Any errors made with anything legal in this book are mine and not his.

DEMON
INSIDE

Chapter One

Megan slammed on the brakes, sending Rocturnus's little green body flying into the windshield. She barely paid attention. Demons were tough. He'd be fine.

Better than the demon inside the nondescript tract home in front of her, if she hadn't made it in time. She didn't need her psychic abilities to know that.

She grabbed Roc by one scrawny arm and yanked him off the dashboard, her gaze focused on the house. To her panicked brain it seemed to loom in front of her, tinged with the awful blankness of death. Her shoes slid in the hard-packed snow covering the lawn as she ran as fast as she could up to the front door, still dangling Roc from her hand. Nobody could see him but her anyway.

"Hello? Hello?" The old paint on the front door flaked off under her pounding fists. She barely heard her own voice over the blood rushing through her veins, the screeching wails of her inner voice. "Please, open up!"

She lowered her shields as far as they would go—so far she picked up faint images from the houses on either side—but still received nothing from the house before her. No sounds, no pictures of a napping resident dragging him- or herself out of bed, or of someone singing in the shower. Nothing at all.

"Oh, God . . ." Megan stepped back from the door and looked at the wide windows next to it, white and empty. The folds of the drapes were like a TV test pattern: no signal.

Nothing moved on the pale winter street except Megan, her shouts echoing through the crisp air as she tried the door one last time. She had a tire iron in the trunk . . . but no. Shattering the big front windows would alarm the neighbors.

Still carrying Rocturnus, she rushed off the porch, only to slip and fall flat on her face. Pain blossomed in her mouth as her teeth sank into her tongue. For a moment her vision blurred; her eyes stung with tears and icy wind.

This isn't the time to start crying! She hauled herself to her feet and started moving again, careening around the side of the house to the back, where a snow-dusted red swing set added the only spot of forlorn color to the winter-dead yard.

The back door refused to yield to Megan's kicks and shoves. The windows in the back were smaller than those in the front; even if she managed to break one discreetly, she couldn't fit through it.

Rocturnus would, though . . .

She looked down to find him glaring at her.

"I'm fine, by the way, thanks for asking," he said, squirming from her grasp. "Let go of me, I'll get the door open for you."

"How—oh, right." At least the blush warmed her

face a little, although she already felt like her nose had fallen off. She resisted the urge to check. Too undignified, even when no one was looking.

Rocturnus disappeared. A second later the door clicked. Megan turned the knob and officially committed a crime: entering a stranger's home without permission.

Her skin prickled. Something in here did not feel right at all. A musty, unpleasant smell like moldy leftovers hung in the air. She reached for the little tube of pepper spray attached to her key ring, but she'd left the keys in the ignition.

Megan sighted a wooden block holding a number of knives on the kitchen counter. She grabbed what appeared to be the largest. Nobody was in the house, she knew that. But it somehow made her feel safer, stronger, to have some kind of weapon. She held the big butcher knife in front of her as she trod carefully through the kitchen and into the beige living room beyond, her gaze cast down, trying to delay the moment when she'd actually see the damage.

She looked up. Worse than she'd imagined.

On the floor at her feet a long green finger rested in a pool of crimson blood, the lurid colors an obscene mockery of the cheerful Christmas decorations on the walls and tables. A foot protruded from under the couch, while a messy pile of green flesh and red . . . she didn't want to look at the rest of it, didn't want to *see* the rest of it, but her eyes refused to close. Blood splattered the walls and furniture and even the darkened Christmas tree by the front window. Here and there more . . . pieces: clinging to a picture frame, flung under the tree, hanging off a pine branch like a homemade ornament crafted by Ed Gein.

"I'm too late," she said. Her voice disappeared in the accusing silence. "Again."

"It's not your fault. You came as fast as you could."

Megan nodded, but knowing she'd done her best didn't help. Thinking of how she'd abandoned a client in the middle of a therapy session in her desperation, and how her partners would feel when they found out . . . that definitely did not help. And the pain in her tongue and elbows from her fall put a nice miserable cap on the whole depressing mental ensemble.

"Even if you hadn't been working, you probably wouldn't have made it. I guess he"—Rocturnus indicated the remains—"didn't have much warning either."

"Just like the others."

The demon nodded.

Tinsel glittered in the faint air flow from the central heating, like tiny swords waving in the air. To any other human the room would have looked perfectly clean and friendly, a family home anticipating Santa's visit in eleven days' time. Human eyes wouldn't see the carnage, human bodies wouldn't feel the demon blood seeping into their clothing as they sat on the couch or squelching between their toes as they stepped in it. Human noses wouldn't smell that horrible odor in the air.

Megan wished she didn't have to see or smell it either. But three months before she'd become leader of the local Yezer Ha-Ra—the personal demons, tempters and misleaders of mankind—and it was her responsibility to take care of them as best she could.

Three times in as many weeks, one of her demons had exploded like this. No warning, no explanation. Just . . . gone, reduced to bits of squishy flesh, and she had no idea how or why.

"Maybe he was trying to call more of you and he did it wrong?" she asked, just as if she and Rocturnus hadn't gone over every possibility in every discussion they'd had already.

"I don't think so. I think . . . well, you know what I think."

Megan shivered. "I don't want to talk about it."

She walked into the kitchen to find some cleaning supplies. The demon's body, such as it was, would be sent back to the demons' home on the astral plane. But the blood, and the mess . . .

She couldn't just leave it, even if the occupants of this house would never know it was there. The thought of them unwrapping gifts under that abomination of a tree made her stomach churn.

"You're going to have to make a decision, Megan," Rocturnus said. "You know I don't think this is your fault, but—"

"I said I don't want to talk about it." The butcher knife clattered to the counter—she didn't trust herself to put it back neatly into its slot. A minute or two of hunting through the cabinets produced garbage bags; they rustled in her shaking hands.

"It's a simple ceremony."

"And it turns me into some sort of human-demon hybrid, Roc. I don't want to do it. I don't want any of this!"

She clutched the bags to her chest, turning her back

on the grisly scene and the small demon watching her. She didn't want to see his beady eyes go black as he tasted her pain.

Every human had a personal demon. Since before humanity became capable of complex speech and higher thought the demons had existed, tempting people into the kind of petty meanness that made life such a joy, then feeding from the misery they caused.

Every human except Megan. She'd managed to kill hers at the age of sixteen, to bind it somehow to the Accuser, a minor Legion of Hell who'd nonetheless almost killed her twice. Now he was gone—but a piece of him still lived inside Megan, a ghastly souvenir of the time he'd possessed her.

It was that piece of demon inside her that connected her to the Yezer Ha-Ra. It was that piece of demon inside her that forced her to be here today.

But her humanity still defined her, and her emotional pain—like any human's suffering—still nourished Rocturnus; Rocturnus, who'd become her unofficial personal demon. He didn't mislead her or tempt her to sin, but he couldn't stop being what he was either, and what he was treated her negative emotions as food.

"At least he managed to warn us," Rocturnus said. "So his human already has a new demon."

"Of course." Megan wiped her eyes and turned around. "I knew there had to be a bright side."

"It *is* a bright side, Megan, it's what we do, what we *need* to do to survive. If things start to slip—"

"I *know*!" She threw a bag at him. "Help me clean this up."

Not wanting to get her coat dirty, she removed it and set it on the kitchen's little breakfast bar, then grabbed a roll of paper towels. Whichever demons had been assigned to the house's occupants would keep them out as long as possible and would let Megan and Roc know when they were on their way back. She had some time. She hoped it would be enough.

"We need to do this fast, too," she said. "Can you . . . can you take care of the big pieces?" Her stomach gave a warning lurch.

Rocturnus started moving, his little hands waving in the corners of her vision as he transported chunks of the dead demon back to the Yezer's house Megan sopped up blood, wrinkling her nose against the smell, shoving the used paper towels into the garbage bag as fast as she could. If she pretended it was just Kool-Aid or something, maybe a red-wine spill . . .

But Kool-Aid or red wine didn't coagulate like that, didn't smell like that. She gritted her teeth and kept working.

Three dead in three weeks. Rocturnus said in the old days Yezer Ha-Ra were killed by explosion as punishment, and from what Megan had seen of demon punishment she had no trouble believing it. But she wasn't punishing them, and she was supposed to be in charge, so who—or what—was doing this?

Who had so much power over demons who were supposed to be hers? How much power did she actually have over them herself?

She managed to take care of the worst of the largest blood pool, but there were more. The smaller splotches she'd worry about if they had time, just like the stains. For now, she half-crawled a few feet to her right and started on another puddle.

The front door burst open. Five large bodies invaded the room, guns drawn. Five uniformed police officers.

"Get down! Get down!"

Megan obeyed, dropping the garbage bag in front of the couch. A splotch of blood she hadn't cleaned yet seeped through her trouser leg, but she ignored it. Guns were pointed at her, big, real guns, and a strong hand gripped the back of her neck and forced her all the way down.

"Please," she said. "There must be some misunderstanding." Her mind raced. What kind of cover story might explain why she'd entered a stranger's home and started cleaning?

She didn't even know whose house it was.

Rough hands held hers in the small of her back while cold metal snapped around her wrists. She was being arrested, she was really honestly being arrested and her entire career flashed before her eyes as those hands started patting her down. She was a psychological counselor, she was supposed to be sane and normal and well adjusted, not some sort of tidiness bandit.

"She's not armed," one of the cops said. Megan tried to look up at him but all she could see were feet. Armed?

"Get her up."

Aided by two men, one on each of her arms, she struggled to a stand. Was it normal for five policemen to come to a simple breaking and entering? That's all this was, right? A response to some sort of silent alarm maybe? Or perhaps one of the neighbors had seen her enter the house and had called?

She hadn't even *broken,* really. Rocturnus had opened the door. She'd just entered.

"Officers, please. This is all a big—"

They ignored her. One of them opened the garbage bag and pulled out a handful of wet towels. "What is this?" he said. "You're stealing balled-up paper towels?"

"I'm not stealing anything. I just—"

"You just tore up these people's yard, abandoned your car in the middle of it, broke into their house, and started throwing away paper towels," the cop said. "Was it padding for the things you planned to steal?"

"What? No, I wasn't—"

"Hey, you're Dr. Demon Slayer . . . Megan Chase," another officer said. "I recognize you from the papers."

"The radio lady?"

"Yeah. She caught that guy, you know, the Satanist guy from the hospital."

"Right, right."

The eyes regarding her now were slightly friendlier, but only slightly. "So what are you doing in here?"

"I . . . I must have the wrong house, I was coming in to surprise a friend—"

"We got a call that there was a body here."

Megan blinked. "What?"

Two officers came down the hallway now, their guns holstered. Relief flooded her body. "There's nothing here, Jim," said one of them. "It's clean."

"So why did you break in?" The first policeman—Jim?—held up the bag. "And what's all this?"

"I thought this was my friends' house," Megan repeated. "I was cleaning as a favor. Something to pass the time while I waited for them."

For the first time in months she actually wished she hadn't asked all the personal demons to hide themselves as a matter of course. It might be nice to see some smiling faces, even if those faces did have too many teeth. But not so much as a spot of color showed in the air above the policemen's shoulders.

"See?" she continued, aware her voice was getting higher with nerves. "Just a mistake, Officers, nobody's dead here, I got the wrong address. Can't we—"

Jim shook his head. "We still have to contact the owners of the house, see if they want to press charges. We're going to need to take you in, Dr. Chase." He turned to the cop who'd recognized Megan. "Get her coat for her?"

"Please, Officer, it was a mistake. I didn't even break in, the back door was unlocked. Can't I just go . . . ?"

The looks on their faces were her answer. Megan sighed. "Okay. But I want to call my lawyer."

She was completing her umpteenth lap of the small holding room when a policewoman finally came and opened the door. "Megan Chase!" She scanned the room and spotted her. "Come on, you're free to go."

Trying not to smile at the others who weren't as lucky, Megan brushed past the officer and out the door. Every fiber in her body screamed to be outside. Only two hours had passed, but it felt like a lifetime. Worrying about going to prison, worrying about her career, worrying about her demons, and, as time stretched, worrying about why Greyson Dante hadn't shown up yet.

The worry deepened when she got to the small check-in area and saw the man standing there, holding a briefcase and smiling: Hunter Kyle. Definitely an attorney, but definitely not the one she'd called. They'd met a few months ago at a charity party and she'd seen him once or twice since, but . . . why was *he* here?

The officer behind the desk grabbed the manila envelope containing her possessions and handed it to her. "Check to make sure everything's there, please, and sign here."

She did. "What's happening? I mean, did I have to post bond, or . . . ?"

"The owners of the house declined to press charges." He gave her a tight smile, an unfriendly one. "Lucky you."

"Yeah . . . thanks." Did it just bother cops when anyone got to go, or what? For a moment she contemplated reading him, but it didn't matter. Who cared what he thought? She was free. She had to suppress the urge to skip through the bulletproof glass doors separating the booking area from the rest of the building. Innocent psychologists didn't skip.

"Are you okay, Megan?" Hunter asked, taking her arm solicitously. "I got everything started as soon as I could, but it took some time for the homeowners to agree to drop the charges."

"I'm okay, thanks." They burst through the double doors into icy darkness, broken only by dim streetlights.

The temperatures had hovered around freezing for weeks before finally sinking lower two days before. Her entire face felt chapped, stretched by the fierce wind. "Where's my car?"

"I had one of the boys drive it to my place." Greyson Dante emerged from the shadows outside the circles of light, like a villain in a James Bond movie. Megan hadn't seen him in four days. It was a little embarrassing, how her heart leaped at the sight of him, his dark hair shining, his strong-boned face twisted in a little half smile as if he knew the effect his appearance had on her.

Which he probably did.

He extended his hand to Hunter. "Thanks, Hunt. I owe you one."

Hunter smiled. Megan didn't think he had any idea what exactly he was being promised; Hunter wasn't a demon and so wasn't familiar with the complex system of favors and promises they used. Greyson was powerful, even more now than he had been when she'd first met him. To be owed a favor by him . . . a lot of demons would have killed for that opportunity. Maybe some of them did.

Then again, maybe Greyson said it because he knew Hunter wouldn't realize. Greyson never said or did anything without having more than one reason for it.

Her suspicion was confirmed when Hunter merely replied, "No trouble at all, I'm happy to help."

Megan stood in the cold and bit her lip while the two men chatted for a minute, until Greyson slipped his arm around her waist and made their good-byes.

His black Jaguar wasn't far away and she was grateful when they reached it. Her toes were numb.

Not so numb Greyson couldn't still make them tingle. His lips, like the rest of his body, were blissfully warm, and the kiss he gave her sent shivers of flame up her spine—just like the real flames he could create from thin air any time he wished.

"You okay?" His thumb caressed her cheek while tiny sparks of red showed in his eyes.

She nodded. "A little freaked."

"By being in jail, or by what happened to your demon in that house?"

"I . . ." Shit. She hadn't told him what had happened, only that she'd been arrested by mistake. She hadn't told him about the other demons either. "Both."

He nodded and put her in the car, then got in on his side and started the engine. "When were you going to tell me?"

"I wasn't. How did you—"

"Come on, Meg. Where do you think I've been?"

"What do you mean?"

The parking lot disappeared behind them as he sped down the street, past deserted office buildings with the white wires of Christmas lights draped across the windows. It was not yet eight o'clock, but nobody was in this section of downtown. Even the homeless had deserted the streets and found shelter from the cold.

"I went to convince those people not to press charges. It looked like a fucking abattoir in there."

"I tried to clean up."

"How thoughtful. Why haven't you told me what's going on? I hear this is the third one."

"Why are you so mad at me? You said yourself, how I run my Meegra is my business."

"Yes, how you run it. But when your demons start getting killed and demons in other Meegras start getting killed, it's not just up to you anymore."

"But I—what do you mean, other demons?"

"I mean, you've lost three. I lost one two days ago. House Concumbia have lost four, House Caedes Fuiltean two, everybody's had at least one loss. I only found out about it today."

"None of the others told you, then, so why—"

"I'm not sleeping with any of the others, either. I would have— *Shit!*"

Something thudded at the trunk end, like a large rock kicked up from the pavement. Greyson swerved so hard Megan fell against him despite her seat belt. Cold air flooded the car as he downshifted violently and sped up, jerking the wheel to the right and roaring down a narrow side road.

"What's—"

"Get down, damn it, that was a gunshot!"

Chapter Two

"What?" Megan jerked up in her seat, instinctively trying to look behind them, but his hand forced her head back down. Her ear pressed hard against the padded console.

Another shot. This time Megan heard it, heard the rear windshield shatter. She screamed, the sound ripped from her throat as Greyson cursed again and spun the wheel. She fumbled with her seat belt, wanting absurdly to crawl onto the floor and hide like a small child under her bedcovers at night.

Orange light filled the car, pulsing, disappearing and coming back as Greyson sent balls of flame into the car behind them.

He cursed. She popped up, unable to resist looking, and saw the flames extinguish, saw the black car behind them still racing along as if nothing had happened. Another tiny explosion happened inside their car. Again it disappeared and they advanced.

What sort of creatures were these, impervious to fire? Were they *vregonis* demons, like Greyson himself?

As if in answer to her question, the Jag filled with smoke, black and foul smelling. It filled her nostrils, stuck to her skin.

"Stay the fuck *down*! Cover your face!"

She ducked just as fire filled the car, burning away the smoke. Sweat broke out on her skin from the brief, intense blast of heat. "What was—"

"Open the glove compartment, get the gun."

The car bounced over something, a pothole or speed bump. Megan's arms flailed in the air. She'd tried to reach for the dashboard but the impact had sent her back against her seat.

Greyson made a sharp left. The Jag's tires complained loudly about such rough treatment. Megan clutched at the center console to keep from hitting the door.

"Open the glove compartment, Meg, come on."

"I'm trying!" The engine roared. The interior was bleached white by the headlights of the car behind them, switched on high. Greyson flipped the console lid up and grabbed his sunglasses, snapping them open and sliding them on to block the glare.

The car bounced again. Another gunshot broke the air, then another. Loud thunks came from the car and it shook with the impact; they were shooting the trunk, the roof, as Greyson swerved back and forth, trying to avoid the shots.

"*Fuck!* My *car*!" For the first time she felt his anger, a breeze colder than the air outside brushing over her skin.

Megan grabbed the handle with clumsy fingers and yanked open the glove compartment. Inside, Greyson's leather gun case rested on the owner's manual.

Light flared behind them. Megan turned and saw flames erupting from under the hood of the pursuing car as Greyson tried to make the engine explode. Even as she started to breathe a sigh of relief, the flames disappeared and the car lunged at them. She could almost see the figures inside, two shapes, pale flashes in the dark exterior. Maybe if she lowered her shields—

"Megan!"

"I'm trying to read them."

"You won't get anything. They're not human. Just open the case."

It took her three tries to grasp the slider and pull it down and another second to force herself to look at what lay inside the case. She knew he carried it, she'd seen it several times. But she'd never really thought about it before, about why he needed it or what he might do with it.

"Take out the gun. Be careful, it's loaded. Take off your seat belt."

"I can't."

"Do you want to die?"

"No!"

Greyson swerved again, riding up on the curb. They'd turned onto a busier road; horns honked and tires squealed around them. "Then get the fucking gun out *now*!"

Her mouth was so dry she didn't think all the water in the world could help, but tears poured freely from her eyes. The gun sat heavy and cold in her hand, dwarfing her palm. She didn't like guns, had never liked them, and Greyson once told her he didn't particularly care for them either.

She turned around so her chest rested against the seat back.

It's them or us, it's them or us . . .

"Okay. Steady your arms on the back of the seat and look straight down them. Use your dominant eye and close the other one."

She obeyed. "Okay."

"Good. See those notches at the end of the barrel? Line up what you want to shoot between them. Then squeeze the trigger—don't yank it, just squeeze it. Be ready, it's going to kick back on you, so don't lock your arms too hard."

This felt unreal. She could do this, she could, she'd destroyed two zombies once with nothing more than a showerhead and some hair spray, she could definitely shoot these fuckers trying to kill her . . .

She took a deep breath and fired.

The Jaguar was going too fast for her to recoil far. Inertia, like a large hand, forced her body against the seat, but her arm kicked back. The gun's report echoed in her ears, thundering all the way through her body. She couldn't see where the shot had gone.

More black smoke filled the car. This time she acted instinctively, ducking forward while heat flared behind her back.

The car behind them swerved and sped up, its front end only inches from the Jag's rear. Greyson jerked the wheel to the left. Megan fell against the door, her hair blowing wild around her face, obscuring her vision. The Jag bounced and lurched, cutting into the next lane, flying across the center divider and down another side road. Metal crashed against metal behind them.

"Okay, get my phone and hit one," Greyson said. She couldn't believe how calm his voice was, how through all of this he'd barely yelled at her despite the rage she felt simmering below his surface. Even now his face in profile didn't reflect any anxiety save the slight tightening of his lips and a faint furrow in his brow. Whereas had she looked in a mirror she doubted she would have been able to recognize herself.

She obeyed, the sleek little phone much friendlier in her hand than the gun now resting on her lap. The other end rang once, twice, before a familiar Cockney voice answered.

"Malleus! Malleus, we're being chased, they're shooting—"

"Tell him where we are and we're heading for the reservoir," Greyson interrupted. "Tell him to meet us at exit twenty-two."

She'd barely finished repeating this when Malleus hung up.

"Are they gone?"

Her answer was another gunshot. The aluminum accents on the dash broke with a sharp, loud crack. Megan's hands flew up to cover her face. Greyson said something, but she didn't understand him.

"Shoot them again." Roughness underscored his tone.

"What's wrong?"

"Just shoot!"

She braced her heels against the underside of the dash and raised the gun again, shaking with adrenaline and fear.

"Shoot the grill!"

She did, aiming as best she could, but just as she squeezed the trigger the car shot forward. Greyson jerked the wheel to the right and Megan fell onto him. His gasp was audible even over the screaming engine and the rushing of blood in her ears.

The world spun dizzyingly around the car; they were turning in a full circle, leaving ink-black tire marks on the street. Before Megan even had a chance to duck they'd sideslipped the black car and passed it, heading back the way they'd come. Flames leaped up behind them, completely obliterating the road.

They went right, taking the turn wide, almost ramming a truck coming through the intersection. The truck's horn added to the cacophony of sounds around them.

"Did we lose—"

The black car flew around the corner, its tires still burning. Without being told she raised the gun, her fingers working of their own accord as they pulled the trigger. This long smooth stretch of road was the best chance she'd have.

This time she hit something. The black car lurched sideways, the dim shapes inside moving. A ball of blue-white fire came out of nowhere and slammed into the grill, through the grill, flames licking the top of the hood from beneath. Black smoke poured out, then as Megan watched, the smoke formed itself into a shape like an arrow and aimed at the Jag, only to vanish in another conflagration.

Her eyes burned from the horror and heat. She

shot again, not knowing how many bullets were even left in the gun. More smoke, white now, came from the car behind them. Still it burned. Hope blossomed in her breast.

"Hang on," Greyson said, spinning the wheel. The Jag slipped up an entry ramp onto the highway, the black car still following but slower now, lurching forward. Its tires exploded in a mass of flames. The car leaped in the air, forced up from the blast, and landed on its side against the retaining wall of the ramp. Megan watched until Greyson merged into traffic, but the car didn't move again.

"Oh my God, oh my God, who were they? Why were—"

Pale gray light from the streetlamps flashed into the car and out, like a slow-motion strobe, highlighting the black splatter of blood on the charcoal dashboard, the gleaming river of it soaking Greyson's sleeve.

"I'm fine," he said again, just as he had so many times in the last hour as they drove all over the city to make sure they weren't being followed. Megan stopped just inside the dimly lit white entry hall of Iureanlier Sorithell, the mansion on the outskirts of town belonging to the Gretneg of Greyson's Meegra.

Right now that was Greyson, at least in theory. Since his takeover of the position had involved handing the former Gretneg, Templeton Black, over to the supernatural law enforcement agency known as Vergadering, some members of his Meegra doubted his integrity. The other Gretnegs were still debating whether or not to allow him to have that much power and authority.

It was a battle she knew he was still fighting, but one they didn't discuss. She'd never asked, and she doubted he would give her a straight answer if she did. It was his business, just like the changes she'd been implementing in her Meegra were hers. Although she knew he didn't approve of them, he'd never once told her so, or tried to change her mind when she made a decision.

"You're getting blood all over the floor," she said, following him through the small crowd of *rubendas*— members of his Meegra—who stood waiting. Clearly the wound wasn't serious, but the sight of it still made her nervous. Uncomfortable.

Especially since something deep inside her, some small part she refused to acknowledge, liked seeing it. Liked the contrast of dark red blood on the white marble floor. Wanted to touch it, to raise fingertips smudged with it to her lips and taste it, spicy and tinged with smoke.

Horrified, she looked away, swallowing hard. Her eyes caught those of one of the *rubendas* and saw the same yearning reflected there.

Her heels clicked on the floor as she hurried to catch up with Greyson, staring resolutely at his sharp profile. Malleus strode along beside him, carrying the overnight case he'd gone to her house and packed for her. Through the open door of the kitchen she saw Maleficarum and Spud opening a large bag and setting out silvery instruments on white cloths.

Malleus, Maleficarum, and Spud were guard demons—brothers—terrifically strong and tough, with self-healing powers accelerated even beyond those of normal demons; she'd seen them lose enough blood to kill a man and do a jig three hours later. But they'd spent some time learning emergency medical procedures as well, especially over the last three months. They were among the few demons Greyson really trusted, so their duties under his rule had increased from simple bodyguards to something more like personal assistants.

"Mr. Dante?"

Megan and Greyson both stopped. Megan turned around to see the *rubenda* who'd caught her eye earlier step cautiously forward and gesture to the droplets on the floor.

"Mr. Dante, can I have your blood?"

Angry mutterings broke out in the small crowd of demons near him. Megan's mouth fell open, but when she looked back at Greyson he stood perfectly calm, as if the other demon had asked him about the weather.

"No," he said, and strode into the kitchen without looking back.

Her feet sank into the soft pale carpet as she paced back and forth, trying to somehow walk the adrenaline out of her system. Whiskey had taken the edge off, but her mind still raced.

From the way Greyson's eyes tracked her movements she knew he was well on his way to being drunk. He slouched in his heavy chair by the wall, shirtless, his bandaged arm resting on pillows beside him. His other hand clutched yet another drink.

"I really don't think painkillers and booze are a great combination, Greyson, why don't you—"

"Why don't you let it go?" he snapped. That, more than anything else, told her how unnerved he'd been by their experience. Greyson almost never lost his temper.

She stared at him for a minute, then kept walking. Tension hung in the air between them, weighing Megan down even more fully than she was already. She'd found another of her demons exploded all over some suburban home, she'd been arrested, she'd gone to jail, she'd almost been killed . . . and she'd had the bizarre and unfortunately not unfamiliar desire to lick her boyfriend's blood. A desire shared by at least one demon in the house, if not more.

"Sit down, *bryaela*," Greyson said softly. "You're making me dizzy."

"I can't sit. I'm too nervous."

"We could lie down."

Her laugh sounded slightly hysterical in her ears. "Is this really the time?"

"It's as good a time as any, isn't it?" He stood up and crossed the room to her, capturing her between his hard warm body and the heavy dresser behind her. "You're here, I'm here . . . I believe you're familiar with the bed—"

"We almost got killed tonight. After I went to jail!"

"Mmm, that's so sexy." His lips tickled her ear, then traced a path down the side of her neck, stopping so he could scrape her skin with his teeth. "You bad, bad girl."

She didn't intend to respond, but did, meeting his lips with a ferocity that stunned her. Her arms slid up under his so her fingertips could run over the tiny *sgaegas*—dull little spikes—covering his spine. Goose bumps broke out on his skin under her hands.

He gripped her waist with his right hand and pulled her closer, pressing his erection against her belly while his left hand tangled in her hair. She raised herself on tiptoe, forcing him to kiss her harder, wanting to forget everything and lose herself in him.

Heat exploded in her chest, in her stomach, working its way to points lower. Her fingers yanked at his belt. The entire night—the shame, the terror, her failure to protect her demons—disappeared in a haze of need so strong she thought she might die from it.

She shoved his pants down and grabbed his cock, hot and heavy in her palm. His breath rasped into her mouth, onto her throat, as he pulled away enough to lift her shirt.

One quick move slid it over her head, and another adroit twist unfastened her bra. It slid down her shoulders and he pulled it all the way off, then pressed his chest to hers, forcing her hips harder against the dresser. She caressed his back, down the hard muscles of his behind, forward again to stroke him where she knew he'd appreciate it the most, and all the while her heart beat with fire and fear and the need for oblivion.

He lifted her up, his powerful hands curving under her thighs, and propped her on the edge of the dresser.

"Your arm," she gasped. "Be careful."

"Hush." His mouth caught hers again while he undid

the button of her trousers and lowered the zipper. Underneath she wore a tiny scrap of black silk he'd bought her on his last trip to Paris. Greyson liked to give gifts, especially gifts he could remove later.

She started to lower herself from the dresser but he stopped her, bracing her back with one hand while he used the other to peel the panties off and drop them on the floor.

"I thought you wanted the bed," she whispered.

"Changed my mind."

Her head fell back as he thrust into her, gripping her hips with both hands. She clutched the short, soft hair at his nape, twisting it between her fingers and bringing him closer. His mouth hovered not half an inch from hers, his eyes glowing red and staring into her, through her.

"Meg . . ."

He dove closer, capturing her lips, invading her with his tongue, and the flames in her body leaped higher. Their mouths fused together as he thrust, keeping his pace steady, but she felt his arms shaking and the loose urgency of his lips and knew this wouldn't last, couldn't last, that the fear and pain which made her want to escape acted like an aphrodisiac for him.

Her hips left the dresser. She braced herself with her hands on the smooth, cool surface and wrapped her legs around his waist while he held her up, moving her pelvis in slow circles so he hit all the right spots deep inside her. She tensed, her thighs urging him on, begging for more.

His grip shifted, freeing his right hand so he could

slide it down between them, and that was all she needed. Her back arched, shoving her hips farther forward, and she cried out as her body shuddered and clenched with release.

He joined her moments later, his fingers digging into her skin so hard it hurt, his entire body shaking, her name on his lips.

They stayed like that for a long, lost minute, their foreheads pressed together and their breath slowing in unison, until her arms started to cramp and she lowered her feet to the ground.

He brushed her cheek with his fingers, then bent to retrieve her panties, handing them to her as he pulled his trousers back up.

"How's your arm?"

He shrugged, but the quick smile he gave her warmed her heart just as surely as he'd warmed her entire body moments before. "Hurts like a bitch, but I'll be fine in the morning. Good thing too. I have to go to New York on Monday, and there's a bunch of stuff to organize before that."

"But—I mean, aren't you worried?"

He picked up the half-full glass he'd left on the little table by his chair and drank it off. "Why? Harrel's a good pilot, and—"

"Somebody tried to kill us, Greyson. Aren't you worried about that?" She grabbed one of his T-shirts from his drawer and yanked it over her head. Exhaustion started sinking into her bones, and the bed had never looked more inviting—almost never, anyway. But although the memory of the car chase and its attendant panic had faded, thinking about it didn't do her nerves any good.

"They weren't trying to kill us, darling. Don't be so dramatic."

"They did a pretty good imitation."

"No." He poured himself another drink, and a shadow crossed his face. "That was just a warning."

"How do you know?"

"Because they were witches. If they'd wanted us dead, we'd probably be dead."

Chapter Three

I don't understand."

"There's no way I could have defeated those witches so easily if they'd really wanted to kill us," he said. "Not unless they were just a couple of kids hunting demons for a lark, which we know isn't the case."

"How do we—oh. The jail. They knew I was there."

He nodded. "And they knew I'd come for you. They were too powerful to be kids, too."

"The police said someone called them and told them there was a dead body in that house. Do you think the witches might have called? That they're the ones killing the demons?"

"I don't think so, no. I think our little friends just took advantage of the situation." He emptied his glass again. Worry started creeping up Megan's spine. He looked as if he was bracing himself for something, as if he was trying to forget. Even with a demon's metabolism, which she knew was pretty good, four Percocet and half a bottle of Bushmill's couldn't be helping him think faster.

What was bothering him so much?

"Why did they come after us? Why would witches want to ki—warn us?"

"*Me,* not us, if I'm right—and of course I am. I'm taking care of it, so don't worry."

If she pressed him he would tell her, but now it felt like an invasion of his privacy. Which was probably his intent.

"So who is doing it? Killing the demons, I mean?"

He shook his head. "I don't know. Nobody knows."

The chill air swirling around her legs was starting to make her uncomfortable. Greyson kept the room ice cold, and usually she preferred it that way too because he was so warm all the time. But there was no point in standing here shivering. She climbed into bed instead, not realizing until she slid between the heavy silk sheets how hard it was to keep her eyes open. "Rocturnus said they used to be punished this way, with the explosions."

"Did he?" He poured another glass.

"Yes. Why?"

"So for the Yezer this is normal?" She could almost see the wheels turning in his head.

"I wouldn't say 'normal,' but I guess it's not unheard of. Isn't it the same for the rest of you?"

"Did he say who used to do it? Was it the Accuser or—"

"Are you going to answer my questions, or what?"

"If you answer mine. Who used to punish them that way?"

"Roc didn't say. Do you all blow up? I mean, should I expect you to explode one of these days?"

"Only if you don't do everything I say, all the time."

Her fist gripped his pillow. His reflexes were a little

slower, maybe, from the injury and the chemicals. She might be able to hit him with it if she moved fast enough . . .

His eyes gleamed. Damn it. "Where is Roc, anyway?"

"Checking on the others. I kind of wanted some privacy while I was—"

"Rotting in jail."

She smiled in spite of herself. "You put it so nicely."

He raised an eyebrow, but didn't take the bait. "Do you remember anything else he said?"

"No. Why?"

He glanced at the clock by the bed. "It's past one. You should get some sleep."

"Aren't you coming to bed?"

"Eventually. I have a few things to do first."

She expected him to get up and head back down to his office, but he didn't. He was still sitting in his chair, drinking and watching her, when she drifted off to sleep.

Wings of fatigue beat behind her eyelids three hours later as they walked into the casino. Her entire body ached. All she wanted to do was go back to bed.

Unfortunately, for reasons she still couldn't seem to get straight in her sleep-muddled head, that wasn't possible. Instead she was here, making her way across the floor under scarily intense white lights and the watchful gazes of at least a dozen demons.

She'd been to the casino only once before, when

Greyson was doing some work and called her to meet him for lunch. It had been daytime then, the casino a dark silent room waiting for the crowds.

Now the crowds were there. The floor roared with bells and shouts and the harsh bright rattle of poker chips hitting each other. So much noise in such a small space made her head hurt. She didn't even know how all of these people knew about the place. The demons, yes. But at least half of the shoulders crammed up against the craps and card tables had Yezer Ha-Ra perched on them. It bothered her. She didn't know much about Greyson's various legal enterprises, and even less about the illegal ones, but she'd assumed this one—illegal— was demon-only.

He stopped when she did, and followed her gaze. "You're not the only human who knows demons," he said quietly. "Just the only one who knows what we are."

She tried to smile. "I knew I was special. Where's Gerald?"

He nodded toward the back. "They managed to get him into one of the storerooms. Come on."

His hand in hers reassured her as he led Megan through the room, past a roulette wheel and a long, well-lit bar where several pretty young ladies served drinks. They smiled as Greyson walked past, their big eyes following him. To Megan they gave the barest of nods, not daring to ignore her completely.

Two guards stood outside a nondescript doorway. "Mr. Dante," said the first. "He's inside."

"This is Dr. Chase," Greyson replied. "He asked for her?"

"Yeah, he seemed, I don't know, really off," said the second. Both of them kept their eyes averted, she noticed, and shuffled their feet. "He sounded like he was speaking our language, but . . . not."

"Like a weird dialect," the first added. "Then English again."

Greyson and Megan exchanged glances. One of her clients speaking the demon tongue? She couldn't even speak it, not more than a couple of words anyway. *"Bry-aela,"* of course, although why anyone but Greyson or John Wayne would call someone "pilgrim" she had no idea. He said it was because she was like a little explorer in a new world, but that wasn't exactly a satisfactory explanation. *"Sheshissma,"* she knew, but he only used that one when he was feeling particularly amorous, so she'd never had the guts to repeat it.

In fact, now that she thought of it, the only words she knew seemed to be essentially useless outside the bedroom. Maybe he'd agree to give her lessons, or if he wouldn't, Rocturnus would.

Speaking of whom, where was he?

"Did he say anything else?" Greyson asked.

The second guard shook his head. "No, sir, he just started crying and asking for Dr. Chase. He didn't want to come in here at first, but . . ." he glanced uneasily at Megan. "We, uh, convinced him. He was strong too."

"Let me in," she said, hating the way he waited for Greyson's nod before opening the door. Bad enough she'd managed to get herself involved in this demon underworld of violence and crime. Now innocent people were mixed up in it, people who came to her for help and instead got roughed up in a storeroom.

A storeroom in a casino, which didn't make any sense. Gerald wasn't a gambler. She'd never even read the slightest interest in gaming from him, unless you counted the occasional football pool at his office, and even that was simply his trying to fit in. Which was good, because he lost every time.

Still he was a nice man, a good man, and he deserved better than this. A kind, gentle—wait a minute.

"Did you say he was strong? That you had to fight to get him in here?"

The guard nodded. Muscles bulged from every inch of his body. He was like a demon Conan, with a smaller chin. Gerald—the Gerald Megan knew—would have been a snack for him.

She pushed the door open and entered the small, dingy storeroom, half hoping, half expecting to see a stranger in there, someone pretending to be Gerald.

But no, it was Gerald. Cowering in the corner, his bare feet scraped and dirty and a bruise marring his narrow little face.

"Megan! Megan!" He scrambled across the floor toward her like a broken-legged crab, his limbs jerking under his clothes. She jumped back. The unnatural movement sent shivers up her spine.

Gerald stopped, glancing up at her. His expression was innocent, fearful, but something in his eyes . . . Megan lowered her shields to read him. Maybe he was on some kind of drug, maybe he'd gotten hold of something . . .

Nothing. No images came, no stray thoughts, no flashes of emotion. Fear chased the last of her sleepiness away. This wasn't right, not at all. She'd always been able to read Gerald, he was a heavy transmitter, and the only times she'd gotten nothing at all from a person were when they weren't actually people at all, but demons . . .

Gerald's eyes glowed. Just for a second, but long enough for Megan to see it. Without thinking she turned the energy she was using to read him into a shield, a weapon, and aimed it at him.

The pressure of the hit reverberated through her entire body, but Gerald only wavered in place. Trying not to let fear overwhelm her, Megan braced herself, certain she was about to be hit back, and hit hard. The place deep inside herself that she saw as a door, the one she'd only opened once before in her life, seemed to throb and glow, wanting her to open it, to reach into it and through it to the personal demons. This was where they connected to her, this was where she knew without thinking that she could harness their power. It would be so easy, so simple to open it and let the demon inside her take over . . .

But so wrong. So scary. Just the idea of it made her shake. Instead she forced everything she had into shielding herself and ducked down, her knees slamming against the dusty cement floor, the doorjamb against her shoulder.

Screams filled the room, high-pitched squeals of delight that sent shivers up her spine. They reached a piercing crescendo, hurting Megan's ears, making her scrunch herself into a tighter ball, her heart pounding with terror and her entire body braced for the pain she knew was coming any second—but something inside her wanted to scream too, wanted to leap in the air and dance. The desire beat in her chest, so strong and fierce she screamed herself and wrapped her arms around her ribs. She couldn't hold on, couldn't keep herself from bursting into flame—

Silence.

Large bodies pushed past her, knocking her into the wall. She was too afraid to open her eyes. Where was Greyson? He didn't usually leave her like this, didn't force her to stand by herself, especially not when she was certain it was obvious to anyone looking that something was very, very wrong with her.

"He's dead." The other guard's voice, the non-Conan one, sounded strangled somehow, confused. "Mr. Dante, the human's dead!"

In the space between the male feet crowded around it, she saw one hand on the floor. Gerald's hand, fingers curved up like a dead spider, pale and unmoving. The image filled her mind. Even when she closed her eyes it stayed, burned in like a photographic negative, luminous against the blackness of her eyelids. Her client was dead. Her nice, sweet, nongambling client died on the floor of a storeroom in a demon casino, with his eyes glowing and an unearthly scream—a scream almost like a laugh, she realized now—on his lips, and none of this made any sense and she thought she might faint.

"Get Dr. Chase out of here," she heard Greyson say. "Take her to the car." She wanted to argue but her tongue and lips didn't seem to be under her control. Gerald was dead and she knew it was her fault. Knew it as surely as she knew her own name, knew it as surely as she knew Greyson wanted her to get in the car not just because he didn't want her to have to look at that hand on the floor, but because he needed to get the body out of his casino before someone noticed it and called the police.

An annoying hum woke her up, and it took her a minute to remember where she was—and for other memories to flood back: the bitter taste of the pills Maleficarum had given her when he put her in the car, she and Greyson sleeping squeezed together across the big backseat, Malleus carrying her up to bed.

The room was dim when she opened her eyes, thanks to the heavy blackout shades on the windows, but there was enough light to see her stupid cell phone buzzing angrily on the bedside table.

She picked up the phone and fumbled with it, trying to find the catch to slide it open. Greyson had bought her the damn thing and she still couldn't figure out half of the spiffy tricks it was supposed to perform, much less open it with a flick of the wrist the way he and the brothers could.

"Hello?" It hurt her throat to talk.

"Hey! I'm running a little late, do you want to meet me at four instead of three?"

Tera Green sounded chipper and well rested, the way she always did, as opposed to Megan, who, at the moment, probably sounded as wrung out and hungover as she felt.

She pulled the phone away to look at the time. It was twenty to three in the afternoon. She and Tera had a date to go shopping and have dinner. She'd totally forgotten.

Rather than admit that, though, she nodded vigorously until she remembered Tera couldn't see her. "Yeah, of course," she said, trying to put some enthusiasm in her voice. "I was just—just getting ready."

"Great. I'll see you at four, then."

Megan echoed the response, although "great" was the last word she thought it was at the moment, and dragged herself to a sit.

"Tera?"

He sounded tired, but not as tired as she felt. She looked at him, his hair rumpled with sleep and his eyes still heavy, and nodded. "We're going shopping."

"What fun." He yawned and reached for her, pulling her closer so he could rest his head in her lap. "Why don't you stay here instead? I have some things to do but I'll be free in a few hours."

"And sit by myself in your room all day? No thanks." She didn't move, though. Memories of the night before started coming back: Gerald on the floor, the scream, the pounding in her chest . . . she shivered.

Greyson's arms tightened around her. "It wasn't your fault."

"Yes it was and you know it. I appreciate your not saying, 'I told you so,' though." Her attempt to keep her tone light wasn't very successful.

He paused. "I worried something like this might happen, but that isn't why I want you to give up your practice. It still isn't why." He sat up and wrapped his arm around her, pulling her down a bit so she could rest her head on his chest. Beneath the smoky scent of his skin she still smelled last night's whiskey and whatever Spud had put on his wound. She glanced at his arm. The bandage was gone, but a small puckered scar remained.

"Meg, people die all the time. Would it have been your fault if gentle Gerald's problems had overwhelmed him and he'd killed himself? If he got hit by a car crossing the street because he was thinking of something you said and forgot to look both ways?"

"A demon possessed him and led him there to die, I think that's a bit dif—"

"No, it isn't different, it's exactly the same. It's too bad the guy's dead if it bothers you, but all of your clients could die and I wouldn't give a damn. The only life I'm interested in saving is yours. And mine, of course."

"Of course." She didn't know if she believed him, didn't know if she really felt less responsible, but the black cloud over her head seemed to lift a little just the same.

"Which is why I want you to take Malleus with you today."

She pulled away. "No, I can't."

"Yes, you can. Tera will just have to deal with it. And don't tell her why."

"She's going to know something's up if she secs him."

"She can think what she wants to think. What did I just say? I want you to stay safe. Malleus can make sure you do."

"I thought the witches were just after you."

"Call me paranoid."

He looked, sitting on the bed framed by the black satin pillows and sheets, like a medieval king granting favors, but his eyes were tired and serious.

"If I didn't know better I'd think you really cared," she said. It wasn't an unusual joke or one they'd never made before as they edged carefully around the issue of their feelings, but this time it fell flat. Her face flooded with heat.

He blinked. "Yes, well, I've got you rather a nice Christmas present, I'd hate to see it go to waste." The covers whispered as he shoved them off and got out of bed. "Malleus will be waiting for you when you are ready to leave. He brought your car over last night."

"Greyson . . ." But there was nothing to say.

He fastened his pants and came over to her, planting a kiss on her forehead. "I'll try and come by tomorrow night. I have to leave early Monday, though, so don't wait up."

Without meaning to she reached for him, curling her fingers around his arms, stroking up and down the hard, smooth muscles. Just the feel of him under her palms made her warm.

He kissed her again, on the lips this time, lingering just a moment longer. "Unless you want to cancel on Tera after all . . ." His hands traveled down her ribs to her waist, where they paused.

She shook her head. Much as she wanted to stay, she was looking forward to going out into the normal world again. As normal as it could be when you were shopping with a witch and had a demon bodyguard following you. "She'll be hurt if I cancel."

"Just make sure you have your phone on. And be careful."

He started to move away, but she grabbed him. "What did—what did you do with him?"

"Gerald?"

She nodded.

"Took him back to his place, put him on the bed. Someone will find him."

The cold feeling started creeping back. He sounded so nonchalant, like he moved dead bodies around—or ordered them moved—every day. Which she supposed he might. "Who did this to him? Was it someone from a different Meegra, or—"

His knuckles under her chin forced her to look up at him. "We'll figure it out. Meanwhile—"

"I know. Be careful, don't tell Tera anything, and keep Malleus with me."

"See? It's so much better when you just obey me."

He ducked away before she could swat him.

Chapter Four

The minute Megan saw Tera she looked down to see if she'd spilled something on her shirt. She hadn't, of course. The only blot on her image was the dark shape of Malleus behind her, his gold pinkie ring flashing in the bright winter sun coming through the skylight.

Tera looked, as she always did, perfect; cool and immaculate in jeans and a black sweater, with her trapeze coat swinging behind her and her platinum hair falling in a shining curtain down her back. She was designed to make other women feel inadequate. Megan would have wondered why they were friends if the answer wasn't so obvious—neither of them had any other friends.

Besides, she genuinely liked Tera, despite the fact that the witch had the social skills of a gnat.

They hugged and started walking through the pre-Christmas Saturday crowds. Maybe shopping wasn't the greatest idea. Megan had expected to relax, surrounded by people to make her feel normal again. Instead she found herself itching to read them all, to open up and read the entire building, to make sure no one who shouldn't be lurked in the corners.

Here and there little demons winked at her or waved from human shoulders and she tried to acknowledge them without looking like she was greeting everyone she passed. Where was Rocturnus? She hadn't expected to see him when she woke up this morning—one embarrassing incident had been enough for her to forbid him from ever appearing in bedrooms, and he couldn't enter Greyson's place alone anyway—but she'd thought he might at least put in a quick appearance here to let her know he was okay.

"So." Tera looked back over her shoulder, her blue eyes scanning Malleus, who stared purposefully ahead. "I see you have a guard today. Grey thinks you might get busted again?"

Megan's stomach sank. So Tera—and thus Vergadering—did know about her arrest. "You know me, always in trouble."

"What were you doing? Trespassing in a regular family's house?"

"I thought it was somebody I knew."

"And some Good Samaritan called the police and said you were murdering people."

"Geez, Tera, did my mug shot get sent over to Vergadering as well?"

Tera waved her hand. "They didn't take a mug shot. And I keep my ear to the ground."

"That must get uncomfortable after a while."

Tera smiled. "More than you know. I'm glad you're okay, though." She looked at Malleus again. "Hi, Malleus."

His head barely dipped. "Miss Tera."

Megan bit her lip. After three months he and his brothers still refused to use her own first name, insisting it was disrespectful.

If Tera knew she'd just been insulted, she either didn't care or didn't show she cared. "Look at that blouse, what do you think?"

Megan dutifully looked. Pink and white stripes ran vertically up the tailored shirt. It suited Tera. "Sure, try it on."

Tera tried. Tera bought. The process repeated itself several times, while Megan grew more and more uneasy. The mall, with its garish every-religion-in-the-world decorations and piped-in cheery music was never her favorite place anyway, and now she was feeling claustrophobic. Life among the crowds had never made her especially happy and the relentless pushing and shoving forced her to shield so hard she lost the train of her rambling conversation with Tera.

"I'm sorry, what?" she asked again. Tera sighed.

"Come on. Let's get a snack or something and sit down. There's a new store by the food court. I want to check in there and then we'll have dinner."

"We're getting a snack right before dinner?"

"Some of us like to eat."

"I like to eat."

"When you remember to." Tera looked her up and down. "Your life of crime keeping you too busy to eat?"

Megan waited while Tera ordered a gooey cinnamon bun, then said, "It was just a misunderstanding and nobody pressed charges. As you know."

"I still think it's weird."

"You know me, weird Megan the crazy demon woman."

"You're not a demon." Tera shoved a piece of bun

in her mouth. "Despite being hip deep in them all the time. Or the other way around, so to speak."

Megan blushed. "I can't just magically disconnect myself from them."

"But your demons aren't the same. They just do their thing and stay out of the way. You can do whatever it is you do with them and stay yourself. You can keep your practice. You can keep your life."

Megan didn't tell her about the discussions she and Greyson had been having lately—the closest thing to arguments they'd ever had—about her practice. "I still have my life."

"Right. That's why you were arrested for breaking and entering."

"It wasn't breaking and entering, it was trespassing. I didn't break in."

Did Tera really not know why Megan had been in that house? Did she really not know about the other demons exploding, about—Megan swallowed—about Gerald?

Somehow she'd managed to forget about Gerald as they wandered the mall. Now the memory rushed back, so vivid and painful Megan had to brace herself against the cheap Formica table to keep from curling up into a ball. Her involvement with the demons had already killed one innocent person, if her instinct about what happened the night before was right. Whatever Greyson said about the inevitability of death or the possibility of accident, something demonic had gotten hold of Gerald, and it was related somehow to her.

"So you were trespassing. Want to tell me why?"

Megan blinked. "Is this an official inquiry?"

"No. The normal police bought your story, so Vergadering isn't investigating. But I'd like to know. I worry about you, Megan. I'm your friend. Aren't I?"

"Of course you are." Megan shrugged. "I was trying to surprise a friend. Someone from the station. I had the wrong house, that's all."

Tera's eyes narrowed. Megan forced herself to look into them and think innocent thoughts. She didn't want to lie to Tera. Tera knew a lot about a lot of things. She'd worked for Vergadering for a dozen years now, and Megan would have loved to spill it all to her, to tell her about the demon explosions and the assassination attempt and Gerald and see if the witch could make sense of it.

Just having an actual discussion about it would be nice, an opportunity to think out loud to another person. Nobody played their cards as close to the chest as Greyson did, and while Megan was used to it—even liked it, most of the time, because she did the same— there were moments when she wished he was more forthcoming.

But if Greyson was right and it had been witches trying to kill them in that mad car chase . . . she didn't want to talk about that with Tera. Couldn't talk about it with Tera, much as she wanted to try and pick her friend's brain. If Tera didn't know anything, it could be awkward, and if she did . . . that could be even more awkward. Not to mention dangerous.

"I thought you trusted me," Tera said.

"I do. Tera, what is going on? You don't usually grill

me about this stuff. Aren't you going to tell me more about Roger or Todd or whoever else you're dating now who you don't really like? Or tell me how my top isn't the right color or something?"

"It's not. It washes you out." But she smiled. "I'm sorry. I get a little cranky around the holidays, I guess, and we've been hearing some odd—well, I just don't want to see you get so involved with demons that you forget who and what you are."

"I'm not forgetting anything." She glanced up. "What odd things have you been hearing?"

"Oh, nothing. Just that there's some unrest in the demon world." Tera was a good liar, but even without being able to read her Megan still knew. It saddened her a little, the same way she imagined her refusal to open up saddened Tera. In the three months they'd been friends, they'd never run into a situation where they really couldn't discuss something.

"Come on," she said, getting up. Malleus stood as well, his beefy arms still crossed, his expression grim. His contempt for witches was ingrained, had been ever since he'd been born and named. "You wanted to check that dress shop, right?"

The air between them seemed to clear a bit as they threw away the remains of Tera's snack and shoved through the crowds. Or rather, Malleus shoved, and they followed in his wake.

"I'm beginning to think I was wrong about him," Tera murmured. "He's pretty handy to have in a crowd, isn't he?"

Malleus's shoulders twitched, but he said nothing.

Megan seized the opportunity and lied, "That's why he's here."

"A favor?"

"Sort of."

"And how will you be repaying that favor, hmm?"

Megan blushed. Tera laughed and patted her on the shoulder. "Hey, better than—"

"Mr. Brown!" Malleus's public code name. Who was—

A short, stylish little man threw himself across the shop as they entered. Megan started to jump out of the way, but the broad grin on the man's face and his outstretched arms stopped her in midjump, turning it into a sort of awkward jerk that made Tera raise her eyebrows.

"Mr. Brown, so good to have you here, I'm so honored! Is Mr. Dante—oh!" His shining eyes lit on Megan. "Dr. Chase, isn't it?"

Megan nodded, her face burning. She didn't need to look at Tera to imagine her friend's expression.

The man reached for her hand, then thought better of it and bowed instead. "Dr. Chase, I'm so pleased—so pleased! Come in, come in, sit down. What would you like today? A dress? A purse, some shoes?"

"I'm just looking," Megan managed as the little man ushered her through the shop without actually touching her and indicated a padded bench for her to sit on. Tera sat next to her, smirking.

"Nonsense! You don't need to look, we'll look for you, you just sit here."

"You stay here, m'lady," Malleus added, plunking his

weight down on her other side. "You let 'im show you things."

It was a reminder as much as a genuine desire to see her treated well, she knew. Malleus never forgot whose servant he was and what was expected of him in that capacity. Those rules apparently extended to her. The man now thrusting various garments at her wasn't a demon, but just the same she didn't need an interpreter to know what was going on.

It would be an insult not to smile and finger the clothing. It would be an insult not to finally select something and allow the man to box it up for her as carefully as he would the Hope diamond. It would be an insult to try and pay, especially when the little man kept grinning and telling her to remember him to Mr. Dante, to tell Mr. Dante how honored he was that Mr. Dante had sent Dr. Chase to his store and that if Mr. Dante ever wanted anything he shouldn't hesitate to ask.

Megan finally left the shop with a designer gown, the shop owner's business card, and a face bright enough to send satellite signals.

Tera smiled beside her. "Sure," she said. "You're not getting too wrapped up in the whole demon thing at all, are you?"

The bag with the gown in it banged against her leg like a toddler demanding attention as she walked into her house. She'd managed to have a good time, all things considered, especially when the conversation turned away from her and toward Tera's various casual dates.

"Hi, Megan."

The scream died in her throat when she saw Rocturnus lounging on her couch. "Damn it, I've asked you not to—"

"You asked me not to jump out at you and I'm not. I'm just sitting here."

"You scared me."

"Sorry." He didn't look sorry, but then demons never did.

She set down the bag and switched on the lamp by the couch. "Where have you been?"

"Checking on everyone." His beady little eyes shifted. Not a good sign.

"And?"

"And they're all alive. No more explosions."

A breath she didn't realize she'd been holding escaped. "Good."

"But . . . maybe you should sit down."

Megan knew people often told other people to sit down when they had good news for them too. It just hadn't ever happened to her. There was no point in trying to put a brave face on things as she sat. Rocturnus would be able to feel, taste, and smell her every negative emotion anyway. "Okay, what?"

"Well . . . some of us aren't very . . . happy. About the changes. And about what's been going on. The deaths."

"I didn't think having your buddies explode would put you guys in the Christmas spirit," she said, "but—"

"Actually we quite like the holidays. Lots of depression, feelings of inadequacy, jealousy . . . we're very busy this time of year."

"Mmm, just like Santa's elves," she said. "What about the changes?"

The frown on his wizened little face told her what he thought of the "elves" joke. "It's confidence," he said. "I know you don't feel entirely comfortable with us. With what we do. But you have to remember, it is how we stay alive."

"I'm not trying to kill anyone. I think it's fair to ask you to exercise a little restraint, don't you?"

"There's another family."

"What?"

"Another family. I mean, some of us have always had loyalties to other families. Not all of us in this city or even this country belonged to the Accuser."

She nodded. He'd touched on this subject before, but she hadn't paid much attention. It was enough to know several thousand demons in the city belonged to her. What the others did didn't matter much, at least that's what she'd thought.

Apparently she was wrong. "Another family is forming in the city. Some of yours . . . they're uncomfortable. They don't like your new way of doing things."

"They'd rather be tortured and beaten?"

Rocturnus nodded. "And be able to live the way they always have."

"But they aren't giving it a chance!" She stood up—so much for sitting down—and started pacing, then realized she was still wearing her coat and scarf. No wonder she felt so warm.

"They don't think you can protect them," Rocturnus

said. "They think you didn't want us to begin with, and now you're trying to starve us and you don't care about the explosions."

"That's not true, you know it isn't true. I do care. I went to jail last night for you guys; if I didn't care I wouldn't have bothered to go in that house and—"

"I know that."

"Have you told them?"

He nodded.

"But they don't believe you."

"It isn't all of them," he said. "It's not even a lot of them . . . yet. But enough to make me worry. They just—they don't think you're strong enough."

She brushed aside the little voice in her head warning they they might be right. "I want to help them!"

"They want to be ruled, not helped. It's the way demons are." She raised an eyebrow and he amended, "It's the way Yezer Ha-Ra are. The big ones, they have their own needs. They still want a strong leader though."

She never thought she'd live to see the day when she was rejected by a bunch of little demons who fed on human anger and misery. By rights they should be drawn to her like flies to . . . well, like flies to just about anything. She'd never heard of a discerning fly.

They should be drawn to her like she was drawn to the bottle of vodka in her liquor cabinet. It sloshed into her glass, cracking the ice sticking to the bottom, turning a lovely jewel pink when she poured cranberry juice over it and added a splash of Rose's lime. A tropical drink for a very cold and frosty night. Hey, something should be warm and tropical. Her insides certainly weren't.

Half the drink was gone before she felt ready to talk again. "So who started this other family?"

"What do you mean?"

"Who started it? Who's in charge? Is it one of you guys or is everyone joining a different Meegra or what?"

From the way his mouth twisted she almost expected him to say the others were joining Greyson's Meegra. But that wasn't possible, she knew it. Greyson wouldn't betray her like that.

At least she thought he wouldn't.

Shoving that disturbing little doubt out of her mind, she repeated the question. "Who's in charge, Roc? Come on, if I'm going to be in direct competition with someone I'd like to know who it is."

"I don't know," he said finally. "They wouldn't tell me."

"Can't you—wait, what do you mean they wouldn't tell you? Who wouldn't tell you, the ones who left or the ones who're still with me?"

He looked at his hands.

"Okay, so my demons—the ones staying with me—are now refusing to tell you where the demons who are no longer with me are going?"

"That's the gist of it, yes."

"Fuck." She stood up and held out her hand. "Okay, then. Let's go see them."

"Now? They won't be there."

"Then I'll call them there." Why this was suddenly so important she didn't know. Hadn't she spent half the day wanting to be rid of the little demons, to be herself again? To come down to it, hadn't she spent most of the last three months wishing this whole leader-of-the-personal-demon-pack thing hadn't happened? As much as she liked Roc, being pulled in two directions like this wasn't exactly comfortable.

But now she was hopping mad, fighting mad. It wasn't that they were leaving, it was that they weren't even telling her where they were going. That anger burned in her chest, burned through her entire body. If they wanted to leave, that was fine. But to not tell her where they were going, to treat her so disrespectfully . . .

It wasn't until she'd closed her eyes and reached with her mind for the high-ceilinged room in the sky where they lived that she realized she was thinking exactly the way Greyson kept telling her she should think.

Chapter Five

She had no idea what to say.

Faced with a sea of little bald heads in a confusing Impressionistic variety of colors and squinty lashless eyes, she started to regret her impulse. It would have been better to let it go. It would have been better to let the ones who didn't want to stay with her just leave. If they weren't even interested in trying things her way, in giving being a little less vicious a chance, they should go.

But the people . . .

And that was why. She couldn't let them all just leave her and move on. Not when she'd spent so much time formulating a plan. Not when she was able to sleep easier at night knowing the humans her demons affected slept a little easier as well, because her first rule had been no more suicides, no more abuse. They could make their people miserable, but they were not to harm others.

Even that made her uncomfortable. But she couldn't let the Yezer starve either.

"I called you here because I know some of you are leaving," she said finally. "And going to a different house."

The crowd shifted uneasily. She glanced at Roc, but

his expression was unreadable. She hated not being able to use her gifts with demons. Having spent her early life getting hunches about people and then her entire life beyond her teen years being able to simply open up and know all sorts of things about what a person was feeling or thinking or doing, she felt disarmed these days. Naked, and not in a good hot-demon-in-bed kind of way, but in a showing-up-to-work-undressed-and-being-laughed-at way.

"I want to reassure all of you that I'm doing everything I can to stop the . . . ah . . . the attacks on you. I will find out who's doing it, and I *will* make sure they're punished."

A ripple of interest moved through the crowd, and her spirits rose a little. "It's happening in other Meegras too. Not just to you."

"So if the others can't protect their *rubendas,* how are you going to protect us? You're not even a demon."

"Yes, when are you going to do the ritual?"

The words echoed in the cavernous space for a moment, bouncing off the wooden cabinetlike doors of their bedrooms and the incredibly high ceiling. Normally this house felt oddly peaceful, a happy place despite the human despair its inhabitants fed on. But now . . . the demons were angry. With her. With the Accuser for having bound them to her. At the unseen, unknown killer stalking them.

"We're not here to discuss that," she said, then, remembering what Roc had said, "I didn't come here to be questioned. I give my orders and you follow them."

A few of them seemed to settle down, either at her

strong tone or the words themselves. But unrest still hovered in the air.

"Do you doubt I have the power to protect you? Is that why you're going somewhere else?"

Murmurs. Mutterings. But none spoke up.

"I'm connected to you. You're connected to me." Her face reddened. She felt like a bad actor in a melodrama. But Rocturnus nodded slightly beside her and the numerous eyes glinting in the white light from the ceiling were trained on her. Bad melodrama was just the sort of thing they liked, along with sugary snacks and twee home decor. They were like vicious little old ladies in that way. "Any more of you leave and you'll all be—punished. Punished severely."

The crowd sighed and shifted a little. Shit, Roc was right. This was what they wanted. Did they know it was bullshit? That she didn't think she could bring herself to punish any one of them demon style? The only example of such treatment she'd seen had turned her stomach; she still woke up some nights alone in her bed with the image of Greyson's bloody back in her mind, with the sound of the whip echoing in her ears.

What she could do, though, was hit them with her power. The telekinetic ability Tera had taught her didn't always work; in fact, it hadn't been working very well at all of late. Tera said it was because despite Megan's abilities being so closely aligned to those of witches, she wasn't a witch. She simply didn't have the genetic power.

Megan suspected it was more than that, but she didn't want to think about it. She'd been doing very well with it before the Yezer Ha-Ra had connected to her.

Demons weren't telekinetic.

But she didn't need to move any solid objects here. She just needed to let them know how strong she was, how capable. And since they were bound to her, it would be easy.

Deep inside her was a door and behind it lurked her power. Lurked the piece of demon lodged in her chest. Lurked the anger and the fear and—her heart pounded in her chest, red heat spreading from it through her body. In her mind the door bulged and shook, wanting, waiting, ready to—

She opened it.

For the first time since the night she'd been bound to them she opened it and power, shiny bright and cold-hot, burst from it, into her, through her, filling the room.

The little demons screamed in unison. Megan screamed too, but whether it was from triumph or fear she didn't know. All she knew was her throat ached, her head fell back, and before she could stop it she was pulling the energy back in, pulling it in mixed with theirs, her body acting of its own accord just like the last seconds before an orgasm—

Their power thrust itself into her. Every bit of misery they caused, every shameful thought and deed that fed them, ran through her mind like a triple-speed film played on the backs of her eyelids.

And it was *wrong,* it was so wrong because it felt good, it felt better than anything, it was power and danger and food and sex and everything she'd ever wanted, and it filled her until she thought she might explode.

"No!" She fell, crouching herself into a ball, trying to fight. The door had to close, the flames inside her had to recede, had to, because if she stayed like this much longer she might decide never to stop it, she might go ahead and— "No!"

With a final, almighty mental shove, she slammed the door shut, locking it tight, and just before she realized she'd fled the Yezer and gone back to her house something came to her, words that turned her shivers into quakes of terror though she didn't know what they meant.

Ktana Leyak.

"Megan, are you sitting down?"

It was so much like Roc's question the night before that she shivered and gripped the phone more tightly. "Yes."

"Gerald Caroll died."

Megan bit her lip. She almost said "I know" before she remembered she wasn't supposed to know. "Gerald?"

"Yes, your client Gerald." Althea Sprite's voice, full of compassion, made Megan want to cry. Althea was, at this point, the only one of her practice partners—except Neil Fawkes, and that was simply because Neil didn't have an opinion about anything—who didn't turn away from her in disgust when she spoke up at their weekly meetings. Her radio show had not made her popular with them.

Megan knew she was holding on to her membership

in the group by a thread and that one of these days it would likely break.

So why not just leave? a voice said in her head. It sounded suspiciously like a certain demon she knew.

Because I don't want to leave, because I worked hard to build that practice, because it's something I'm good at . . .

"Megan, are you okay?"

"Yeah, I'm just—how? Who told you?"

"The police called the service; they found an appointment in his diary but it didn't have your name on it. The service called me and I said I'd call you."

"Did they say how . . . it happened?"

"Heart attack, looked like," Althea said. "They can't be sure, of course, until the autopsy. The police want to meet you at the office tomorrow morning, to get a look at his file."

"But they know I can't just show anybody those records, it's—"

"They're bringing his next of kin. So technically you're not."

"That's fine." Her voice shook a little. Next of kin. Gerald had a sister, she remembered.

"Are you going to be okay? Do you want some company?"

Althea, despite being the closest thing Megan had had to a friend until Tera entered her life, had never offered to come to Megan's house before.

Then again, Megan had never had a patient die on her before, had she?

"I think I'll be all right. I just . . ." She took a deep breath. "I feel like it was my fault."

"It wasn't your fault, honey. It was just his time to go. Sometimes it's fast and sometimes it takes a long time, but when it's your time to go there's nothing anyone can do."

Megan tried to take comfort in this, but somehow the idea that Gerald's end via demonic possession— whether it had caused a heart attack or had taken his life in some other, more sinister fashion—had been written in the stars just didn't hold true for her.

"Yeah. Well. Thanks for calling me, Althea. Did the police say when they'd be there tomorrow?" With her luck it would probably be the same ones who'd busted her on Friday.

"They asked if nine was okay, but I told them eight's better, that way there aren't any clients in the office."

"Great."

"And, honey . . . I feel just awful springing this on you at a time like this, but . . ."

"Just say it, Althea. Don't worry."

"The partners . . . that is, some of us . . ."

"Which means everyone but you, right?"

Althea cleared her throat. "Some of us want to talk to you. About what happened Friday."

"Do you mean my interrupting a session?" Did Althea's refusal to answer mean she was included in this group this time? When the partners had suspended her three months before, Althea had been the holdout. She'd been the only one purely on Megan's side. Was she not any more?

"Well, yes. And the, ah, arrest."

"Jesus, does everyone in the city know about that?"

"Someone called us."

"Someone?"

"She didn't give a name. Just said you were in jail. By the time I got there, though, you'd been let go."

"Nobody pressed charges," Megan said. "It was a mistake." Who the hell had called her office to tell them she'd been arrested? Nobody knew about that. Nobody but the arresting officers, Greyson, Hunter Kyle, and . . .

And whoever it was who'd made that phone call about the supposed body and tipped the cops off to begin with.

Not to mention probably all of Vergadering, but the chances they would have involved themselves in something as mundane as this were slim to none. Tera said they weren't investigating, so the idea that they would have been responsible for an anonymous phone call to get Megan in trouble at work was really stretching it.

"Honey, I just want to warn you. I'm sure the police thing was just a big misunderstanding. But you know one of the things that makes our practice different is the way we organize things and, well, ever since you started that radio show you haven't been very organized. We had to suspend you for that one week, then you took two weeks off, and now it seems you're taking long weekends almost every month . . . we just don't feel like your heart's in the practice anymore."

"Are you . . ." Her throat felt like someone had filled it with glue. "Am I being asked to leave?"

Pause. "We just want you to think about whether you really want to stay. If you still want to make that kind of commitment to us."

Funny. Everyone seemed to want her to make some kind of commitment to them these days. Everyone except, of course, Greyson Dante.

Two minor domestic disputes, one rebellious teenager, one disgruntled employee, and a woman who didn't know if she should accept a marriage proposal from a "reformed" felon later, Megan was just taking her last call of the night on her radio show when it happened. Again.

As my-name-is-Pat started telling her about an issue with her mother, Megan opened her shields to read. This had actually become much easier to do over the phone than in person lately, she'd noticed, in large part because so many of the Yezer felt the need to show themselves during appointments, especially when clients described feelings of misery or doubt. They'd nod and wink and wave, expecting Megan to cheer them, she guessed.

She *had* guessed. Now she wondered if they were taunting her instead. Although given what had happened in their home the night before, she doubted they'd be taunting her again anytime soon.

So, relieved that there weren't any little demon faces looking at her, Megan lowered her shields, just as she had for her first ten callers, and reached out.

And got nothing.

It didn't make sense. My-name-is-Pat, whose real name was of course probably not anything like Pat, had the trembly, shaky kind of voice Megan associated with people who were easy to read. Nerves opened them up, as a rule. So did adrenaline, fear . . . the closer to victim-hood people were, the easier it was to break through the weak shields most carried instinctively.

"But she just doesn't seem to appreciate anything I do for her," my-name-is-Pat said. "All she does is criti-cize. And she tells my children she doesn't care about them."

Megan leaned forward in her chair as if she could somehow get closer to the woman by doing so. Why wasn't she getting anything? She'd never not been able to read someone, unless . . . Unless they weren't human. She couldn't read demons.

My-name-is-Pat didn't sound like a demon, and Megan couldn't think of a single reason why a demon would call her show and pretend to be just another human seeking advice. But there was no other explana-tion for it. Either my-name-is-Pat was a demon, or . . .

Or she was possessed by one.

"Pat, this seems to be causing a lot of stress for you," Megan said. "How have you been sleeping?"

Flying blind was definitely not her favorite thing to do, and whatever she knew about demon possession she'd learned from B movies. But she imagined it would be something like Dissociative Identity Disorder, so she came at it from that angle.

"Oh, I seem to fall asleep anywhere," warbled my-name-is-Pat. "What difference does that make?"

"Do you think you're sleeping too much?"

"I didn't know you could get too much sleep. Is that, like, a medical problem?"

Just answer the damned question! "So are you just falling asleep at odd moments or places? You said you seem to fall asleep anywhere."

"Well, sometimes I sit down and the next thing I know it's several hours later." Nervous laugh. "But I'm not getting any younger, you know! We start to need more sleep as we age."

Given that the woman was probably barely forty, Megan rolled her eyes. Still . . . she shifted in her seat. The woman was losing time and couldn't be read. Something was definitely wrong here, and it was a lot more than just a disapproving mother. Hell, Megan's own mother hadn't spoken to her in ten years, unless you counted curt little Christmas cards printed complete with signature facsimile—"Happy Holidays from Diane and Dave"—as talking. Megan didn't.

"Have you been to a doctor? About your sleeping?" What to tell my-name-is-Pat? "You're probably possessed by some sort of demon" just didn't seem right, somehow. Aside from the fact that Megan had no idea how to treat it or take care of it or anything. Greyson had said all that God versus the Devil stuff ceased being relevant centuries ago, and there wasn't even a Hell anymore.

So Megan did the cowardly thing, the only thing she could. She told my-name-is-Pat to give her mother a break and remember how hard the old woman's life must have been. She told her to take vitamins and get some exercise and to cut down on time with her mother if it upset her so much. She told her everything she would have told any client in the same situation, and hoped for her sake this had nothing to do with the red shape behind Gerald's eyes before he'd leaped at her Friday night.

Her cell phone rang just as she was nearing the turnoff for her neighborhood. Thankfully she was stopped at a light, because the damn thing had fallen so far into the bottom of her purse she would have run off the road while hunting for it.

"Hello?"

"It was lost in your purse, wasn't it?" Greyson's voice was sexy and intimate even over the phone. Megan wondered how he managed it.

She laughed. "Maybe."

"I'd buy you a big heavy chain to attach to it, but you'd probably manage to choke yourself with it if I did."

"Probably."

"What are you doing now?"

"Heading home. Are you—"

"Why don't you come here?"

"Where, the house or your apartment?" She preferred the apartment, honestly. More anonymous, less crowded, and with a much better view. But he spent so much time at the Ieureanlier these days, and with Templeton Black gone, it made sense for him to spend most nights there.

"Actually, I'm at Mitchell's."

"Mitchell like a guy, or Mitchell's the—"

"Restaurant, yes. Come over. I'll buy you dinner."

"Haven't you eaten?"

"Earlier. Come on. I'd like to see you before I leave and this way you can have something to eat."

If she waited she could probably get him to say please, and she did love it when he said please. But she wanted to talk to him anyway. After everything that had happened, after her visit to the Yezer and Althea's phone call and my-name-is-Pat . . .

Actually, she probably didn't want to tell him about Althea's phone call, now that she thought about it. But everything else, she did. More than that, he *should* know about it. If the answers weren't already lurking in that twisty mind of his, he'd find them somewhere else.

"Okay," she said. "Just let me stop off and change, okay? I'm not exactly dressed for Mitchell's."

"I'm sure you look fine."

"I'm wearing jeans and a big T-shirt."

"Ah. Put on the dress Mr. Santo gave you yesterday then."

"I—how did you know—oh, of course. Malleus, right?"

His laugh caressed her. "I know everything, *bryaela*. See you soon."

Chapter Six

She wished she hadn't offered to change. Especially not into a dress, because the temperature had dropped even further if that was possible. Just the short walk from the parking lot into the building numbed her legs.

The dimly lit interior of Mitchell's wrapped around her like the inside of a garnet, warm and filled with subtle sparkles from the candles on the tables. She'd never been there before, but she knew Greyson loved the place.

And no wonder. It smelled like every kitchen of childhood dreams and felt even more welcoming.

She stood by the door for a minute, feeling her muscles relax as heat seeped into them and enjoying the atmosphere. Movement in the corner of her eye made her turn her head in time to see a couple of little demons disappear. Good. They were keeping themselves hidden tonight. She slipped off her coat and draped it over her arm.

"Surely a lovely woman like yourself isn't dining alone?"

Megan turned, ready to say who she was and why she was here, but the words died on her lips.

It wasn't just that he was handsome, though he

definitely was. Straight dark hair fell casually over his smooth brow, and the candlelight bronzed his tawny skin.

It was the way his eyes glowed, faintly red at first, then when he picked up her hand and bent to give it a presumptuous kiss, brighter still.

At first Megan thought it was some sort of Pavlovian reaction. She'd grown so accustomed to seeing a man's eyes go red before . . . well, in the bedroom, or whatever place they happened to be substituting for a bedroom, that the mere sight of it often sent a shiver up her spine.

This was different. This man's gleaming eyes caught her, held her as surely as he still held her hand in his strong grasp, and before she knew what was happening her breasts were straining against her gown and her insides were turning to molten liquid and she *wanted* him, wanted him so bad she was ready to tackle him then and there and she didn't care about Greyson or anyone else in the restaurant—

Something slammed down hard, a shield of some kind, and another hand joined hers and the man's in midair.

"Hey, Nick, you want to give my girl a break?"

Greyson's tone was light, his smile easy, but the tightness of his jaw and the coldness in his eyes told her, and the man now dropping her hand as if it burned him, how far from amused he was.

My girl?

The man—Nick—glanced quickly from her, to Greyson, and back again. "This—this is *Megan*?

Oh, shit, man, I'm sorry. Megan, I'm sorry. I didn't know—he didn't tell me you were coming, so I didn't think—"

What was she supposed to say? "That's okay"? What was he apologizing for, anyway? What had just happened?

Nick's embarrassed grin seemed to mollify Greyson. He shrugged. "No problem." But he didn't usually grip Megan's shoulder quite so tightly, or pull her quite so close to his side. "Meg, this is Nick Xao-teng. Nick, Megan Chase."

"Great to meet you." Nick nodded and smiled, but didn't touch her again.

"You too," she managed, distressed to realize her voice was shaking a little.

"We were playing cards until you got here; you don't mind if I finish, do you?" Greyson followed Nick toward the back of the room, then, as Nick turned down a hall, pulled her aside.

"Are you okay?" His dark gaze searched her face, his hands tight on her upper arms.

"Yeah, I just . . . what happened?" *My girl?*

"Nick is half incubus."

"And . . ." Her blush had started to fade. Now it came back with a vengeance. "Oh. I'm sorry."

"You don't have any reason to be."

"But I—"

"It wasn't your fault." But his jaw was still tight. He looked away.

"I'm glad you came when you did," she said. He

might say she'd done nothing wrong and he might even believe it, but that didn't make her feel any less guilty for her last thoughts in that dizzying minute. She had no idea if he was dating anyone else or if he cared if she did, but being absolutely ready to have sex with one man while out with another was fairly sleazy no matter how casual the relationship was or what sort of demon-sex thrall one was under. "How did you know—I mean—"

"I've seen that look on your face before," he said, and then he was kissing her, pressing her back against the wall, his body looming hot in front of her.

His hands roamed from her arms to her waist and around to her back, pulling her closer, while he urged her mouth open with his lips so his tongue could slide inside. He tasted of Scotch and cigars and lust, and she wanted more.

Megan gasped and wrapped her arms around him while heat burst in her body, the flames of his desire and hers mingling in her chest to make her movements almost frantic, to make her wrap her right leg around him in a desperate attempt to bring him even closer.

It went on for only a minute, maybe two, but when he pulled away they were both panting.

"*That* look," he said with satisfaction, and took her hand to lead her down the dark hallway while she used the other to smooth her dress.

The cheery, tingly feeling lasted while they entered a dim, smoke-filled room in the back where several men sat around a table piled high with bills. It lasted while he introduced her to everyone, sat her in his lap, and picked up his cards—and faded abruptly when she saw them.

Greyson was holding aces and eights—a dead man's hand.

The waiter set her plate in front of her and stepped smoothly away, leaving them alone again in the shadowy corner. She tried to let the fragrance of the steak soothe her, to let the excellent wine seep into her muscles and relax her, but it didn't.

"I didn't think you were superstitious," he said, watching her.

She shrugged. She hadn't thought she was either. "Just considering everything that's been going on . . ."

"Stop worrying. I'm not worried."

"How can I not be worried? The—the police are coming to my office tomorrow. To meet me. They want to see Gerald's file. I guess they think he might have killed himself."

"They can't make you—"

"They're bringing his sister. I do have to release it to her, or at least copies of it."

"I'll call Hunter. You should have a lawyer with you. Just in case."

"I thought you were my lawyer."

"Trust me, darling, the last thing you want when you're dealing with the boys in blue is me at your side. Don't give them more ammunition, not when you have a public image to protect."

It was the closest he'd ever come to answering outright a question she'd asked when they first met: "Are you in the Mafia?"

Strange as it seemed, she hadn't given the matter much thought since. She'd started compartmentalizing it, thinking of it simply as "demon business" and so not anything that involved her. Even her experience at the mall with Tera hadn't really concerned her, aside from the embarrassment.

But she hadn't thought about how it might affect her career. Obviously he had.

"Is that why you had Hunter come to the jail?"

"In part. But he wouldn't have been able to convince those homeowners to drop charges as easily as I could either, and that needed to be done. Although it wasn't exactly easy—that lady was tough. I thought for a minute I might actually have to pay her off."

"How nice that you didn't."

"Don't be sarcastic. It spoils the digestion."

She raised her eyebrows, but couldn't help smiling. The steak was delicious too, although something seemed off about it.

"What's wrong?"

"It's overdone."

"Really? I told them medium."

She cut a new piece and fed it to him off her heavy silver fork.

"Tastes like medium to me, Meg. That's the way you usually have it, so—"

Oh God. She did usually have her steak medium, he was right. And this was perfectly cooked.

So why then did she suddenly wish it wasn't? That it was bloody rare and red, the way he ate his?

"Must just have been the piece I had." She shoved another forkful into her mouth. "Yep, that's perfect."

"We can get you another one if—"

"No, no, it's great. Thanks. I think I'm just tired." Desperate to change the subject, she said, "So when will you be back?"

"Hmm? Late Wednesday, maybe, or Thursday, depending. Shall I just pick you up Saturday afternoon? Cart you off to my lair?"

"Your lair?"

"Oh, it's a lair. It qualifies. It's secluded, it's secret, and I do private things there."

She blushed. "Will you have your car back?"

"We're taking the truck anyway. In case it snows."

They were spending the entire week of Christmas at his Meegra's cabin in the woods outside the city. Greyson didn't actually celebrate Christmas, of course, but most demons treated it as a winter holiday just the same.

The first time he'd taken her onto the land she hadn't even known the cabin was there, but it was, and she loved it. Almost as much as she loved the fact that, for the first time in years, she actually had plans at Christmas, real plans that didn't involve her tagging along at Althea's family celebration or watching movies by herself at home.

Althea. She didn't want to think about that now.

"What's wrong?"

"I . . . I went to see my demons last night."

"And?"

She shook her head. "I heard something. It felt like a name, but I don't know if it was, or if it was just words."

"What was it?"

"Ktana Leyak."

If she hadn't been watching so closely she wouldn't have noticed the tiny pause as he lifted his wineglass to his lips. "Interesting. How did you hear it?"

"Are you ever going to just tell me what you're thinking?"

"What do I get if I do?"

"Me not being mad at you. How's that?"

He smiled. "If you put it that way. The words ring a few bells. 'Ktana' means 'queen.' "

"And 'leyak'?"

"It's a type of demon. Not generally a very dangerous or warlike type. It poses much more of a threat to humans than other demons."

"But I am human."

"Hmm." She thought she saw his gaze flicker to her half-eaten steak. "How did you hear that phrase, anyway? Did Roc tell you?"

"No." She gave him a quick rundown of what had happened, eliminating the part where she used the full strength of her power but telling him how the words had popped into her head as she returned home. "I meant to Google it but I haven't gotten around to it."

It was surprising how much information could be found online, how many people in the world knew the truth or brushed up against it, and how many other people didn't believe them. Megan wondered sometimes just how unique she was after all.

He shrugged. "Don't worry about it. I'll see what I can find. You done?"

It took her a minute to realize he meant her food, and she nodded. She hadn't even eaten half of it, but she didn't want the rest, nor did she want the potato or asparagus. The discussion about how it had been cooked and the reminder of yet another new idiosyncrasy, and what it probably meant, wasn't something she wanted to think about.

Service at Mitchell's was certainly fast enough. It seemed to take no time at all before the check was "taken care of"—she suspected the meal had been on the house—Greyson's friends had been bid good-bye, and they were at her doorstep.

"Are you coming in?"

"I can't." He kissed her forehead. "It's almost midnight already. I have to be up at five."

One of the best things about dating a fire demon was how warm he always was, although she suspected that would turn into a definite downside in the summer. If they were still seeing each other then. His comment earlier about her public image . . . She pushed it from her mind.

One of the other best things . . . well, maybe they weren't all such good kissers. She and Greyson stayed on her porch for a few more minutes, saying a leisurely and mostly silent good night, before she finally pulled away. "Have a good trip," she said.

"I'll call you when I get back. And if you need anything call me, or Maleficarum if I don't answer." He paused. "I'm leaving Malleus here. He'll be over in the morning."

She opened her mouth to protest, but decided against it. *Assassination attempt, remember?* "Thanks."

One last kiss, like a faint breeze over her lips, and he stepped back to watch her slip inside the house. She wished he hadn't decided to go. Some nights she liked having her bed all to herself, but this wasn't one of them.

She'd just shrugged off her coat when she heard a key scraping in the lock and turned to see Greyson opening the door.

"Fuck it," he said, striding across the room to take her in his arms. "I can sleep on the plane."

"This is Gerald's file." She handed the photocopies in their new manila folder to Maureen Boehm, Gerald's pale and pink-eyed sister. The woman's pain colored the air and beat against Megan's skin, even with her shields up as far as they would go.

Usually she only felt anger like that, and then only demon anger. Unhappiness like this she could shut off completely—had to be able to if she wanted to do her job.

Megan turned her attention to Detective Walters, cool and silent next to the shaky Mrs. Boehm. Walters had the sort of stocky confidence Megan associated with cops, especially those who'd been on the job for a few years. She wondered for the first time if cops developed shields like hers, if somehow without realizing it they covered themselves up and tried to dissociate themselves from the emotions of the people they dealt with.

It wouldn't have surprised her. Most good cops had some psychic ability themselves, though they never realized it. That was one reason she didn't read them.

Not that she often had the chance. She hadn't been around this many policemen in this short a period of time in fifteen years.

"Please let me know if there's anything else I can do, Detective," she said. "And Mrs. Boehm, I'm so sorry." Her voice shook. Mrs. Boehm would never know how sorry Megan really was. "Gerald was a very sweet, kind man. I liked him."

"Thank you." The woman turned to go, her tightly curled brownish hair in its stiff helmet, making her head look oddly like a mushroom from behind, then stopped. Before Megan knew what was happening, Mrs. Boehm threw herself at Megan, the file pressed between them and her free hand clutching Megan's arm so hard Megan thought she would bruise.

"Why did he do it? Why did he do it? I knew he was unhappy, but . . ." The words became unintelligible, then turned into sobs.

Megan's heart twisted. This was her fault, all her fault; because of her, Gerald had been targeted. Whatever it was that wanted to get to Megan had used him and his poor body couldn't stand the pressure.

"I don't think he did, ma'am," Megan said. "For what it's worth, I—"

"Megan." Hunter, sitting calmly in the corner, straightened up a bit. His warning was clear: *Don't say things like that.*

But she couldn't help it. Not when this woman was

so brokenhearted and Megan could offer her some sort of assurance. She knew the investigation would finally rule natural causes. That would comfort Gerald's sister—when the result came back, which could be several weeks away. Megan wanted her to feel better now. Itched to make her feel better now, with an urgency she realized stemmed from some unnameable discomfort.

"You don't?" Mrs. Boehm straightened up and turned her big, watery brown eyes to Megan's, and before Megan knew what was happening her shield dropped, just a little, like a reflex she couldn't control. The other woman's pain washed over her, cold and wet, and slid through Megan's skin, down her throat, into her pores.

It filled her up, filled her the same way the personal demons' power had filled her two days before. Lights sparked behind her eyes; she had to force herself not to smile. Mrs. Boehm tasted so good, that unhappiness, so rich and thick, like nectar—

Suppressing a scream, Megan pulled herself back. Her chest ached like she'd just run a marathon, her palms felt sweaty, her skin cold.

If anyone else noticed what had happened, they didn't indicate it. She forced herself to smile reassuringly, as if her life as she knew it wasn't ending. "I don't," she said. "And he loved you. He talked about you often."

Mrs. Boehm started crying again; Megan could barely understand her thanks as she and the detective left the office. Megan stood for a minute, breathing in through her nose, out through her mouth, until her heart slowed its frantic beating.

"I'm so sorry you had to go through that, Megan."

Hunter stood up and came closer to her but not too close, as if he wasn't sure what he should be doing. His hand fell heavy on her shoulder. "Are you okay?"

She paused. "Could you wait here for me, please? And get me some boxes from the storeroom next door?"

"Of course."

Megan took a deep breath, blinked back her tears, and walked down the hall to tell her partners she was quitting.

Chapter Seven

From the outside, Vergadering headquarters looked like any other office building, with its 1970s brick facade and large reflective windows. The plastic-letter directory board in the foyer listed several different businesses, but Megan suspected they were only dummies.

She reached for the handset of the pay phone mounted on the wall, waited for the dial tone, and hit 8843, just as Tera had told her to when she'd called earlier, depressed and lonely.

"Tera Green."

"Hi, it's me, I'm downstairs."

"Okay, I'll be right there."

Megan waited, glancing out the glass door to see Malleus still sulking on the sidewalk outside. He'd refused to even enter the building, despite the cold. And if she were honest, she hadn't really wanted him to. He'd been very kind, more than kind, all morning as he and Hunter helped clear out her office. He'd even given her the world's most awkward hug—the first time aside from actually saving her life that he'd touched her to do more than magically set her lipstick.

Too bad he'd made himself uncomfortable for nothing. The ache in her chest couldn't be healed with a hug.

Somehow, without Megan realizing it, she'd become such a danger to her clients that she could no longer involve herself with them.

Because her involvement could get them killed. Because that piece of demon inside her chest, the piece she'd been trying to deny, wanted to feed off their pain. Just like it wanted to feed on rare steak or Greyson's blood or the hot red energy from couples making out in dark corners—

She shook her head, shook her shoulder, pushing it away. She was still in control, wasn't she? That's why she'd quit her job. If the demon was in charge she would have stayed, right? Would have treated her clients like a fucking smorgasbord and licked her fingers afterward.

No. She was in control. She, Megan Alison Chase. Human being.

"Hey." The door behind her opened. Tera's blue eyes scanned Megan up and down. "You look like shit."

"Thanks."

"No, seriously. You really do."

Megan nodded. "Yes, thank you, Tera. Am I coming in, or—"

Tera hesitated. "I—"

"Oh, oh, right, of course. I can't, can I? Because of the demon thing."

Tera smiled as if the sarcasm had passed right over her head. Which it probably had. "Thanks for understanding."

They were halfway to the parking lot and Megan's little Focus when Tera stopped. "Shit! I forgot to—I forgot to sign something, and it needs to be done by three. It'll only take me a second, do you mind?"

Megan shrugged. "Go ahead."

Malleus scowled as they watched Tera retreat. "Just like a witch," he said. "Ain't got 'er mind on 'er work."

"Now, Malleus, Tera is—"

"I know what she is, m'lady, and you oughta too. Mr. Dante says it's none of our mind 'oo you're friends with, but me an' Lif an' Spud, we don't fink—m'lady?"

Megan barely heard him. The Vergadering building loomed over an alley on its right, and at the end of the alley rested a black sedan, gleaming in the lone ray of hard winter sunlight sneaking between Vergadering and the lower roof of the strip mall next door.

Surely she was seeing things. It couldn't be the same car. Logically it couldn't be, whether it had been witches chasing them or not. But it drew her just the same, and she started toward it before she had time to think.

"M'lady, where you going?"

She didn't look back. Tera would be out in a couple of minutes and she wanted to get a look at that car.

The tires weren't even dusty yet. The windshield still had a sticker on it. New black paint shone. It was the same sedan, had to be.

Greyson would be royally pissed when he found out they'd gotten their car back before he had his Jag.

She reached out to touch it, to see if she could get some kind of reading from it. She'd never been able to do it before . . . But she knew someone who could.

He'd probably get nothing, just as she did now. The smooth, slick surface of the hood yielded no secrets.

Witches, like demons, were generally unreadable, although not quite as much so. But there was something else Brian Stone could help her with. She dug in her purse for a pen.

"What're you doing? You come away from 'ere before somebody sees you." Malleus reached for her arm, then pulled back.

"I'm taking this car's license plate number."

Malleus looked puzzled.

"I think—" No. Who knew what his reaction would be if she shared her suspicions? She didn't know if Greyson had mentioned witches in connection with the car chase or not. Better to let it go. "Just never mind. It'll only take a second."

Quickly she scribbled the number on the back of an old receipt and tucked it into the zippered interior pocket of her bag, then strode back up the alley with Malleus trailing behind like a bulky, disapproving shadow.

They met Tera just as she hit the parking lot, and headed off for lunch with a new secret worry buzzing in Megan's head. If witches were involved—Vergadering witches—what did that mean?

"Did you get the address?"

"Yes. Can I take my coat off before I give it to you?"

"No. Come on, I want to go there."

Brian followed her back out the door—trailed by Malleus and, though Brian couldn't see him, Rocturnus. Roc tended to creep Brian out. He didn't like the reminder of what hovered by his head.

They all piled into Megan's car, Malleus squeezing himself into the backseat with a grumble. "Shouldn't be doin' this."

Part of Megan agreed. This probably wasn't a good idea. But she'd just left her job, the practice she'd worked so hard to build up, and if she wanted to do something dangerous she was going to fucking do it. Why not? Who cared? What difference did it make what she did?

"So what's so important?" Brian asked as Megan pulled out onto the street.

"Never mind." She glanced at the slip of paper he'd given her. "Just come on. I need you to try and read a car."

"Are you serious?"

"No, Brian, I'm playing a practical joke on you. Of course I'm serious. Would we be out in the freezing cold if I wasn't serious?"

"What do you expect me to get off a car?"

"I don't know. Anything might help. You can read inanimate objects, right? Connect with them?"

She knew he could. He'd once used a wristwatch to communicate with Greyson.

"I can connect with my own stuff. It has to be around me for a while before I can use it." Seeing her glare, he continued quickly, "But yes, I can read inanimate objects. Sometimes."

"Good. So we go to this address, you read the car, and we decide where to go from there."

"Is this illegal, Megan?"

"Is touching a car against the law?"

"No, but—"

"It's not illegal. Why would we be doing something illegal?"

"Why did you break into a house last week?"

"I didn't *break in*; the door was unlocked, and—oh, never mind. The homeowners didn't press charges, anyway." She glanced at him. "I'm surprised you didn't call me. I imagine you found out about it, what, within five minutes of its happening?"

"About that. Turn here, I think."

She did. "How's Julie?"

Brian's girlfriend Julie was a police officer. Megan was fairly certain she was the one who'd traced the plates, but she didn't want to say anything outright.

Since the week Brian had been assigned to write a profile of her for a gossipy local magazine, his reputation as a journalist had grown. Not from the profile, of course. That was a cheap puff piece, forgotten by the public as soon as it became birdcage liner. But because of his help in defeating the Accuser, who'd been posing as a mild-mannered local therapist named Arthur Bellingham. Megan and Brian had decided to cover the truth by concocting what Megan thought was a rather ridiculous tale about Bellingham's secret Satanism and his using his therapy group to conduct mysterious rituals.

The fake story had, ironically, given Brian what he'd long desired: real journalistic integrity and a reputation for finding a good story. Now he was a full-time staff reporter for the city's biggest daily newspaper.

Too bad, in a way. If Brian hadn't been so—well, so nosy—Megan could have told him what was going on.

If he hadn't been so straight-laced she still might have considered it, but he made no secret of his disapproval of her involvement with demons. Like Tera, he understood she had no choice when it came to the Yezer Ha-Ra. The others, though . . .

"She's fine, thanks," Brian said. "Looks like she might be in line for a promotion. Working a big investigation at the moment, so if it pans out, she'll be in."

"How great, tell her I hope she gets it."

"Tell her yourself. We're spending Christmas Eve together, you could come over too."

"Can't. Thanks, though."

They chatted about Julie and her work and Brian's next story for a few minutes while Megan navigated the cold, silent streets. Christmas lights and decorations sparkled on most houses they drove past, giving their casual conversation a festive air. Christmas always felt like secrets and excitement to Megan, even though it had been years since she'd had a holiday filled with either.

Four-twenty-seven Old Barle loomed in front of them, a large apartment building in a rundown part of town. The area was just starting to be gentrified; here and there rainbow flags flew, but for the most part it was still shabby and dark, a street full of graffiti and car parts.

Their breath puffed clouds of white into the air as they slid silently out of the car, closing the doors with careful hands.

For a minute, Megan thought the sedan wasn't there and silently cursed herself. She hadn't wanted to try

Vergadering first, assuming they'd have guards and eyes on the street at all hours. Maybe that was a mistake.

Then she saw it, parked about half a block down in front of a boarded-up house. She grabbed Brian's arm and pointed. He nodded. Malleus glowered.

Keeping to the shadows, they sneaked along the sidewalk, avoiding bottles and debris as they went. Brian stripped off his glove and put his hand on the car.

A minute went by. Two. Brian shook his head. "I'm getting a lot of stuff about the people who fixed it recently," he whispered. "Tires, bodywork, radiator and engine, paint job. But nothing about anyone who drove it. Sorry."

"I didn't think you would." So Greyson had been right, not that she'd doubted him. They were witches.

But as far as she knew, all witches strictly obeyed Vergadering rules. So why would two witches have been trying to kill them?

Unless another demon/witch war was about to break out, which she simply didn't believe. Tera would have mentioned it. Wouldn't she?

"Can we go now? You promised me hot buttered rum if I got the address for you."

"Megan." A little tug at her sleeve.

She sighed. "Yeah, I guess. At least I—"

"Megan." Another tug, harder this time. She glanced down.

Rocturnus stood next to her on the street, his eyes wide with terror, his finger outstretched to point to another Yezer stumbling toward them in the middle of the road.

Even at a distance she knew something was wrong. It—the little demon—wasn't walking right. Its limbs jerked oddly, as if it was trying to take bigger steps than its body would allow. The movements of its hands reminded her of Gerald and the terrible scuttling movements he'd made in the storeroom. Its skin rippled, the movements in the moonlight horribly like roaches crawling.

"Megan?" Brian sounded very far away. "What's going on, Megan?"

She had to force her mouth to work. "A demon."

"A—oh, damn it! I should have known. What are you mixing me up in this time? I should be—"

"Shut up, Brian." Malleus kept trying to move in front of her, to usher her back to her car, but she resisted. The little demon kept moving, getting closer, its eyes glowing red, like the traffic light blinking on and off at the end of the deserted street.

She took a step forward. She thought she knew what was happening, was certain she knew, and resisted the urge to cringe. Any minute the explosion would come. Any minute the street would be covered in blood and body parts, steaming in the icy air.

"This doesn't feel right," Brian said, in a different voice. "Megan, this feels really off."

He was right. She felt it too, even with her shields up. The temperature around them seemed to have dropped a good ten degrees. She pulled her coat closer, but took another step.

The little demon's grin stretched across its face. Too wide, like someone had carved a bastard smile into the flesh of its cheeks. "The human." Its voice echoed in her ears. Not a Yezer voice, but deeper, louder, with a lilt her mind identified as feminine even though she didn't know how or why. Deep in her chest something fluttered, moved, the frantic beating of a second heart trying to burst out.

A can blew down the street, clanking against the concrete. Megan jumped. She heard Brian gasp beside her. Bless him. He probably hated her right now for dragging him into this but he was standing with her just the same, his strong upper arm pressing against her shoulder.

"Who is it, Roc?" she whispered. "Do you know?"

"Smealtus," he replied. "I think."

"M'lady, we need to go," Malleus said. Megan glanced at him, but he wasn't looking at the little demon. He was looking behind him and to the left, and when Megan followed his gaze she saw two men in black coats and ski masks emerging from the apartment building they'd passed.

The apartment building whose address was on the registration of the black sedan. She lowered her shields and reached out, hoping against hope she was wrong, but she received nothing at all from them.

"Megan." Brian grabbed her arm. "I really think we should go now." Panic laced his voice, transmitted itself to her with her shields down.

Malleus yelled and leaped behind her, shoving Brian sideways. Brian fell on the concrete between two parked cars, his outraged curse unnaturally loud in Megan's ears as time seemed to slow down.

The witches reached into their coats, their movements identical, and produced guns, long and black and terrible.

Megan jumped back, like trying to run through syrup, and almost stumbled over Roc.

Smealtus opened his arms wide, then wider. His head fell back, his mouth stretching in a scream she couldn't hear.

The report of a gunshot. Megan screamed and tried to duck, her arms instinctively rising to cover her head as her knees hit the street. Pain shot up her thighs. The sound of the shot echoed off the dead buildings crouching along the street.

Another sound, a soft, wet thud, as Smealtus exploded.

Chapter Eight

Something hard slammed against Megan's back at the same time Rocturnus gripped her hand and pulled. She ended up on her side in the middle of the road, her face turned toward the spot where Smealtus had spent the last seconds of his life.

A shape, large and black and many limbed, rose from the pavement, slithering into the air, expanding as it grew.

Megan didn't need Malleus's hands circling her waist to lift her or Roc's tug to get up and move. Another gunshot rent the air. Malleus grunted but did not stop moving.

Together they dove behind a van. Blood dripped from Smealtus down Megan's forehead and cheek. More stained her coat, made Malleus's thick jacket slippery and Rocturnus look like an oversize newborn.

The van shook with every bullet puncturing its side, the gunshot echoed by the smaller pop of bullets against metal. The witches were coming.

"Brian's on the other side of the road!"

Her scream was drowned out by male voices, loud, terrified. Megan tried to peek around the van. Malleus grabbed her, tried to force her back down to the grubby sidewalk, but she managed to slip away as Rocturnus disappeared.

More shots, in rapid succession. Megan peered over the hood and saw the witches, not looking at her now, but staring down the road, emptying their guns.

Brian huddled in the same spot where he'd fallen. His mouth opened, but Megan couldn't hear him. She didn't know if the shots had deafened her or if it was the pure, cold terror invading her body, seeping through her clothing, making that heart-which-wasn't-hers pound and shift and writhe in her chest until it hurt.

The witches were shooting at a demon. She knew that's what it had to be, but she'd never seen anything like this before.

It was enormous, big enough to block out the moon, to block out all hope. Arms sprouted from its body at random. It was like a Three Mile Island spider standing upright, a caricature of anything living, with a woman's face and breasts and horrible, mottled flesh that squirmed and quaked and rippled.

Here and there bullets entered its body, leaving gaping holes that were instantly healed, each one with a faint clinking sound it took Megan a moment to realize was the bullets being ejected and hitting the street.

She couldn't breathe, couldn't think. Her mouth fell open and cold air whistled into it, down to her lungs to freeze her chest.

The thing moved jerkily, carefully, as if each step hurt. Three legs supported it, as far as she could tell, thick dark red legs ending in clawed, pawlike feet. As she watched the feet shrank, became human. The arms were sucked back into the body—there was no other way for her to describe it—until the monstrous thing on the street was simply a woman. Only the disgustingly distorted color of its skin and the fact that it—she—was naked gave lie to her appearance.

The witches stood their ground for another moment. Megan could almost feel their shock, knew they kept shooting because their minds refused to accept that shooting didn't work.

The demon woman's eyes, bright green and staring, narrowed. Her head tilted to the side. Megan could barely see Brian huddled on the ground across the street, his lips moving in what she assumed was prayer. Behind him Rocturnus tugged at his coat, struggling to pull Brian into safety, out of sight—if such a thing were possible.

"We need to go," Malleus whispered, tugging her arm almost out of its socket. "M'lady, we need to go now!"

"I can't leave Brian!" The whisper turned into a scream, a scream she knew she shouldn't have let out, as the demon woman leaped forward, her arms and legs somehow closing in and then expanding, and knocked the head off one of the witches with a single smooth stroke of her slender slithering arm.

The body fell. She picked up the head, looked at it thoughtfully, and dropped it on the ground with a dull thud.

The other witch screamed and tried to run, slipping in the first witch's blood, but she caught him easily, her arms winding around him and pulling him close, forcing him to his knees.

"A witch," she said, and her voice made Megan shake even harder. The demon woman sounded like . . . a woman. Any woman. Light and airy, as if she were asking for shoes in a different size.

Her hand stroked the witch's face, then lifted off his ski mask. His screams grew hoarse, his eyes bulged with fear. Megan couldn't tear her gaze away, much as she wanted to.

The man writhing on his knees on the ground had tried to kill her twice. He'd shot Greyson. But nothing, nothing in the world, meant he deserved to have the demon woman's hand drive itself into his chest, deserved to have his still-beating heart ripped from his body and held high in the air.

She didn't see what happened next. Malleus threw her over his shoulder and started running with his legs bent, keeping himself ducked down. How his feet managed to move so silently over the gritty pavement she didn't know, or perhaps it was just that she couldn't hear anything over the never-ending shrieks of terror in her head. All she knew was they rushed past the cars and started to cross the street, Malleus clearly hoping to cross back to Brian—back to her car—before the demon realized it.

Where they would go from there she had no idea. The demon hadn't been moving very quickly, but that didn't mean she couldn't.

The ground shook. The demon had slammed her fist down on the street. Malleus stumbled, knocking Megan's hip painfully against the trunk of the car they'd slipped behind. He righted himself just before they hit the ground and flipped her back over, yanking her down in the same motion so they crouched just a few cars away from Brian and Roc.

Brian seemed to have regained control of himself. He motioned her over, keeping himself in the smallest possible ball behind a beat-up Escort.

"Human," the demon woman said. Her voice reached right into Megan's soul and vibrated there. "You have something that belongs to me. I want it back."

Brian shook his head. "Don't," he mouthed, his brows knitted. "Don't."

Malleus tightened his grip on her arm.

Roc's entire body shook. His eyes were squeezed shut.

"I know you're back there, little human."

A creak, then the twisting crunch of metal as the demon woman picked up the Toyota Megan and Malleus hid behind and tossed it away as if it were an empty box. The car landed on another across the street with a brittle crash. Glass flew everywhere and sparkled on the street, oddly festive in the icy pale moonlight.

Megan, exposed like a child playing hide-and-seek badly, cringed into Malleus. He pushed her sideways, stepping in front of her, rising to his full height with his arms ready at his sides.

Roc took her hand, and Megan realized in that moment how stupid she'd been. She had no hope of defeating this demon by herself. Malleus didn't either, she knew. But with Brian and the power of the Yezer behind her—the power she'd learned only days before she could still harness and reach—she had a chance.

The demon woman's hands came toward her, the fingers still coated with witch's blood. Megan closed her eyes against the sight, found the door inside herself, and opened it.

Power flared in her body, greenish-blue sparks that sizzled along her skin and nerve endings. But nowhere near where it had been before, nowhere near the all-consuming blast she'd felt Saturday night.

She tried again, focusing, concentrating all her might on it. Maybe she wasn't—

"M'lady!"

A shove. She fell against a chain-link fence and shifted sideways, caught by Brian, pulled away even as Malleus rose from the pavement, hoisted by one bloody demon hand.

Megan screamed. Brian held her tighter, trying to shove her toward her car, but Megan fought him, turned the feeble energy from her opened door into a weapon and crashed it into him, tears clouding the vision of Malleus being borne into the air, of his struggles calming as she turned those mesmeric green-light eyes on him . . .

Brian's arms convulsed around her as her psychic weapon made contact. "Shit!" She felt him fumble in her pocket, felt him let go, heard his footsteps as he ran away, but she couldn't care, couldn't even think about anything but Malleus.

At her feet rested a dusty wine bottle. She picked it up and threw it, aiming for the demon woman's chest, knowing the chances it would inflict any damage were slim to none.

Indeed it did nothing, smashing against the rotted-looking flesh but not even making the demon woman blink.

"Ye old bitch!" Malleus shouted. Light flashed off the edge of the blade Megan hadn't realized he had as he lifted it over his head and drove it into one of the glowing eyes.

The demon shrieked, her mouth opening impossibly wide, revealing several rows of foul teeth.

Megan picked up a brick off the ground, grateful for the first time that this street was already like a war zone, and flung it. It bounced off the demon's teeth, but her scream grew louder in acknowledgment. Triumph like sweet blood red wine flooded Megan's breast.

Tires squealed on the pavement. Brian spun Megan's car around, turning the headlights on high beam, aiming them right at the demon woman.

She turned, her eyes widening as the hood of the Focus sped toward her. Malleus pulled back his knife and raised it for another strike—

And fell to the ground just as the car whizzed past. The demon woman had disappeared, leaving the street silent and empty except for the dead.

"Hot buttered rum?"

"Sure, just hold the hot and the butter," Brian gasped, collapsing on the couch. "In fact, hold the glass and give me the whole fucking bottle."

Megan considered it for a minute, then obeyed, grabbing a bottle of bourbon for herself and whiskey for Malleus. Roc took a shot of crème de menthe and sipped it slowly, a habit that usually made her laugh. Tonight she didn't think she could find humor in a Chris Rock routine, let alone the curious drinking habits of a little green demon.

"M'lady." Malleus finished swallowing and rested the bottle on his knee. He'd drunk half of it in one long gulp. "You 'ave to call Mr.—"

"Don't even say it. Just don't."

His brows lowered. "You know you 'ave to tell 'im. You need to—"

"He's right, Megan." Rocturnus spoke so quietly she had to lean forward to hear him. "They all have to know."

"Who all? Why does anybody need to know—"

"Because she's hurt others, from other families." Roc finished his glass and poured another. "Because she'll keep doing it."

"You know who she is?"

"And so do you. You heard her name."

Ktana Leyak.

She opened her mouth, but Roc, eyes wide, held up a warning hand. "Don't say it, don't even think it."

"Why? Who is she, who was she?"

He sighed. His eyes closed. "She's our mother."

The phone rang.

For a moment Megan didn't even understand what it was. The sound, so normal, so everyday, didn't seem to fit into this conversation; it belonged to a different life in a world that hadn't become increasingly more insane over the last few months.

"What do you mean?" she asked Roc.

"Just what I said. She created us. She's our mother."

"So—"

"Are you going to answer that?" Brian's eyes were closed as he slumped back on the couch. With the bottle in one hand and his other hand on his chest he looked like a drunken fraternity boy.

"No, I don't think so." The bourbon was starting to spread its heat and false comfort through her body now, taking the edge off the deep chill.

"M'lady, you should—"

"So what does that mean, your mother, Roc? Why is she killing you, why is she killing other demons?"

He shook his head. "We don't know."

"Is it the ones who leave she's killing, or the ones who stay, or what? Why is she going after demons from other families?"

Megan's answering machine clicked on, then fell silent as her caller hung up.

"We can't tell," Roc said. "We don't really talk a lot as a rule, you know. It's not like we all sit down at the end of the day to have these little meetings you humans seem to enjoy so much."

From her purse came the sound of her cell phone. Damn it. She'd known it was him. Greyson was pretty much the only person who had that number except for Brian and Tera.

"Sorry if we try and communicate with each other," she snapped. This was too much, all too much. She just wanted to crawl into bed and go to sleep. For a week. She'd basically killed one of her clients, she'd lost her job, she'd lost another demon, from the look on Brian's face it was possible she'd lost one of her few friends, and now her damned—well, whatever he was—wanted her to talk to him. She was going to have to tell him what happened and he was not going to be pleased, and she thought if she had to deal with one more thing tonight she was going to start screaming. And keep screaming until they put her in a nice, quiet, padded room somewhere. Hey, straightjackets probably weren't as uncomfortable as they looked, right?

"Don't get snippy with me. I'm trying to help you."

Megan stared at him, trying to keep her anger from overflowing and leading her to do something she would regret. "I appreciate that, Roc," she said, enunciating each word carefully. "But I've asked you to tell me what's going on and you haven't. So do you think I have a right to be angry?"

Now Malleus's phone rang. Megan closed her eyes. She could refuse to answer her own phone but she couldn't stop Malleus from answering his. He didn't work for her. He worked for Greyson, and if he ignored Greyson's call she had no doubt he would be punished.

With a look that was half guilty, half defiant, Malleus picked up his phone and flipped it open. "Yeh," he said. "Yeh. Sorry, I— She's safe, she's right 'ere. We had a little trouble—the lady found the car, y'know, the one them witches—she wanted to—she said she'd go wifout me if I—Mr. Dante, please don't—" He cringed and held the phone out to Megan. "He wants to talk to you."

God damn it. How dare he call her up to yell at her, how dare he order her to the phone like she was his goddamned slave. She snatched the phone from Malleus. "Hello?"

"What's going on, Megan?"

That was a bad sign. He never called her Megan.

"Nothing," she said, trying to keep her voice light. She could practically feel his anger through the satellite connection. "Malleus told you, I found the car. Brian and I—"

"Brian?"

Deep breath. "Yes, Brian. He can read inanimate objects and you know I can't. So we went to see if we could get anything from the car."

He was quiet for so long she wondered if he'd hung up. Then he said, "Let me get this straight. Someone shot at us the other night. You saw the car you thought they were driving, so you grabbed the choirboy and ran over there to see if you could figure out who they were, after I asked you not to get involved, is that right?"

"Well—"

"And you thought that was a good idea."

She gritted her teeth. "No, I thought it was an incredibly stupid idea, that's why I did it. After all, that's what I do all the time, right? Stupid shit?"

"No, you don't," he snapped, echoing her own nasty tone, "which is why I can't figure out why the fuck you'd do something so reckless when you know how dangerous—"

"I don't know anything, because you haven't told me anything!"

"Jesus, I didn't think you would—"

"You lied to me, Greyson."

"What?"

"You lied to me. In the restaurant. I told you about—
I told you that name and you lied and pretended it was
nothing to worry about, didn't you?"

"I didn't pretend anything. I told you what I knew."

"You're *lying*! Again!"

"Why didn't you say the name just now?"

"Don't try to change the subject."

"I'm not trying to change anything. I say I didn't lie,
you say I did; we're at an impasse. But I would like you
to answer my question, please. Why didn't you say the
name? You said it in the restaurant, why not now?"

"What difference does it make?"

"For fuck's sake, Megan. You saw her, didn't you? She
showed up while you were broadcasting your presence
to every sensitive in a ten-mile radius, right?"

"So what if she did?"

"Are you serious?"

"We got away, we're fine, I don't see why you're so
mad at me!" She glanced to her right. Brian was making every pretence of reading her battered copy of *The
Caine Mutiny*, but the speed with which Malleus and
Roc looked away told her they'd been hanging on her
every word.

Now she looked like some dumb little girl in front of
them. "You don't own me, Greyson," she snapped. "It's
not up to you what I do or don't do."

Pause. "Fine. Do whatever you like."

"I will!"

"Good."

"Good!"

This was what her anger and embarrassment had reduced her to. The kind of fights thirteen-year-olds had.

"Just do me a favor, send Malleus home if you've decided to commit messy suicide. He's rather valuable to me."

"And I'm—you know what? Fine."

She slammed the phone shut and tossed it back to Malleus. Her entire body shook.

So that was that. He'd yelled at her, she'd yelled at him, and now she'd actually hung up on him. She waited—along with everyone else in the room—for the phone to start ringing again.

It didn't.

Brian cleared his throat. "It's getting kind of late, Megan, I should probably call Julie and see if she'll pick me up. I'm too buzzed to drive."

She nodded. "Sure, go ahead."

Malleus, of course, wouldn't be leaving unless ordered to, and Roc—Roc was enjoying her pain too much. Little demon bastard. Maybe later she'd stub her toe as dessert for him.

So Ktana Leyak was their mother? She could have them, then. Megan would be well out of it all. She could sever the connection, if that was possible—which it must be—and be done with the whole damned thing, and who cared what happened next?

She could build a new practice, out of her house. Lots of counselors did that. Or she could find a little office somewhere, closer to home, where she didn't have to worry about partners. She could put her rates on a sliding scale, like she'd wanted to before. She could—

Brian had just touched the phone when it rang. Megan watched as he started to pick it up, then glanced at her, realizing what he'd done. She shrugged. Might as well get it over with.

If it was over with. He'd called her back; maybe now they'd both calmed down, they could talk like reasonable adults again, and she'd apologize, and he'd hint at an apology, and all would be well, she thought. They'd never really had a fight before.

"Hello?"

"Megan?"

She knew that voice. She couldn't quite place it, but she knew it, and for a second the world seemed to twist before it fell back into place.

"Mother?"

"Megan, it's your mother," the voice continued, as if Megan hadn't spoken. So yes, definitely her mother. "There's been a—there's been . . ." She cleared her throat. "Megan, you need to come home. Your father's died."

Chapter Nine

Hostile shadows hid in the corners of buildings and under trees as Megan drove through what the residents of Grant Falls referred to as "downtown." Or at least used to refer to as. She hadn't been here in a dozen years.

The heater in her car was turned up full blast but she still shivered. A funeral and the reading of a will and The Lawyer Says You Have to Be There.

Not "Honey, you should come home and say good-bye." Not "Sweetheart, maybe it's time we got back in touch." No. "The lawyer says you need to be there for the reading of the will. Just a formality, of course." Which meant she wasn't inheriting anything, not that she cared.

Megan had left her suitcase back at the dubiously named Bev's Holiday Hideaway on the outskirts of town—although who would ever holiday in Grant Falls she had no idea—and, grabbing a cup of coffee from the McDonald's next door, started making her way home.

To her parents' home, anyway.

Hardly anyone was out on the windswept streets, but Megan still felt eyes on her. She'd left Grant Falls to go to college and never returned. Now it seemed the time away had been just a short vacation, that the town had sat here waiting for her with the patience of a predator at a watering hole.

Her hands slipped on the wheel a little as she made the left turn that would take her to her old home. It was a longer route, but it would allow her to avoid passing the hospital where she'd spent several months of her fifteenth year. She never wanted to see that building again.

Not that she remembered most of it. She'd been possessed by the Accuser at the time, and had blocked the entire experience out of her memory until she'd been forced to confront it all in order to defeat him for good.

A child ran out into the street in front of her. Megan slammed on the brakes. Her coffee spilled all over her jeans.

"Damn it! Ow!" She set the cup down on the seat next to her, wishing for once she was as finicky as Tera, who always accepted napkins no matter where she was.

Megan glared at the child, a boy of about eight, totally anonymous in his red coat and cap. He stuck out his tongue. Brat.

"Michael!" Oh great. The last thing Megan needed now was the kid's mother. She hadn't even come close to hitting him, for fuck's sake, but something about the look of the heavyset woman scurrying toward her and the smug expression on the boy's face told her that wouldn't matter.

She was right. The woman marched over and raised an imperious fist to start tapping on the window. Megan took a grim pleasure in rolling it down before she could.

"You need to watch where you're going! You almost hit my son!"

"Perhaps your son should watch where he's going," Megan said pleasantly. "Instead of just darting out into the street."

"How dare you! You—Megan Chase!"

Oh, shit. Just as recognition hit the plump, high-blooded face of the woman, it hit Megan. Cassie Bryant, from Megan's gym class senior year.

There was no point recalling the specifics of Cassie's cruelty toward Megan. She hadn't been unique in it.

"Yes. Hi, Cassie." Megan forced a smile. "Look, if your son is okay, I'm just going to—"

"He's fine," Cassie said dismissively. She hadn't even glanced at her son since her beady eyes had fixed on Megan. "What are you doing back in town? It's so good to see you! We heard about you, you know, on the radio and everything . . ."

Ah, so that explained it. "Right. Yes. I really should be—"

"You know, we should go out one night! For a drink. I remember where you live, I could come over and get you."

"I'm . . . well, my father died, so I don't really think—"

"Oh no!" Cassie's hands, heavy with cheap gold, clasped over her mouth. "Oh, Megan, I sure am sorry to hear that. When is the funeral?"

"Wednesday. I'm sorry, Cassie, but I really have to go."

"Of course, of course. I'll tell you what. I'll call you later, over at your parents'—your mom's—house, okay? I think you need a night out with the girls to cheer you up. I'm still friends with all of them, you know, me and Amy and Jen, we all still live in town. We could all go out? Sound good?"

It sounded as appealing as an appendectomy with no anesthetic. "If I have time, sure. Sounds fun."

She gave Michael, sulking by the side of the road, a half smile and drove away. Great. The last thing she wanted or needed was for her meager fame outside the town to haunt her even more than her infamy inside it already did.

"Megan." Her mother stood in the doorway, her blonde hair tucked into a smooth chignon, her black dress gliding over a figure still slim. No late-life weight gain for Diane Chase. For a minute time seemed to shift. Megan was acutely aware of the splotch of cold coffee staining her jeans.

"Come in."

No hugs, no watery smiles. Megan hadn't really expected them.

"I see you're alone."

"Yes." What did the woman expect, that Megan would be bringing a dozen friends? Of course she was alone.

At least until tomorrow. Brian and Tera were driving out together in the morning to attend the funeral with her.

Greyson . . . didn't know. She hadn't called him back. Her pride hadn't allowed it. They'd had a fight, maybe a stupid fight, maybe not—as her temper cooled she'd started to see his anger as the more logical of the two, which didn't excuse it—but she wasn't going to emotionally blackmail him into cutting his trip short to be with her. If he even could. Or would.

It wasn't like she was heartbroken. Saddened, sure. But her father had never been much more than a cipher to her, and they hadn't spoken since she'd left for college.

She could get through this alone. She didn't need a crutch. No matter how much she wanted hi—it.

"Take your shoes off, please. The carpet."

Megan blinked. Her mother nodded toward a rack by the door. "Shoes off, Megan."

For a minute she thought about running. Turning around, leaving the house, picking up her bag, and just going home.

Instead she just bent and unzipped her boots, placing them neatly on the rack.

"I've made coffee," Diane said. She still had not touched Megan or looked her directly in the eyes. "In the kitchen."

They trooped past a living room almost unchanged since the day Megan left for what she thought would be the last time. The furniture sitting placidly in the overheated air looked new, but was the same style and color it had been before. The family portraits still hung in the same places on the walls, although Megan noticed the ones with her in them had been moved farther down and some were missing altogether. No surprise there.

"Why am I here, Mother?"

"Sit down."

Megan glanced at the chairs. Their hard wooden seats

and straight backs promised physical discomfort as well as the mental unease of being here to begin with. Why were they even in here? They'd never had meals in the kitchen or even coffee. The kitchen was for unacceptable guests, for contractors giving estimates or—

Answered her own question there, hadn't she?

She sat. And waited. If there was one thing she was good at, it was waiting for the other person to speak first.

Her mother placed a cup in front of her, along with a little china boat of cream and a matching bowl of sugar cubes. Megan shook her head.

The coffee, damn it, was delicious. Diane always had been a good cook; it was one of the few things aside from her looks Megan had inherited.

"Apparently your father made a new will a few weeks ago," Diane said, shifting in her seat. "He—"

"How did he die?"

"Don't interrupt me, please. Our attorney has the new will and he informed me that we all have to be at the reading. That's why you're here. Plus I thought perhaps you would like to pay your respects to the man who supported you throughout your childhood. He deserves your *quiet and unobtrusive* presence."

"What happens if I don't go? To the reading of the will, I mean."

Her mother sniffed and took a dainty sip from her cup. "I didn't ask. I assumed that when I explained the situation to you, you would of course do the right thing and help your family avoid any inconvenience."

Megan's legs tensed, ready to get up and leave. She

didn't want to be here, didn't want anything to do with any of this.

But she stayed. Because if she didn't this would follow her home. Because she had a good reputation as a psychological counselor and news of a huge rift in her family would shed a bad light on that at a time when her radio show was her only income.

"Fine," she managed. "How did he die?"

"Heart attack." Her mother leaned back in her chair and smoothed her skirt. "He'd had several before."

Megan didn't bother to ask why no one had called her then, and it didn't matter anyway because a rattling sound from the living room indicated someone was walking into the house.

Diane's face lit up. She pushed herself out of her seat and practically floated from the room. "David!"

"Mom! Mom, are you okay?"

Megan turned in her seat and peeked out from around the open doorway of the kitchen to see her older brother, his fair head bent as he embraced their mother, who sobbed theatrically and clung to him.

If she'd thought about it, she would have known he'd be here. Dave was the fair-haired boy in more ways than one.

They entered the kitchen, her mother and brother—her family—and Dave helped their mother into a chair. He glanced up.

"Megan. Oh. Hi."

"Hi, Dave."

"I didn't think—well, wow. It's nice to see you."

Her smile felt painted on. "Yeah, you too."

They all sat in silence for a minute before Megan stood up. "Well, I should go. Um, I'll see you tomorrow."

"Don't be late. Eleven o'clock, at our church." The look Diane gave her clearly indicated she thought Megan was planning on showing up drunk halfway through the service.

"Um . . . our church?"

"United Methodist," Dave said. Like Megan was supposed to know. "On Oak."

"Okay, well, I'll be there. See you tomorrow."

"I'll walk you out." Dave stood up. She had no idea what he was doing these days, if he was married or had kids or . . . anything. The last time she'd seen him he was still doing some low-level dealing out of his bedroom.

He took her arm and led her to the door. "Listen . . . ," he said, while she shoved her feet back into her boots. "There's going to be a lot of people there tomorrow, you know? A lot of friends of Mom and Dad's."

"Yeah?" For the first time since she'd walked in the door, she had the urge to lower her shields. Idle curiosity, really. But the memory of Gerald's sister's pain and the reaction it had caused put her off the idea before it even finished crossing her mind. Dave would be upset about their father's death, and she would feel that, and . . . no.

"So . . ." Dave's blue eyes, so like her own, widened. "So it would be nice if you wouldn't make a scene, you know? Maybe just keep to the back, out of the way . . . ?"

She stared at him. Once, when they were children, they'd been close. Only three years separated them. Now it felt more like fifty. "Sure, Dave. I'll try to remember not to pee in front of the altar."

She was out the door and gone before the puzzled expression left his face.

One day she would learn to stop paying attention to the little voice in her head that told her to lighten up.

She'd listened to it this time, and that's why she was stuck in a booth at Kelly's Tap with Cassie, Amy, and Jen, three women who'd had nothing but nasty things to say to her for years and now seemed to think their mutual attendance at the same high school meant they were bonded like Vietnam vets.

Which for Megan wasn't an entirely inappropriate analogy.

She couldn't blame just the voice in her head, though. Her craving for a drink and anything to look at other than the bland hotel furnishings had something to do with it as well. So had Rocturnus, who was actually spending the evening at Megan's mother's house. There was plenty of misery to go around over there.

And here. Or maybe this wasn't misery. Maybe it was filth. She'd never been in such a sticky place. A thin film of whitish grime seemed to cling to everything and everyone. Even the music coming from the aged jukebox—a mixture of soft rock and modern country—sounded distorted and fuzzy, like the speakers were clogged with phlegm.

She shifted in her seat and drank her beer, while the ladies discussed memories they shared, which had nothing to do with Megan. Once they'd ascertained she didn't know any celebrities, wasn't married, and didn't have children, they'd completely lost interest in her.

Not surprising.

She shifted in her seat, lifted her bottle again. This was a huge mistake. As she tuned out the chatter of the women at her table she became aware of other conversations, less friendly ones, taking place around her. It hadn't taken the locals long to figure out who she was. Their suspicion and resentment beat against her skin.

Nine o'clock. The liquor stores would be closed, but there was a gas station not far. She could buy her own beer and sit in her hotel room and drink it. Even being alone with her thoughts—of Gerald, of Greyson, of her family— would be better than feeling the eyes and anger of Grant Falls's drunks focused on her like a lightning rod.

"I have to go to the bathroom," she said. Cassie, Amy, and Jen ignored her. So much for catching up.

The sticky floor sucked at her feet as she made her way to the back of the room and the dull illumination of the cracked bathroom sign. There might be a storeroom, another way out, so she didn't have to walk through the small crowd again.

There wasn't. She ducked through the ladies' room door anyway, to gird herself.

In the bathroom mirror she looked sallow, half dead. The flickering bug light above the rust-stained sink did not flatter. Megan thought of the women who came in here to check their lipstick or brush their hair. What did they see when they turned their drunk gazes on themselves? Did the ugliness of their lives reflect back at them?

Silly thought. They saw what they wanted to see.

She turned back and opened the door, keeping her head down. She could probably slip past the girls without them seeing her; hell, they probably wouldn't even notice she was gone. If she couldn't gossip with authority about various useless heiresses and the general misery of raising children, they weren't interested.

Megan clutched the strap of her purse and entered the bar, only to be assaulted by hostile glares. Coming to the bar had been the wrong thing to do. Leaving it, even worse.

Keeping her head down, she tried to push her way through the crowd, but the bodies would not budge.

"Excuse me," she said, then again, louder. "Excuse me, please."

A few people blinked and moved. Most didn't. Megan glanced up and saw demons, Yezer Ha-Ra, on every shoulder, in every corner.

Not hers. Roc was at her mother's house. These belonged to someone else, perhaps Ktana Leyak, perhaps a different demon entirely. A different family. The Meegras didn't tend to divide land territorially, at least not in the city, but who know what subset ruled here, or in whose power the local Yezer were?

Whoever it was, she was willing to bet they weren't particularly friendly.

"We don't like murderers here," said a man's voice, low and threatening, from the back of the crowd.

Megan glanced at Cassie and her friends. They looked away, as if they didn't see what was happening.

Anger boiled in her chest. Why wouldn't they leave

her alone? She hadn't killed anyone. She hadn't killed Harlan Trooper, all those years ago. She knew it and the judge knew it. She hadn't even been charged.

If I wanted to, I could have you all killed, she thought, and was stunned when the thought didn't shock her, didn't scare her the way it should. She looked at their faces, stony and stubbled, shiny with alcoholic sweat. The power in her chest hadn't worked against Ktana Leyak, but it could against them, this miserable bunch of humans with their heavy boots and beer guts.

She pictured those guts exploding. She pictured the terror in their eyes when they realized they were messing with the wrong fucking demon, they were—

Demon?

She wasn't a demon. She was human. She was *not a demon,* no matter what lump of flesh crowded next to her heart and tried to grow.

She was human.

"Mr. Maldon doesn't like you here," one of the Yezer hissed. Her gaze flew to him as he hunched in one of the booths, bigger than the others. The Rocturnus of his family, she assumed.

"Then I'll leave," she said, her voice loud and clear as a bell in a forest, answering both the man in the back and the Yezer. She summoned as much of her anger as she could, let it fill her and give her strength, and shoved her way through the crowd and out the door.

She'd stopped shaking by the time she left the gas station with a six-pack of cheap beer and a couple of magazines.

Something light, undemanding, gossip about people she didn't know and didn't care about, shiny pictures to look at while she tried to focus and relax. Anything to take her mind away from what was happening to her, away from the death of her father and how she felt about that, away from memories of the coldness in her mother's eyes.

Away from herself. She thought of what she might advise a client to do—back when she still had clients—in this situation, when the misery of their existence and uncertainty as to who they really were closed in on them like rusted iron bars. She might suggest they take up a hobby. That they try and join some organizations to make friends. What bullshit! Jesus, had anything she'd ever said really helped anyone? Had anything she'd ever done in her entire life actually been worth a damn?

And who could help her now? The demon who shared her bed a few times a week? The witch she went shopping with? The psychic reporter who dated a cop and thought what Megan really needed was a good dose of religion?

She turned right and headed back toward town.

Chapter Ten

She hadn't expected the doors to be locked. Weren't churches supposed to be open all the time?

Perhaps vandals were a problem even in a small town like this—a dying town. Perhaps that was the type of place that had the most to worry about from them, from the spray paint and broken glass. Nobody liked to watch their own destruction creeping up their walls and into their buildings, and to realize they couldn't do anything to change it.

She edged around the building, trying every door she found, looking for something, anything. She'd never been here before. Apparently her parents had found religion of some kind after she'd left—Diane and David praise the Lord, another photo for the wall—but who knew how much of that was the desire to worship and how much was social climbing. United Methodist was the church of choice for Grant Falls's movers and shakers, if she remembered correctly. Certainly in this town any other church was regarded more highly than this one, Holy Innocents; undeniably Catholic, from the illuminated statues of Mary to the stained-glass image of the Sacred Heart she could barely make out.

Brian was Catholic. Brian was very happily Catholic.

He'd once told her he had a priest, as if it was a normal thing, to have a priest who talked to you regularly about everything from women to psychic abilities. Maybe it was.

She just wanted someone to talk to her about something. To look at her with eyes that didn't judge or hate. So she'd thought of Brian and his stubborn insistence on doing the right thing, and come here, and found it locked against her. The metaphor was so good she almost laughed.

"Can I help you?"

She turned, startled, and found a man standing, silhouetted by the safety light behind him. "Um—I was just—"

"Trying to get in," he finished, moving slightly so she could see him better. A priest, his collar gleaming.

"I wanted to talk to someone," she said. "I thought maybe here . . ."

He looked at her for a long minute while hope rose inside her. He was a priest, after all, it was his job—no, not even his job, his *calling*—to help people, to counsel them and show them the way, wasn't it? To believe in God and demons and angels? Maybe he could explain to her why she had to keep reminding herself that she wasn't a demon, why she even wanted to still be human when it seemed all they ever did was try to hurt each other?

"It's a little late, isn't it?" he asked.

"Well, yes, but—"

The priest shook his head. "You'll have to call and make an appointment if you want to talk to someone."

She blinked, expecting him to say something else, to smile, to change his mind. But he just stood there.

"I'm sorry, F-Father," she managed. "I didn't mean to disturb anyone, I just—do you believe demons exist?" The words came out in a rush. She wanted to hook him, to make him listen.

He shook his head. "You just need a good night's sleep, I bet," he said. "Good night."

He turned and walked away. He didn't look back.

Megan stared after him, her blood heating her cheeks, becoming aware of how stupid she must look. So much for that idea. There was no help, there was no sanctuary, there was nothing but the icy wind whipping around the corners of the building and insinuating itself through her coat.

The feeling of letdown lasted as long as it took to pull into the parking lot at the Holiday Hideaway, replaced by a different emotion, one she couldn't quite analyze, when her headlights skimmed over one very familiar black Jaguar parked outside her room.

She didn't know what to say.

She'd wanted him here, wanted him as badly as she'd ever wanted anything, but now that he was . . . she fidgeted, she couldn't meet his eyes, she thought about hiding.

Not that hiding was possible, not when Malleus, Maleficarum, and Spud practically leaped on her, so eager were they to express their sympathy. Spud didn't speak, of course, just patted her back—hard enough to make her cough—with tears in his eyes. It took several minutes to free herself, and another deep breath before she forced herself to meet Greyson's eyes. His were completely unreadable, remote.

"How did you . . . how did you find out I was here?"

He shrugged. "They called me."

"They?"

"The local crew here."

Ah. "Mr. Malton."

"Maldon, yes. His boss, Winston, called me."

The brothers kept shooting little glances in their direction, like they were waiting for either a fight or some explosive sex. Or both.

"Why did he call you? I mean, why you?"

"He didn't have a number for you and he was pretty sure I would, Meg."

"Oh. Right."

She felt his gaze on her, tasted the awkwardness in the air. He didn't know what she wanted, or maybe he did and didn't know if she wanted it from him.

Neither did she. She wanted to be held. She wanted to be kissed, to be reassured that the world outside this shitty little town existed and that she had a place in it. Was welcome and wanted in it.

But her soul cringed at the thought of his arms around her while he checked his watch behind her back. Of a kiss given with perfunctory ease because it was expected. She wanted his empathy, not his sympathy, and it was an emotion she didn't know if he understood or was willing to give—if he cared enough about her for her problems to really matter to him, enough for her to penetrate that smooth, hard veneer.

For the first time since the night she'd let him take

her home, she wanted him to be someone or something other than what he was. Not a demon. Not someone who looked at the foibles of humanity with a sardonic eye because they didn't affect him. But just a man.

He took the six-pack from her hand, and the chips. The chips he tossed to Maleficarum; the beer he kept, and with his free hand he grabbed hers, enveloping her fingers in heat.

"Let's go for a walk."

"It's too cold."

"Come on." He set out across the parking lot, pulling her after him.

They walked in silence for a while, down the deserted street, past the scanty forest marking the edge of the town proper. The street continued, all the way into the heart of Grant Falls, but Megan stopped. "I don't want to go there."

"Why not?"

She looked away, down at her shoes, until his hand under her chin forced her to look up at him. Damn it. Her lids fluttered. "They . . . they remember me."

He was silent for a moment, digesting that. "Why didn't you call me?"

She shrugged. In her head she heard her own voice, reassuring a client, floating into people's homes and cars from the radio. *Never be afraid to talk about your feelings. Speaking up is bravery. If they don't know how you feel, they can't respond to your emotions.*

Bullshit. "So I guess whoever this Maldon guy is, he isn't very happy I'm here. He sent some of his Yezer to the bar, I was at this bar in town, and they—"

"Why didn't you call me, Meg?"

"You were in New York."

"Didn't you think I'd come back?" He paused. "Or did you not want me to?"

She shrugged. "You were mad at me."

"And *you* were mad at *me*." He let go of her chin and sat down on the curb. Glass clinked loudly in the crisp air as he pulled two beers out of the pack and opened them, their caps ringing on the sidewalk. "Are you still mad?"

She tucked her coat beneath her to try and guard her behind from the freezing pavement. "No. You?"

"No." He drank his beer and made a face.

"It was all they had," she said, smiling for what felt like the first time in days.

"No wonder you went to a bar. What happened?"

She told him, as quickly as she could, not wanting to think for too long about the sullen faces and bulky bodies in her way. When she got to the part about the Yezer appearing, he interrupted.

"Where was Roc?"

"He's at my par—my mom's house."

"You should keep him with you. Especially when you're not in the city."

"I just . . . didn't want to deal with him tonight."

Greyson nodded. "Maldon isn't happy you're here. He wants to meet with you."

"Oh, for—"

"Yeah, I know. I tried to talk him out of it but . . . honestly, *bryaela,* he's probably pissed off because of me. He doesn't care for me too much."

"Why not? Do I want to know?"

"I seduced his wife."

She choked on her beer. "Really?"

He nodded. "Five years or so ago. They were in town for some kind of meeting. I was bored."

"Well, at least you found something to amuse you."

Why did she love his smile so much? In spite of everything she'd been thinking only ten minutes ago—and it was all true and she knew it—he could smile at her like that and she didn't care anymore, despite the tiny, almost unacknowledged stab of jealousy. "Such as it was. Yes, I did."

"I guess when I go meet this guy you won't be with me."

"Oh, no. I definitely will be."

"But if he hates you—"

"He hates me, yes. But he also knows I'm more powerful than he is. Which, by extension, makes you more powerful than he is. I don't want him to forget it."

"Why do I have to go at all?"

"Because it's courteous and you have enough to deal with here without his Yezer—or who knows what else—following you around."

She sighed. "When do we have to do this?"

"When is the funeral?"

"Eleven, tomorrow."

He checked his watch. "We might still be able to catch him tonight. If not, we'll try for morning."

"Do we have to? Tonight, I mean?"

"Best to get it over with." He opened another beer. "Besides, he'll probably have decent scotch."

*   *   *

An hour later they arrived at Maldon's house, a bland split-level in a new development. Megan, accustomed to the homes of important demons being as opulent as imperial palaces, felt like she'd arrived at the gates of Hell and found Heck instead.

Not that the grand Iureanliers actually resembled Hell, or that Hell even existed—apparently it didn't, but she hadn't yet learned the true story. The analogy suited her anyway and won another smile from Greyson when she whispered it to him.

"Maldon does have some power, though, and his boss is Winston Lawden of House Caedes Fuiltean," he murmured as they approached the guards out front. "So try not to piss him off, won't you?"

The pig-faced guards communicated in low grunts, but seemed to understand Greyson well enough when he spoke the demon tongue. Megan assumed they, like the other non-human-looking demons, were invisible to most people. Lucky her, she was able to see most of them. It certainly made walks in the park more interesting.

They stood outside for so long Megan was starting to think they'd be refused entry. Her legs—she'd changed into the black dress and jacket she planned to wear the next day—were numb. She was cold, she was tired, and with every minute that passed she grew more and more irritated.

Finally one of the grunting beasts nodded and bowed, sweeping the front door open behind him. Greyson ushered her through the door, into another very ordinary earth-tone foyer. She half-expected the Brady kids to come down the stairs any minute.

"Grey," a voice boomed. "And you must be Dr. Chase."

Megan didn't notice, or pay attention to, Greyson's power as a rule. It was just there, something humming in the background, much like her own. But she remembered meeting his old Gretneg, Templeton Black, and the easy strength emanating from his stocky frame. Lord Maldon had the same kind of energy, but Megan knew without even having to think about it that Greyson had been right. Maldon wasn't as strong as Templeton had been, or as strong as Greyson was now. The knowledge made her simultaneously more sympathetic—her presence here really was a threat—and more pissed off. Who did he think he was, sending his minions out to threaten her?

Especially not when he looked like a mangy dog, with his messy dirty blond hair and grizzled face. His entire body, in fact, seemed slight and a little too loose limbed for reality, but she had the distinct impression he could move quickly if he wanted to. Like a ferret.

Greyson towered over him. "Orion," he said, nodding. Neither man offered his hand to the other.

Maldon glanced at him, then looked back at Megan. His eyes, a vibrant, shocking blue, raked her body from head to toe. "So you're Greyson's little human," he said, his voice—loud and calm—at distinct odds with his meager frame.

"She's Gretneg of House Io Adflicta," Greyson corrected. "She's not my little anything."

"That's not the way I hear it." He reached out to touch her hair, but Megan, moving with a speed she didn't know she possessed, grabbed his hand before he could. His skin was cool and smooth, hard like an apple.

"Is touching part of this?" she asked innocently. "Because I don't generally allow men I don't know to fondle my hair."

Greyson's lips twitched, but he didn't speak.

Maldon's eyes darkened. "And I don't generally allow others to do business in my territory without greeting me."

"I'm not doing any business. I'm just here for a funeral."

"Yes, I know about your father. Doubly important, then, that you give me my due."

"Excuse me?"

"I allowed him to stay here, even after you left. After you defeated the Accuser the first time and handed over your Yezer—some of whom were *my* Yezer—to him, stealing from me. I allowed your father to run his business, to keep his home, everything he had was due to me."

"Give it a rest, Orion," Greyson said. His anger brushed against her skin, then withdrew, but the edge in his voice still seemed to echo in her chest. "Dr. Chase owes you nothing. She's come here to apologize for not informing you she was coming. She's done so. That's all."

"You know that isn't true, Greyson." Maldon's eyes didn't leave hers for a long moment, then he blinked and turned away, becoming once again just a wiry little man, vaguely threatening, like a small-time hood but nothing to worry about.

If anyone knew how deceptive appearances could be, it was Megan.

A servant appeared with a tray of drinks. Megan accepted one after Greyson, but did not sip until he'd done so.

"I was just about to sink some putts," Maldon said, holding out one arm. A servant appeared, or perhaps one of his *rubendas,* and handed him his coat. "In the yard. Join me."

Greyson gave her a look that said, *I'll go to the mat on this one if you want.* She shook her head. If the demon wanted to play golf at night in the December cold, that was fine. She just wanted to make him happy so she didn't have to worry about him anymore.

And some of *his* Yezer? Were the defectors returning to him, as well as to Ktana Leyak?

She wanted to find out. So she followed him, her heels sinking into the tawny carpet, while Greyson rested his hand reassuringly on the small of her back.

Maldon hadn't been lying about putts. He selected a long, slender steel club from a rack outside the door and trotted off into the yard, where a strip of AstroTurf seemed to glow in the dead brown of the grass.

"This is bizarre," she whispered to Greyson. "Like *Alice in Wonderland.*"

He nodded, but his eyes didn't leave the small form now teeing up in his bulky coat. "Just remember the Red Queen, *bryaela.*"

"So," Maldon said when they reached him. "What do you propose to offer me?"

"I—" She stopped when Greyson gave a slight shake

of his head. "I've already offered it. My apology. I'll be leaving on Thursday."

"Not good enough." Maldon watched the little ball roll down the artificial grass. It missed the hole. "Damn!"

"Why don't you just tell us what you want, Orion." Greyson sounded bored, lazy, but his arm next to hers was tense.

Maldon glanced at him. "So curt," he said. "As if you're the one giving the orders. As if this is your land."

Greyson didn't respond.

"What do you think is an apt price to pay, Greyson? For invading another man's territory?"

Shit.

"That debt's been paid."

"And now I'll take another one. The human shouldn't be here. She stole my demons and I couldn't do anything about it because she bound them to the Accuser. Now they're bound to her. She'll pay me for them. In cash."

"Fine."

Was he crazy? She didn't have any money, especially now she didn't even have her practice. Her radio paychecks weren't *that* good.

He didn't know about her practice, she remembered. She hadn't had a chance to tell him.

"And she'll pay for her trespass."

"She apologized."

"Not enough." He looked at Megan, his eyes glowing faintly red in the dim light. "I have another form of payment in mind. An hour in my bed."

"No—" she started to say, but Greyson's voice sliced through hers like an icicle.

"Do you want to fight me, Orion? To start a war you can't win?"

"Those are my terms." But Maldon's gaze faltered as he spoke.

"You don't have the authority to make a request like that of a Gretneg and you know it. You could be censured just for suggesting it."

Maldon glared at them. Anger thrashed around him, hitting Megan, hitting Greyson. She stood firm, her eyes steady. The thought of this demon's hard little hands on her body made her stomach clench.

"Fine," he spat. "But I can request blood. You know I can."

Silence. Megan wanted to speak, to run, but she concentrated on standing perfectly still. Blood . . . Greyson's *rubenda* had asked if he could have it . . . she herself had wanted it . . .

"You can have mine," Greyson said.

Maldon's face split into a grin. "No. Hers. I've *had* yours."

Greyson took her arm and led her away, out of earshot. "You don't have to do this," he said. The lights from the windows of the house reflected in his dark eyes. "We can try to talk him down further."

"But you want me to."

"Hell, no, I don't want you to. But he's not lying. It's an excessive request, but the bastard's within his rights to make it."

She looked at the ground, at her shoes disappearing

into the shadows made by her legs. "Is he . . . why does he want it?"

She thought she already knew, and she was right.

"He's a blood demon. He wants to feed on it."

"Oh God." She pressed her hand against her mouth as the Scotch threatened to come back up. Already in her mind she could see it, the sharp knife, her blood flowing into a silver bowl . . . Orion Maldon lifting the bowl to his lips.

"I'll talk him down," Greyson said. He turned away, but she grabbed him.

"Would he touch me?"

"I won't let him."

"What will he do if . . . if we don't?"

He sighed. "It depends. He could make us stand out here all night—to hurt you, you know, he knows the cold doesn't bother me much—and eventually just let us go. Or he could stick to his guns, in which case we either give him what he wants or he talks to his boss, who talks to me, and we have to give in or we have a minor war on our hands."

"He doesn't strike me as the giving-in type."

"No."

Tears threatened, but she blinked them back. "Okay," she said. "But I want another drink first."

Chapter Eleven

This, at least, looked like the lair of a demon. The crimson walls of Orion Maldon's basement changed from blazing red by the flaming torches to deep and shadowy—the color of blood—between them.

In an odd way, the color, and the ornately carved gilded furniture, had a calming effect on Megan. It would have been utterly bizarre to make a blood sacrifice in the comfy earth-tone living room in front of the plasma-screen TV. The basement felt like a movie set, filming about to begin on a scene in a biopic that grew increasingly more bizarre by the day.

Girded by several more drinks, Megan allowed Greyson to lead her into the corner and set her in a surprisingly comfortable armchair. She'd barely settled in it when Maldon advanced, holding a wicked-looking knife.

"You asked for blood and you'll get it," Greyson said, stepping in front of her, effectively blocking her from sight. "You didn't ask to cut her."

"It was implied."

"It wasn't agreed to."

Silence reigned for a moment while Megan pictured

the two men staring each other down. Then Maldon stepped back and stabbed the knife forward.

Megan gasped, but Greyson caught it before it touched him. "Now, now," he murmured, and turned back to Megan.

Tension laced her muscles, her entire body, as he knelt on the black-tiled floor at her feet.

"Give me your hand."

It wasn't the thought of the pain that made her nervous. Pain she could take, and it would most likely be fleeting anyway. Greyson's healing abilities were excellent, and she doubted he'd let her walk out the door with a bleeding cut, especially in a house full of blood demons—at least, she assumed they were all blood demons.

But then, she'd assumed Greyson's Meegra was all fire demons and she'd apparently been wrong.

She'd never asked. She'd never asked a lot of things and had ignored Greyson's casual attempts to teach her. Now it was biting her on the ass—or to be more precise, it was about to slice into her skin with a sharp silver blade.

No, it wasn't the thought of being cut making her heart pound in her chest. It was the thought of bleeding. It was the memory of the overcooked steak that was in fact perfectly done, of Greyson's blood on the white marble floor, of the time he nicked himself shaving and she'd been about to lick the wound before she caught herself.

If she asked him about it, he would probably know what was happening to her.

She just couldn't bring herself to admit anything was, and until she was ready, it was her secret to keep.

His eyes searched her face. "Are you okay?"

She nodded.

Instead of the bowl she'd been expecting, Maldon placed an ordinary crystal wineglass on the floor by Greyson's knee, then said, in his booming voice, *"Krenagr hin alishta caercaeris."*

Greyson's face darkened as footsteps sounded on the stairs, and he glared at Maldon. "You're not sharing anything."

"I can share the moment," Maldon replied. "I can have witnesses."

"What's—" she started, leaning forward, but Greyson shook his head.

"Let's just do this."

Megan had no idea where in the house all these demons lived, but in a matter of seconds the basement went from a dank underground temple to a kinky convention room, full of demons in various states of undress. A few of them had the high pompadour hairdos Megan had come to associate with demons hiding horn stumps; a few more had *sgaegas* like Greyson's down their backs, or third nipples, or odd bony protrusions on their shoulders. All of them looked very pleased with themselves. Sweat trickled down her back.

Greyson picked up her left hand and stared at it for a moment. Megan closed her eyes. Best not to look. Bad enough to be taken with crazy vampire urges when it was the blood of someone with whom you enthusiastically shared other bodily fluids whenever you got the chance, but when it was your own . . . that was just weird.

Unlike everything else about this situation, which was perfectly normal if you ignored the basement, the torches, the furniture, the knife, the demons, and the goblet. Just an ordinary small-town evening, in an ordinary small town.

Which was apparently run by Orion Maldon, who supposedly knew her father . . .

The touch of Greyson's lips on her palm stopped her thought before it had a chance to form. He hadn't kissed her yet, not once this whole night. The gesture was possessive, romantic even, but the icy touch of his anger and the expectant air of the room told her something was wrong.

The room went silent. Something rustled. Greyson's fingers tightened around hers, and the blade sliced into her palm, so sharp and fast she didn't realize it had cut her until she heard the knife clatter on the floor and felt her blood run down her hand.

He turned her wrist and pressed the glass against her palm for a moment, the rim cool and smooth against her skin. It took only a second longer for the stinging to start, and only another before the glass was removed and something soft shoved into her hand instead, her fingers closed over it with a little more force than she would have expected.

Megan forced her eyes open, squinting into the dim room, afraid to see too much. Greyson's handkerchief was balled up in her palm. She bent her elbow, trying to ignore the pain now radiating from the wound as she used her other hand to apply pressure. Cool in a crisis, that's what she was. She glanced at Greyson, hoping for a smile, a look, some sort of reassurance, but his face was turned away, as if he were studying the floor.

To her right Maldon lifted the goblet—the goblet now filled about a quarter of the way with her blood. *"Caercaeris bochylem!"*

Nope, didn't want to see that. She closed her eyes again while great waves of red and black undulated behind her eyelids. Heat radiated from Greyson's body against her legs, but he did not touch her, leaving her alone to deal with this. Ordinarily that would have pleased her, as she didn't particularly enjoy being vulnerable in front of him. But this was too much. She reached out, pressing her injured hand with its wadded-up cloth against her thigh and groping for him, hitting his shoulder feebly until finally his fingers closed around hers so tightly it hurt.

He moved, the scent of his cologne and the smoky fragrance of his skin filling her nostrils, his lips tickling her ear and his voice cold as his energy against her. "Come on, Meg. Let's go." He started to lift her from her chair. "Let's go. We're done."

"I wanted to ask him about—"

"Another time."

Was there going to be another time? She didn't ever want to come back here.

"Oh come now, Grey, there's no need to rush off like that, is there?"

Megan opened her eyes. Maldon was smiling, the empty glass still clutched in his hand. Jesus, had he licked it clean?

"You got what you wanted, Orion."

"Oh yes, I did."

His laughter followed them up the stairs.

Her healed hand still tingled a little, an irritating itch under the skin she couldn't scratch, as she lay in bed later with Greyson's chest against her back and his strong arms encircling her body. The bulky forms of Malleus, Maleficarum, and Spud rested in front of the window, horned silhouettes against the curtains.

Her father was dead.

Funny, it wasn't until now, as she lay thinking of what the next day held, that it really hit her. They hadn't been close, not in years.

But in those dim, long-forgotten years of her early childhood, he'd been someone special and so had she. He'd taken her out for long rides in the car. He'd carried her on his shoulders to watch the Fourth of July parade in the center of town. He'd bought ice cream and candy and smiled and laughed. He'd called her his little girl.

She thought she'd mourned those years a long time ago, but it seemed there was still something left of them in her heart after all, because the dim, tobacco-stained wallpaper blurred with her tears and her throat ached. She'd been someone's beloved daughter once. When did that change? When did she become an embarrassment, something to be hidden?

Not just when Harlan Trooper died. It started long before that. She couldn't help thinking that if she could figure it out, she would find something important.

Something related to why she was here now, why she felt so cold inside despite the heat of Greyson's body wrapped around her.

She wondered if she'd given up first. If her parents had turned from her because she'd pulled away from them, retreating into a world where the emotions of others didn't color her thoughts, where touching people didn't put confusing pictures in her head, because there were no people to touch.

Was she still hiding? She'd become a counselor. Her job was to help people, to reach out to them and try to heal their pain.

But part of that meant shutting herself off from them, meant tuning out of their lives the minute they walked out the door, and not thinking of them again until their next sessions.

Part of that meant comforting herself with the thought that she was a good person because she helped people, not a cold person who didn't care what happened to them. It gave her license to stay uninvolved.

Greyson had asked her once why she did what she did when she knew better than anyone how cruel and inhumane people really were in their hearts.

She didn't know if she had a good answer for that anymore, because she didn't know if her choice of profession was really as altruistic as she'd imagined. If that little second heart, that little bit of the Accuser, had nestled beneath her ribs for fifteen years . . . who was to say she hadn't been feeding on her clients since the day she started working?

Who was to say she really wasn't someone so . . .

so *bad,* her own parents couldn't even love her? She shivered.

Greyson's arms tightened around her. "What's wrong?" he whispered.

"I thought you were asleep."

"I was. Mostly."

It wasn't a question she could ask, not with the boys so close by. She opened her mouth to say it was nothing, but instead she asked, "What do you feed on?"

He didn't move, didn't change his position at all, which in itself told her the question had thrown him. "What do you mean?"

"You heard me."

"You mean *vregonis* in general, or me specifically?"

"Both."

"A lot of us smoke."

"But you don't. Not often." She knew he did some-times—though not generally around her—but she'd never really thought of it as something he would do for . . . well, for his health. The thought would have amused her if she wasn't so nervous.

"Not as a rule, no. Too obvious."

"But, I mean, how does it . . . work?"

"It's energy." He shifted position, leaning back a little to glance at the brothers. They hadn't moved. "Some things have more than others, but we all need to con-sume some of it. Like calories, but power instead."

"So earlier, with Maldon . . . it was energy he wanted or just blood? I mean, do blood demons just feed on blood, or do they get energy from other places too?"

"He wanted blood."

"Because he's a blood demon or because—"

"Blood demons like blood."

She ignored the flatness of his tone. "But the other night when you got shot . . . is one of your demons a blood demon? Because he wanted your blood, remember?"

He paused. "Some demons consider it a . . . an honor, to be allowed blood. An intimacy."

It fell into place then. His refusal to look at her, his tension, his anger—it had seemed excessive, hadn't it, over something that hadn't appealed to her but hadn't seemed like such a huge thing, especially not in the demon world.

"He took something intimate from me," she whispered, turning so she could look at him. When he didn't reply, she continued. "Something you've never had."

Silence stretched between them, prickly and rough, before he spoke. "Yes."

"Do you, I mean—"

"Why Miss Chase, are you trying to seduce me?" He smiled, but she hadn't missed the quick gleam of red in his eyes before he blinked. "Don't worry about it, Meg. It's not a necessity. It's not something I think about."

He'd never really lied to her before. She had no idea if he'd just started.

The lukewarm water in the shower did nothing to improve her mood in the morning, nor did Greyson's snide comments about the quality of the room or the stagnant sodium odor of the boys' fast-food breakfasts. She just wanted to get the day over with so the next day would end too and she could go home.

At least she'd remembered her own toiletries and, even better, at least Spud was waiting with hair dryer and brush when she stepped out of the dingy bathroom. She might be a pariah, but she didn't have to look like one.

Megan had never considered herself a vain person, or one for whom appearances were that important. But she couldn't help feeling a little smug. With the exception of Malleus, Maleficarum, and Spud, who always looked like they were about to start cleaning their fingernails with knives, everyone she was bringing to this funeral was eminently presentable. She was the least attractive of the bunch.

The thought might have made her smile on any other day, when the memories of last night and her own confusion didn't hang over her like carcasses in a butchershop window. Instead she watched herself solemnly in the mirror while Spud fixed her hair, and wished she was somewhere else, anywhere else. That it was this time next week—which she realized with a shock would be the day after Christmas—and she was alone in the woods with Greyson, drinking cocktails and watching the fire with his head in her lap.

She kept that image in her mind, focused on it, and held it there while she put on her dress and shoes, while she sat on the edge of the bed and watched Greyson shave, while they drove to the church, the brothers following in her car.

The white cross reaching into the winter-gray sky

reminded her, with a sharp stab of humiliation, of her adventure at Holy Innocents the night before. It felt as if years had passed since then, but she didn't think she would ever forget the image of the priest turning his back on her. Just as well, really. In the hard light of day she couldn't imagine what she'd thought she would gain from it. If God really had power over demons, her escorts wouldn't be preparing to walk into United Methodist with her.

If God really had power over demons, she wouldn't be able to walk in herself. It had been foolish, really, one last momentary childish desire for reassurance, and if life had taught her anything it was that looking for others to help her gained her nothing.

She looked around for her mother and brother, but didn't see them. Instead she saw what looked like hundreds of pairs of eyes, drawn to her like iron filings to a magnet. Vaguely familiar faces frowned in disapproval. She clutched Greyson's hand more tightly and leaned back against the car, letting Malleus, Maleficarum, and Spud close in a tight little half circle around them.

"Do you want to go in now, or wait?" Greyson's lips brushed the top of her head. "Get in the car and go home?"

"Don't tempt me," she replied shakily. "Let's wait a couple of minutes, okay? I want Brian and Tera to come with us."

He gave her hand a quick squeeze and she went back to watching the crowd, a familiar anger rising in her chest. Who the hell were they to stare at her in disapproval? To pass judgment on her? This was her father's funeral, damn it. She had a right to be here. Every right in the world.

The sun broke through the clouds, weak but welcome just the same. Megan rummaged in her purse for her sunglasses, and slipped them on just as Brian's car pulled into the crowded lot.

It took only a moment for him to park and another few for him and Tera to get out and head for them, but even at this distance Megan saw Tera's face set in tense, angry lines. Tera was her friend, but Tera was about as empathetic as a spider; what on earth about this funeral angered her?

Witches were almost as difficult to read as demons, but Megan didn't need her abilities—as little used as they were these days—to feel Tera's anger. It expressed itself in every stiff muscle in her body as she hugged Megan and nodded to everyone else. It wasn't until Brian's lips brushed Megan's cheek that Tera spoke.

"Two of my witches died the other night, Greyson. What do you know about it?"

Chapter Twelve

E xcuse me?"
    "Don't 'excuse me' me, you know exactly what I'm talking about."

"What makes you think—"

"They were Templeton Black's nighttime guards, Grey. Now they're dead, and it looks like a demon killing. Their . . ." Tera swallowed. "Their bodies were mutilated."

Greyson shrugged. "What a great loss to the world."

"Wait a minute. Templeton Black's guards? But they—"

She didn't need Greyson's hand to tighten painfully on hers to stop talking. The church and the funeral about to begin inside had disappeared. Instead she was back on the cold city street while Ktana Leyak reached into one man's chest and ripped out his heart; she and Brian exchanged worried glances.

"M'lady, we oughter get inside," Maleficarum said, shifting on his feet and nodding toward the church. The parking lot was almost empty of people now.

Tera glanced at the church, then back at all of them. "We're not done talking about this."

"Of course not. That would imply sensitivity to Megan's loss," Greyson said.

Tera ignored him. "But we should go in."

Together they made their way up the sidewalk and through the wide, polished double doors of the church, closed to the winter air. Megan gasped.

About half the pews were full of mourners, their backs in dark clothing looking like fat crows perched on planks, but she barely saw them. Her gaze was drawn upward instead, to the railings of the choir loft, to the ornate pillars in lengthwise rows up the sides of the building.

Every one of them was covered with demons. Her demons, crouching on rails, clinging to ornate stone, with multicolored light from the stained-glass windows playing across their slick skin. They'd come to support her at her father's funeral.

Tears stung her eyes. Feeling a little childish, she ducked her head, pressed it against Greyson's sleeve so she wouldn't start sobbing. Yezer didn't feel love, as far as she knew; their anger at the recent losses of life had more to do with fear it might happen to them than any sense of sadness. So they weren't here out of caring, but out of respect. Somehow it meant just as much. Somehow it meant more.

Unless they were just here because funerals offered excellent feeding. Which was entirely possible. She preferred to think of it as respect.

"We need to sit down," Brian murmured beside her, and she realized people were starting to turn and look at them—exactly what she'd been warned not to allow to happen.

Safely sandwiched on the bench between the two

men, she was able to look up at the little demons again, and nod slightly, hoping they could see her gratitude. She thought they could. They nodded back, almost as one, a choreographed routine nobody else could see.

"Don't you want to sit up front?" Brian whispered. Funny, of all of her escorts he looked the most uncomfortable. The demons and the witch all sat calmly, staring obediently ahead as if they were in a very grandiose schoolroom, but Brian fidgeted and glanced around. Of course. Not a religion thing; he felt her demons.

"My mother told me to be unobtrusive," she said, not bothering to hide her bitterness. "Oh, and my demons are here."

He visibly relaxed. "Thanks for telling me. I wondered why I felt kind of weird."

"You didn't think it was the blasphemy of being in a Protestant church?"

"I figured if I made it through the door without being smited, I had a chance."

If the officiating pastor hadn't stepped up to the podium at that moment, Megan probably would have laughed. As it was she just smiled softly and settled back in her seat, her right hand firmly in Greyson's. Brian reached over to take her left, a gesture that touched her.

". . . David was an accountant, known to most everybody. A family man, survived by his beloved wife Diane and his son David Junior, who will be taking over his firm and his place on the town council. You all know the good works that his company has done for the town—donating new benches for the park, sponsoring school fund-raisers, helping to keep our streets clean.

"David also had a daughter named Megan. I knew David as a good man, one who always wanted to help others . . ."

Megan knew she shouldn't have expected anything else, but she still felt like someone had hit her in the chest. Her eyes stung. Brian's hand convulsed on hers, but Greyson didn't move. She glanced over at him. His face was impassive. Was he even listening?

She turned around, checking to see how clear the path to the door was. Not so clear. The church wasn't crowded, but just inside the doors stood Orion Maldon, staring right at her. Their eyes met and he grinned.

She turned away quickly, to where the pastor was now giving the lectern to her brother. Great. If there was anything she didn't need right now, it was to listen to anything Dave had to say.

"Those witches were Templeton's guards?" she whispered to Greyson.

"Hmm? Yes. I assume they came after you on Monday while you were messing around with their car?"

"We weren't messing around, but yes. And K—she killed them." Megan glanced past Brian to Tera, whose eyes were focused straight ahead.

". . . the best father anyone could ever ask for. Dad was always there for me . . ."

Greyson nodded and put his arm around her, pulling her closer so they could continue their barely audible discussion. "Don't worry about it."

"How can I not worry about it? Tera thinks you did it."

"Tera can think whatever she likes, but without proof

it won't do her much good. I wasn't even in town that night, remember? Besides, I have more sense than to go after witches and she knows it."

"Should I tell her what happened? Brian can back—"

"Good God no, are you insane? It's none of her business. Eventually she'll get tired of poking around and go back to whatever else it is she does all day."

"What if she doesn't?"

"Don't you have other things to think about just now?"

"*. . . when I was eleven, and he helped me build a soapbox derby racer for Boy Scouts . . .*"

She tried to tune out Dave's speech. "Like what, how everyone is embarrassed to even say my name?"

"Did you expect anything else?" *Ouch.* "No, I mean Maldon over there in the corner."

She shifted in her seat, refusing to look at Maldon again but feeling his gaze on her, while her brother continued droning in the front of the church. "He came just to get at me—at us?"

"I don't think so, no."

"Then why?"

Greyson paused. "I don't think he was lying about your father. I think they did know each other."

"Apparently most people did, right? The town council, the accountancy firm . . ." Another surge of bitterness, cold and sharp in her chest.

"*. . . when I finally got it together to go to college, and he and Mom supported me every step of the way . . .*"

"Doesn't that strike you as odd? They'll barely look at

you, but your father went on to become a pillar of the community, such as it is. *You* went to a bar last night and got threatened, but he bought benches and led parades."

"He's not the one who—"

"Stop playing the martyr and think, darling. What could have happened, who could have been powerful enough to make sure your father stayed in business, stayed everybody's friend, while you twisted in the wind? Whose influence could have been brought in to play here?"

Duh. "My dad made a deal with Maldon?"

"Looks like it to me."

"*. . . the position in the firm was just waiting for me. He had my name put on the door before I even got there—a gift to me . . .*"

"I suppose we need to go over there later and find out."

"That's my girl." He kissed the back of her hand and looked toward the front of the church. "Does your brother ever shut up?"

She laughed before she could help herself, a quick nervous bark. Heads turned, and she quickly looked down. "Shit."

"What?"

"What do you think? Here I am, Megan the murderous ghoul, giggling at my father's funeral?"

Now he laughed, thankfully much more softly than she had. "What do you care what they think?"

"My mother—"

"Is a bitch. You don't need these people, *bryaela,* not for anything. They can think whatever they want."

The words sank into her, through her, a spark of truth she didn't yet know that she could fully accept. He was right, absolutely. The thoughts and opinions of the residents of Grant Falls should be no more important to her than the results of *American Idol*.

Shouldn't be, but still were. Was she that much of a wimp? Anger rose in her chest, insinuating itself through her brain, but she couldn't tell if she was mad at them or herself. Or mad, again, at her father, who certainly had not been "the best father any girl could ever ask for."

Dave finally ceded the floor to someone else, a face vaguely familiar to Megan and a voice more so. Bill Ryan, a golfing buddy of her father's. She had a few dim memories of the two men drinking and talking about sports in the backyard, before she reached her teens and they did their drinking elsewhere. Bill was followed by a few other speakers, then the pastor again. Megan wanted to listen. She felt like she was at the funeral of a stranger, someone she'd never really known, and wondered if perhaps somewhere in their words she would find him.

But a small voice in her head refused to let her, a voice that sounded suspiciously like Greyson's. What did it matter? The man was dead. He'd never really been much of a father and now he was gone. Why should she try to know him when he'd never tried to know her?

The man they buried today had died to her thirteen years ago when she'd gone to college. Before that, even. This was just the final period on a sentence that ended long before, so what did it matter?

That wasn't right. She should care. She should be sad.

Instead she was bored. And that thought, more than any other, brought tears to her eyes.

Beside her Greyson turned and murmured something to Malleus, who got up and crossed behind them. Going to set things up with Orion, she guessed.

Rustlings and gentle scrapings indicated that everyone else in the church was getting up too. Was the service over?

No. The mourners were lining up in the center aisle, getting ready to go say their good-byes.

Megan tensed in her seat. Should she go up? If she did everyone would watch, but if she didn't they would all wonder why she wasn't going, and would stare even more.

"Are you actually supposed to get up and just stare at his dead body?" Tera whispered, leaning across Brian. "I mean, isn't that a little weird?"

"It's . . . you're supposed to say a prayer, or something," Megan said.

"But you don't put anything in the casket with him, or touch him or anything?"

"Well, not as a rule, I guess."

Tera rolled her eyes. "Regulars are so confusing."

Several people glanced at her as she said it; Megan bit her lip to keep from laughing while a rush of affection for her friend flowed through her. The combination of Tera's comment and Greyson's earlier about not needing these people seemed to coalesce in her head in that moment and a weight she hadn't really known was there lifted. She was no less hurt, no less angry or scared, but she had people who cared about her.

It wasn't only that either. The service was over, she'd made it through the worst of it, her last public appearance in Grant Falls. Relief made her giddy. Her chest swelled with warmth, her vision seemed sharper.

The church emptied around them while Megan sat and enjoyed, for the first time in days, the feeling of being absolutely in control, absolutely safe. Her demons still crowded the ceiling, there for her. Six people flanked her sides, there for her. It felt good. She smiled to herself and squeezed Greyson's hand.

"Are you okay?" he asked.

"Fine." She didn't look at him, though. She was too busy looking around, thinking about how she'd never have to see this place again, about all those people with their petty worries and miseries, the blackness in their tiny hearts, how insignificant they were compared to her.

"I'm ready." She stood up and smoothed her skirt.

"Meg, maybe—"

"I'm fine," she said again. "Just need to pay my respects, right?"

Greyson's hand tightened on hers, but she shook it off and squeezed her way past Brian and Tera into the aisle. Her mother and Dave stood there; Dave's arm was around Diane's shoulders and her head was bent, her handkerchief pressed to her face.

"Megan," Dave said. "I, uh . . ."

"Sure, Dave. Excuse me." She brushed past them, lowering her shields a tad as she did so she could feel their shock and pain. Ha, served them right. Silly little things, so worried about their stupid miserable lives, about the opinions of others and their social standing in this piss-ant town . . . just like her father had been. Just like they all were.

It seemed to take no time at all to reach the front of the church, as if she had glided up the aisle rather than walked. Behind her she heard her friends talking to each other in low urgent whispers, but she ignored them.

Smooth, cold wood pressed against her palms as she curled her fingers around the edge of the coffin. There he was. Her father.

Older than she remembered him, of course. Despite the yearly Christmas photo she still tended to think of him as he'd been when she'd last seen him. Now the years sat plainly on his still, cold face. Even plainer was the truth; this wasn't her father. He was really gone, and in death he was no less remote to her than he'd been in life.

So sad. She started to whisper it, thinking it might be funny to hear it out loud, to let him know she was too strong for him to hurt now, when the truth of what was happening hit her.

She squeezed the wood, suddenly terrified. This wasn't her, having these thoughts, standing over the dead body of her father and wanting to laugh. This was someone else, someone cold who lurked inside her, someone who'd taken advantage of her relaxed and wandering mind to lower her shields and open herself to the energy of her demons.

She'd sat in that pew and fed on the mourners. It was their sadness, their pain, making her high.

Footsteps beat a muffled, quick tempo on the floor of the aisle behind her. Her knees gave out, and she fell into Maleficarum's arms just a second before the world disappeared.

"It was tribute, Megan. They didn't know it would upset you," Rocturnus said again. Megan turned around to look at him, perched on the backseat of Greyson's car. "They were trying to make you feel better, to pay you for letting them be there."

"Yeah, I feel great now."

"They thought you might punish them for staying through the whole service if they didn't."

"They know I'm not going to punish them," she snapped. "Why can't they just get—"

"They don't know that, and even if they did they would still wish it wasn't so, and you know it. They need their lives to be run in a certain way."

"Then maybe we should just let them. Let them go be with someone who'll beat them regularly, and leave me alone."

"I don't think that's a very good idea," Greyson said, speaking for the first time since he'd put her in the car. She cringed, thinking of it. Everyone gathered outside, waiting for the casket to be loaded into the hearse for its trip to the cemetery . . . Just as well she hadn't planned on going.

"Why not? I don't want to do this anymore. I'm tired of it, the misery being pushed on me and I'm supposed to be pleased, and the crazy urges—"

"Urges?"

Shit, she hadn't told him about any of the other stuff,

had she? One more thing she was hiding from him. "Their crazy urges to have me punish them. What did you think I meant?"

He shrugged, but she didn't like the quick sidelong glance he gave her. "Just asking."

"So why isn't it a good idea?"

"Well, aside from the very real possibility that you could die, there's a distinct chance you'll die."

"Why?"

"Because, and I thought we all understood this, they're connected to you. Physically connected. They're part of your body. Remove them, remove that piece of demon inside you, and you remove your heart. Aside from the metaphysical issues—you could conceivably lose your soul—the physical effects would be devastating."

Fuck. "But some of them have been leaving, right? And a few have died themselves. So I don't get it."

"They're connected to you as a whole, not individually. Think of it as—as a flower, for lack of a more manly example. A few petals can fall off and it still looks like a flower, but if too many petals go, it's nothing."

"So without them, I'll be nothing."

"Yes."

Roc shifted in his seat, breaking the gloomy silence. "Megan, they'll be waiting. Can I give them your thanks?"

"What? Shit. You might as well. Tell them it was great to see them there, and, um, I'm pleased they came." She was, even though she felt like someone had just slapped her. They really were trying to help.

Roc nodded and disappeared again.

"Greyson . . . what happens to a flower when a few of the petals fall off?"

"The other petals have to work harder to get sunlight, I think. Why?"

"Just wondering." Maybe that was why her unusual desires had been stronger lately. Four of her demons had died. Several more—she wasn't sure exactly how many—had gone to Ktana Leyak. So if she'd somehow been getting strength, or whatever it was, from them since September, and she needed that now to live . . .

That might explain why the experience in the church had been so different from the other ones too. Not a sudden, violent craving or aversion, but more like the few occasions in college when she'd smoked a joint. That light, floaty feeling, stealing through her body . . . it had been excessively pleasant.

Which made it even scarier.

Chapter Thirteen

"No, no," Greyson said into the phone. "*Kadagia.* Yes. *Goraner lisket ti bressma,* okay?"

Megan stepped in front of him, her back to him so he could unzip her dress. This he did, giving her bra strap a tiny tug when he was done—a habitual gesture that made her smile.

They had about forty minutes before they would meet Brian and Tera for lunch. Just enough time for him to make some calls and her to—well, to flip through a magazine or watch lame daytime television.

Maybe she should get used to it, get herself hooked on a soap. She had nothing else to do during the day, after all. When Megan was little her mother had followed *Guiding Light*—she still remembered sitting next to her, watching. One of the only memories she had of feeling close to her mother.

Damn it! Why were these memories still hurtful?

"I need *hin beranto etcha bayena,* and *sint restor.* By tonight, *escazer.*"

She opened her suitcase and grabbed a black sweater and jeans, while Greyson kept ordering around his minions or whatever it was he was doing. The demon language flowed through the motel room like water, soothing and oddly comforting at the same time, a backdrop for her thoughts that was better than the talk show set to low volume.

Once she'd gotten past the initial terror at the thought of feeding from her demons, it didn't seem so unmanageable. Creepy, yes. But she didn't eat much as a rule. She could handle this. None of the urges she'd had so far had come to fruition, after all, which meant they didn't have to.

Today it had been forced on her. It wouldn't be again.

Fooling herself? Very possibly. But it made her feel a little better, and right now she would grasp at just about anything that would make her feel better. It was easier too, in the unreality of Grant Falls, so far away from her real life. Here the fact that she'd lost her practice didn't seem as important. The worries plaguing her receded.

The Christmas season always had an air of time suspended anyway, especially at the Serenity Partners office, where they tried to give their patients a sense of family and celebration. There, and at every other job Megan had ever worked, the last couple of days before the holiday were spent eating rumballs and doing shots—which were basically the same thing, if Megan was doing the cooking—opening presents, running into other offices in the building with cookies and snacks . . . it was as if a bubble existed, and in that bubble responsibilities disappeared.

Death was kind of the same way, although with far less tinsel and photocopying of private parts.

Speaking of which . . .

Greyson hung up, then immediately started dialing again. He glanced back at her, still standing in her bra and panties, and raised his eyebrows, but lifted the phone to his ear just the same.

She could have blamed it on her fear, and the need to be held and comforted. She could have blamed it on her sadness and the need to forget. She could even have blamed it on that strange biological urge to reproduce that takes over so many people when a death occurs.

But those were all excuses, and she knew it. And she didn't care.

Her bare feet made no sound as she crept up to him, circling his waist with her arms. He kept talking, but his free arm stole around her, his palm resting possessively on the small of her back as she stood on tiptoe to nibble at the smooth, smoky-scented skin of his throat. His fingers found the top of her panties and insinuated themselves underneath. She felt goose bumps rise on her back.

"What? No, tell them no. Not until they hear from me."

Good, but not quite good enough. One by one she undid the buttons of his white shirt, then lifted his T-shirt to expose a slice of hard, flat stomach. She scratched it lightly. His breath hitched in his chest. Megan slid her hand down far enough to know his mind wasn't entirely on his conversation anymore.

His voice didn't falter until she'd undone his belt and tucked her hand under his waistband, closing her fingers around him. Her bra came loose; he'd unfastened it with his free hand. Sparks flared throughout her body, tiny spots of tingling heat adding to the warmth already there.

"Oh, I know, I . . . what?"

She sank to her knees in front of him and pulled down his zipper.

"I'll call you back," he said, and the phone fell to the floor.

Afterward she lay collapsed on top of him, her forehead nestled under his chin while he stroked her back. Every inch of her body felt relaxed, all the tension gone. Which had kind of been the point, really.

"We should get up," he murmured. "We'll be late."

"Mmm."

"And I didn't get to finish my call."

"Are you complaining?"

"I'm not a complainer."

She slid sideways to lay next to him, one leg thrown casually over his. From that angle, looking up at him, his cheekbones seemed to cut the air around his face. "Greyson?"

"Hmm?"

"Do you . . . do you think you were a good son? To your father, I mean?"

"Couldn't give a fuck, *bryaela*." He reached down and stroked her thigh. "In fact, I rather hope I'm not."

"He's still alive?"

"Unfortunately."

"But—where? Georgetown?"

"Mm-hmm." Where he grew up, she knew. He'd told

her once about watching his parents dress for an inaugural ball when he was a little boy. He'd never mentioned them in the present tense, and she knew his mother had died when he was young—she'd just assumed they were both dead.

"Do you ever see him?"

"No."

"Why not?"

"Why haven't you been back here for thirteen years?"

"Point taken."

"Come on. I'm hungry." He kissed her forehead and started to slide away, but she grabbed his arm.

"Why?"

The bed shook a little as he dug his fists in the mattress and pushed himself up to a sitting position, his dark eyes opaque as he studied her face. "Okay. I'll tell you a story about him and then we need to get dressed."

She nodded.

"Right after my mother died, I found him in my bedroom, going through my stuff. He was taking everything she'd ever given me, all my books and clothes and—well, everything. I asked him what he was doing, and he said, 'Well, the whore is gone, so we can get rid of her shit too.'"

"Oh my God."

He shrugged. "The sentiment behind it wasn't surprising. They never liked each other. It wasn't the words, you see, or even what he was doing. It was that he didn't think I might not see it the same way. It never occurred to him that I wasn't him. And until then, it hadn't occurred to me either."

"How old were you?" she asked softly.

"Nine."

"What was—"

His lips on hers cut off her question before he slid off the bed, unfolding his long, lean body and opening his suitcase. "Don't you get enough of this at work?"

"I quit."

"What?"

Megan pulled the thin hotel sheet up, covering her bare breasts. "I quit. Monday morning. I left."

His brows furrowed for a minute as he stood by the cheap dresser. "Just like that?"

"This business with Gerald . . . I didn't want to stay anymore." It was mostly true, right?

He nodded, but she thought she saw something else in his eyes. Suspicion, maybe, or just curiosity?

"I can still pay my bills," she said, not sure why she was being defensive but being it just the same. "The show pays me enough."

"You don't have to explain it to me." He slipped a white T-shirt over his head, then a charcoal V-neck sweater, one of her favorites.

"But . . . I mean, don't you have an opinion?"

"Yes, and you know what it is. What did you expect, that I'd be shocked and disappointed? I've wanted you to leave that damned practice for months."

"That's not why I did it."

"I never would have assumed it was." He buckled his belt and leaned over to kiss her forehead. "Come on. Unless you want to stay in bed? You do look fetching under that flimsy sheet." His teeth scraped her throat.

"We could send the boys out for food, and spend the day—"

"No. Brian and Tera are waiting." This was so typical. He opened up, then retreated. Now she was doing the same. She wanted to talk to him, to tell him why she'd left, how scared she was, that her radio pay would cover the bills but not much else. That she didn't know if she could ever do her job effectively again, that in her darkest hours she'd found herself actually considering taking up the station's offer of a TV spot on their evening infotainment show because at least there she wouldn't find herself accidentally sucking out people's pain like oysters from a shell.

But something held her back, as firmly as a hand over her mouth. If she told him he'd want to help. He'd offer to cover her bills. He'd as much as offered several times already, and she just . . . she didn't want to be kept.

She didn't want to look weak.

"Ah, yes. Our friends Brian and Tera. How long do you think it will take before Tera brings up those witches again?"

She smiled in spite of herself. "About two minutes."

"That long?" He took her hand and tugged her gently up from the bed, encircling her bare body with his arms so his palms rested hot on her back. "And speaking of time . . . we have ten minutes or so, don't we?"

They were fifteen minutes late, in the end, long enough for Brian and Tera to be thoroughly annoyed.

"We were worried about you," Tera said, for the second time. "You should have called."

"I—we fell asleep."

"You told me you never nap."

"I did today," Megan said lightly, grabbing a menu from the stand. This restaurant—a tidy little diner off the highway—wasn't close enough to town for her to run into anyone she knew, at least so she hoped, and it was crowded enough to make her think the food might be decent.

Tera raised an eyebrow, but didn't comment. Instead she turned to Greyson. "So, Grey, about those witches . . ."

"I win," he muttered. Megan elbowed him.

"I just have a hard time believing it's a coincidence," Tera continued.

"It probably isn't, but I don't see why I'm your chief suspect when the one you should be looking at is already in custody."

"Templeton? He couldn't have done it."

"How do you know?"

"Because he's—he's in prison. He couldn't have gone out and—"

"And I was in New York, but you're perfectly willing to believe I was behind it all."

Megan had seen the implication earlier, outside the church, but it wasn't until that moment that it fell into place. The witches were Templeton's guards. The witches had tried to kill them—or at least warn them, if shooting at them from a speeding car and chasing them through the city flinging foul, oily smoke at them could be considered a warning.

Templeton Black must have been behind it.

Jesus, was there anyone who didn't want to cause trouble for her this week?

"Look, Tera, if there's a problem I'll come to your office after the holidays, but you know as well as I do that I'm not stupid enough to go after witches, and I don't think there's any need to bore Brian with this anymore, do you?"

Tera glanced at Brian, who was studying his menu. Medieval monks transcribing holy texts could not have concentrated harder.

"Fine," she said. "But I—"

"C'n I take your order?"

Brian practically leaped out of his skin. Megan smiled, but her laugh died in her throat. She felt awfully jumpy too. She'd thought it was just the tension from Greyson and Tera's conversation, but the butterflies in her stomach didn't want to settle even now, when Greyson and Tera seemed to have reached at least some kind of accord.

In fact, as everyone ordered, they were only getting worse with each passing second. Megan asked for a Caesar salad she knew she wouldn't eat. The thought of food, so appealing ten minutes before, now made her queasy.

"Brian," she murmured, leaning over the table toward him, "what's wrong?"

"I don't—I'm not sure."

"There's a demon in here," Greyson said.

"Of course there is." Tera raised her eyebrows. "You're here and your men—"

"No." His voice was barely above a whisper as he leaned back, glancing casually around the restaurant. "Not like us."

Malleus and Maleficarum also leaned back, shifting their chairs so they faced more toward the restaurant than the table. Spud got up entirely and plunked himself down next to Megan.

"Is it—" Megan started, but she didn't need his warning glance to tell her not to finish the sentence.

"I think that's a pretty good guess, don't you?"

She nodded.

"What are you talking about?" Tera asked. "Who?"

"A demon. One we don't want to mess with. Maybe we should go." Megan tried not to look around the room, but couldn't help stealing one glance.

No one else in the diner seemed to notice anything wrong. All around them were smiling faces, people chatting as they ate, families with little children playing tic-tac-toe on napkins or paper place mats. Megan folded her arms across her chest in a fruitless attempt to warm herself. Was one of these people, these happy diners, possessed? And if so, would they survive?

Gerald hadn't.

"Whatever it is, I'm sure it's aware of us," Greyson said. "But it might not know we're aware of it."

"Is it the waitress?" Tera asked. "I mean, you guys didn't seem to get really nervous until she came, right?"

"I don't know. I don't think so."

"How do you not know? Don't you guys all recognize each other?"

"Whoever she . . . it is, it's possessing someone. So

no, I feel it, but I don't know who it is. I'd have to look into their eyes or touch them to really know."

Megan caught Brian's eye. He tilted his head back and to the right. She nodded. He'd read that side, she'd read the other.

"Don't," Greyson said. "Don't warn it."

"But if—"

"No. I know what you guys are thinking, but we don't know who or what it is. Let's not—"

Their waitress appeared, balancing their tray on one hand while she flipped open a wooden stand with more force than seemed necessary with the other. She shot a glare back toward the kitchen.

"Here." She set the tray on the stand and started handing out plates, her brows knitted in a grouchy frown.

"Is something wrong?" Megan asked.

"No, it's just the cook." The waitress smiled faintly. "He's got a bee in his bonnet today, you know? Like none of the rest of us work hard. He practically threw your plates at me, at least your food is hot—"

The words turned into a scream as a knife flew past her face and embedded itself in the wall next to Megan's head.

Megan started to jump back, but before she could move more than a few inches Spud was on top of her, his bulky body pressing her hard against the floor of the diner. A dried scrap of bacon sat only inches from her nose; she made a face and tried to twist away, but Spud's weight was unmovable.

Screams erupted around the room. The floor shook

as diners got up, scattering chairs and knocking over tables, sending plates crashing to the tile. At least so Megan assumed. She heard the sounds and felt the tremors but couldn't see much beyond the petrified bacon.

"God damn it, Spud, get off me!"

"Megan!" Tera's voice, calm but with an edge of panic. "Are you okay?"

"Sorry, Spud," Megan muttered, and brought her fist up with as much strength as she could muster into the side of his head. Pain shot from her fingers all the way up her arm. His head was like granite.

He pulled back a little; the reproach in his eyes would have made Megan laugh if she hadn't been so mad.

"I'm sorry, but get the fuck off me! Now!"

"Let her up, Spud," Greyson said, sounding very tired and far away. Spud moved.

The restaurant was almost empty, save for one elderly couple calmly chewing as if nothing had happened. Megan grabbed the edge of the table and pulled herself up.

Greyson, Tera, and Brian were standing in a line together, watching the entrance to the kitchen, with Malleus and Maleficarum flanking them. In the doorway to the kitchen stood the chef, his chest heaving, his eyes red, and a handful of knives clutched in one muscular fist.

Megan barely had time to take this in before he noticed her. His mouth opened, lips curled in a snarl, as he hurled another knife.

Spud's hand snapped over the blade two inches from her face.

Megan jumped back as the chef wound up again.

This time the blade disappeared, dissolving somehow into a harmless trickle of water before it was out of the chef's hand. They all turned to look at Tera, who shrugged.

"He surprised me last time."

The chef, obviously frustrated, eyed them with the air of a cat who didn't understand why the ball of yarn wasn't dead already. His arm swung back, but froze on a muttered word from Tera.

"You witches come in handy," Greyson murmured. Tera frowned but didn't take her eyes off the chef.

"Is he the one? The demon?"

"I don't know, I—"

"Larry? Larry!"

They all turned—except Tera—to look as the elderly woman in the restaurant, the dedicated eater, started screaming. Her entire body shook as she backed away from her husband, dropping her fork with a clatter that seemed much louder than it should have.

Larry stood up as well, his thick body expanding, his head waving from side to side like he was trying to shake away a fly. Megan watched in horror as his shoulders broadened, as his torso stretched long enough for his shirt to come untucked, exposing a long line of fish-belly-white skin.

"I'm guessing it's him," Greyson said.

Chapter Fourteen

Whatever talents Ktana Leyak might have, Megan thought in the next dizzy seconds before all hell broke loose, the ability to pile on the distractions had to rank near the top.

Larry turned to them, his papery face stretched shiny, his eyes burning pits. Once again Megan heard the voice of Ktana Leyak erupting from a mouth that had no business shaping it.

"Hello again, Megan." Larry's expression turned coy. It was so bizarre to see an old man simper Megan might have laughed if she hadn't been so utterly terrified.

Malleus and Spud rushed forward to the chef and hustled him out of the doorway, taking advantage of his inability to move. A steel door slammed, barely audible over the panicked screams of the old woman. Her hands pressed against her cheeks, her eyes open so wide they seemed to float from their sockets.

"Larry! Larry!"

Larry glanced at her. Almost as an afterthought his arm swung back, slamming the woman across the face, throwing her back against the wall. The windows rattled. The woman did not scream again.

"And a witch." The giggle made every hair on Megan's body stand on end. "Good. I'm hungry again."

It all seemed to take such a long time, but in reality Megan knew only seconds had passed, that the door had slammed at the same time Larry's hand was delivering the blow to his wife, that Malleus and Spud were just reentering the room as Larry moved quickly, his body jerking and creaking, toward Tera.

Flames erupted around him, filling the air with the terrible smell of burning flesh. Still he advanced. The flames grew higher, turned blue-white, as Greyson tried to stop Ktana's advance, but her tinkling laugh floated through the air and the flames died.

Larry's body was charred, blackened, horribly blistered. Megan's stomach twisted and roiled in her belly. Not a man in front of her, not anymore. A thing, a demon-powered corpse worse than any zombie because somehow she knew Larry was still alive in there, that he was still able to feel and think.

Ktana tried to move forward, but Larry's legs were curling, his arms bending, as his muscles shrank from the intense heat. Megan closed her eyes and covered her face, knowing what was coming.

"Get down!" Greyson shouted. Someone jostled Megan, pushing her down, as Larry exploded in a creaking, horrible splat like the breaking of a rotten egg.

Tera started to shout something, a spell or a command, but her voice stopped abruptly. Megan looked up and saw Ktana holding her by the throat.

More flames, white around Ktana's head, disappearing quickly when Greyson saw they were doing no good.

The metallic click of the gun being cocked followed, and a shot, but Megan had already seen how little good bullets did.

Tera's face was turning blue. The sight galvanized Megan, seemed to galvanize all of them, because they rushed forward as one. Megan grabbed Ktana's arm, the flesh rubbery and somehow fragile under her fingers, as though it was only a thin layer of flesh over something putrid that was about to burst. It did split a little as she dug her fingernails in, trying to break the demon queen's hold on her friend. Clear, reddish-brown liquid seeped out from the wounds, stinging Megan's skin.

Brian fought Ktana's other hand as it went for Tera's chest, trying to catch it between his arm and his side so he could bring his hand down karate-chop style on the back of her elbow. She kept managing to slip out of the makeshift vice but he refused to let go, his movements increasingly frantic as the choked sounds coming from Tera's throat grew fainter. Malleus and Maleficarum joined the fight, hitting Ktana, punching her, but nothing seemed to make any difference.

Megan looked around, desperate to find something that could help them, looking for Greyson and Spud. Spud she finally spotted, crouching over the body of the old woman on the floor. He stood up, caught her gaze, and looked away guiltily; fresh blood dripped off his knife.

Before she had time to even consider what that meant, Greyson pushed her aside. His eyes burned, his rage froze her to the bone, but his expression was impersonal, almost curious. Malleus and Maleficarum's arms tightened around Ktana Leyak's waist and neck; Tera gave one last choked gasp, and Greyson put his hands on Ktana's grinning face.

Megan felt the heat first, heard Ktana's laugh of triumph turn into a shriek of agony.

Then she disappeared, while Tera slid bonelessly to the floor.

"Tera! Oh my God, Tera!" Megan's knees hit the tile with a painful thud as she checked Tera's pulse, finding it—thready, but there. She put her hand under Tera's neck and lifted, trying to open her airway at least a little bit.

Why wasn't anyone helping her? Tera was alive, but what if she had a heart attack or something? Could witches have heart attacks? She assumed so, but they didn't catch human diseases, so—

"What are you doing? What the fuck are you doing?"

Megan tore her gaze away from her pale, unmoving friend to see Brian surrounded by Greyson and the boys. Spud's bloody knife was at his throat. Greyson's hands hesitated on either side of Brian's face. "Are your shields up, Brian?"

Brian caught her eye. "Megan, tell them to get off me!"

"She could come back! Are your shields up, do you still feel her in the room?"

Brian's eyes widened. "I don't—" He glanced down at the knife, then back up. "No, I think she's gone."

Tera coughed. Megan glanced down at her, wanting to help, but she couldn't seem to move. "What do you mean, come back?"

Greyson lowered his hands and the boys relaxed

too, stepping away and leaving Brian to slump against the wall.

"She's a parasite, she could have tried to invade you, or that old woman if she'd still been clinging to life," Greyson said. "Leyaks usually don't—they're imitators, not possessors—but she gets more power this way, I guess. I don't know. But she disappeared before, and she's disappeared now—"

"Before?" Tera croaked from the floor. "Before when?"

They all stood there, grouped together in the wreckage of the diner, until Tera broke the stillness by throwing up on Megan's shoes.

Maldon wasn't putting in the yard tonight. Greyson had been right about that—it was a show put on for her physical discomfort. Unfortunately, just sitting in the same room with him made her more uncomfortable, especially now that she'd come begging, needing information from him.

Sitting in a hotel room watching public-access television with a very grumpy witch who sounded like Wolfman Jack was definitely preferable to this, and that was saying a lot. Lucky Brian got to take care of her instead, while Megan and Greyson ate dinner with Maldon and a few of his *rubendas*. His wife, Megan noticed, was nowhere to be seen.

Megan took another tiny bite of her fish. It was excellent, perfectly cooked, but her stomach was too full of butterflies for anything else to fit.

"So, Megan," Maldon said, setting down his fork.

"What information are you looking for? Your father's business affairs? Your brother's rehab? Your mother's social clubs?"

Megan forced her features to stay still. Another ploy, designed to make her think Maldon knew everything about her family, possibly everything about her.

All the same . . . Dave's rehab? If she hadn't been so loath to admit she needed anything from Maldon at all, she would have loved to have that discussion. Not that she bore Dave any ill will—or at least not much—and not that she wasn't glad he'd gotten help if he needed it, but still . . .

"I'm interested in what you did for him," Megan said, repeating the line she and Greyson had gone over in the car. "How you helped him. What he did for you in return."

Maldon smiled. "I thought you might be. Now let's see . . . You need two pieces of information from me. Two things you want. So do I get two things in exchange?"

She took a deep breath. "I'll owe you a favor."

"Two."

"Not an equal exchange," Greyson said. His hand on her thigh sent waves of reassuring warmth through her body, while the rest of her shivered. God, Maldon hated Greyson. The emotion was so close to anger she felt it, ghostly cool against her bare arms.

Dressing up had been the last thing she'd wanted to do, but demons loved formality, so here she was, in a black cocktail dress Malleus had picked up for her at the mall while Tera settled into bed and the rest of them had a few tense words going over what Tera did and did not need to know about Ktana Leyak.

"Two bits of information, two favors."

Greyson dipped his head to the side. "Are the pieces of information totally unrelated?"

Maldon looked away.

"Good. One favor." Greyson gave her thigh a squeeze. "Ask your questions, Meg."

Whatever Maldon's other faults, his bartender did excellent work. Megan fortified herself with a sip of vodka tonic and took a deep breath. "What did you do for my father?"

"I gave him acceptance. I pulled strings, greased a few palms—with his money, of course." Maldon shrugged. "People who had things against him and your mother suddenly forgot. People were persuaded. Not difficult, but time consuming."

"But why? Why would you do it for him?" Wheels spun in her head but didn't manage to touch ground and move forward. There was another question to be asked, she knew it, but she couldn't seem to formulate it in her head.

"He helped with my books, which are quite complex. He had a good head for figures, your father. I'm sorry he died. He'll be difficult for me to replace."

"He helped with your books as payment or he helped with them before?" She didn't remember seeing Maldon around when she was young, but that didn't matter. The acquaintance, if it was based on her father's needing help to get past the town's anger at her, would have begun when she was well past the age of noticing or caring what her parents did.

"After."

"Was that the deal? That you helped him, and he did your books in exchange?"

"Yes." But Maldon's gaze was too steady and Megan recognized a lie. Her clients did that too—or had, when she'd had clients.

What was he hiding? It couldn't be loyalty to her dead father that stilled his tongue.

The question clicked into place. "How did he know you? I mean, how did he know to come to you to begin with?"

"Everyone in town knows me."

"No, no they don't. I didn't, when I lived here. I never heard anyone talk about you. When did you move here?"

Maldon sighed and shifted in his chair. "You were fourteen, I believe. Miss Chase, my time this evening is limited, and we still have to discuss your payment for the demons you stole. Can we hurry this up?"

Shit! She'd forgotten about that, and she couldn't possibly pay him. "I—"

"She'll give you ten grand for them," Greyson cut in, so smoothly she wasn't sure at first he'd even heard her start to speak. Was he crazy? Ten thousand dollars?

"She will or you will?"

"Does it matter?"

"It does if I'm deciding whether to treat her as head of her own house, or as your *ornita*."

Megan didn't need to know the literal meaning of the word to understand what had been said. Gasps sounded around the table; one or two *rubendas* pushed their chairs back in shock, and fury and embarrassment rose in her chest despite their obvious disapproval.

"Hit him," Greyson muttered.

"What? I—"

"Show him your power. Now."

No time to worry, to wonder about what might happen if she did. He was right. Megan closed her eyes and gathered her strength, seeing the door inside herself, finding her connection to her demons and the source of her own power. Like a rushing underground spring it welled up inside her, filling her chest, flames burning cold into her head. She saw it, tasted the ozone flavor of it, and let it form itself into a wave and pour from her, over the table, over the floor, smashing into Orion Maldon and knocking him from his seat.

She stood up, aware that the others around the table had leaped out of the way and were now staring open-mouthed at her.

"Does she feel like an *ornita* now, Orion?"

"Bitch," Maldon spat from the floor. He wiped blood from his lips and licked it off his fingers.

"Don't do it," Greyson warned. Tension laced his pose as he stared at Maldon. "Insult a Gretneg and get punished. Attack one . . ."

"Eska brenti Gretneg, kallahept!"

Megan blinked. The sensation of cold from the anger in the room seeped through her skin, into her body, as if the blood in her veins was running cold . . . running more slowly . . .

Her knees buckled and she grabbed for the edge of the table with stiff, numb fingers. She couldn't seem to hold it, couldn't put any strength into it . . . Why was it so hard to breathe? The room started swimming as blackness filled the edges of her vision.

Greyson's hand closed over her arm, his fingers dragging bruises from beneath her skin. "Meg, come on, don't give in," he said, but she couldn't hear him very well through the haze of voices and the loud, slow beating of her own heart. *Ba-bump . . . ba-bump . . . ba . . . bump . . .*

"Damn it, Meg, reach for it!"

Ba . . . what was he saying? Did it matter? The cold was starting to feel pleasant now, the way she'd heard it did when you started to freeze to death. Maybe that's what was happening, maybe she could just slip off into sleep now and—*bump.*

What? No!

Her panicked brain rebelled, woke up, and she knew what Greyson was telling her, begging her, to do. Heat burned the arm he held, warming her freezing blood enough to keep it beating, but she needed the heat inside, all the way through her. Somehow she forced herself to open up, envisioned tentacles coming from the demon inside her and reaching out, reaching through her skin, until she found Greyson's power and grabbed it with every bit of strength she had left. It roared through her body, obscuring everything else. For a moment she didn't just see the flames, she *was* them, bright and glorious as she rose to the ceiling and burst apart.

Greyson tugged at her, dragging her away from the table. Her vision cleared, the flames subsiding enough to see it wasn't just in her mind, it wasn't a hallucination built on power. The room was on fire, the curtains already gone, the crystal glasses on the table shattering from the heat.

They made it almost to the edge of the dining room before Maldon grabbed her other hand, almost yanking her away from Greyson. The shaggy blond hair on one side of his head was gone, burned away. His cheek on that side was red, his eyebrow singed.

"T'gau li!" His voice, thick with rage, chilled even Megan's overheated skin as his piercing blue stare bored into her.

But more than his gaze on her, she felt his power. Not being aimed at her, but resting in his body. His abilities, like hers with reading images in people's minds or Greyson's with fire. She felt his connection to blood, felt an answering bell somewhere in her chest and knew that if she wanted to she could attack him in the same way. She could turn his power back on him, combine it with her anger and Greyson's fire, and make him explode from inside. For one moment she wanted to, needed to. Desire burned in her breast and raced through her veins.

Then it was over. And she would never know if it ended because she wanted it to, or if it ended because Greyson punched Maldon squarely on the nose and sent him sprawling across the carpet.

The sliding glass doors behind the dining table exploded. Megan started to turn toward them but she was already falling, being shoved down to the carpet a few inches from Maldon's feet. Demons ran everywhere, down the hall to her right, escaping from what, Megan didn't understand.

Maldon stirred. Blood poured from his nose down his face as he tried to sit up, but Greyson was already grabbing his lapels and using them to lift his upper body.

"You set us up!"

Maldon swung his fist. Greyson's head snapped to the side but he held on, managing to hit Maldon again in the process.

Porcelain shards filled the air as a vase shattered only a few inches from the men's heads. Greyson dropped Maldon and ducked. Megan ducked too, covering her head and screaming as a wall of flame rose behind her.

"Megan! *Go!*"

Glass and china tore her stockings and cut the skin on her knees and palms as she scuttled away. The front door filled her vision, the front door and the promise of freedom from the hell this modern suburban home had become. Over the subtle roar of the fire and Greyson's shouts she heard more gunshots.

No time to waste wondering who was doing the shooting. She had to get out, now, immediately, before the heat overcame her. Sweat poured down her forehead to sting her eyes, but she dared not stop even to wipe it away.

It felt like an eternity before she made it. Her hand slipped on the knob once, twice, three times before she realized the door was locked. She fumbled with the dead bolt, aware that as she stood in front of the ivory-painted door in her black dress she might as well have had a target painted on her back.

Other fingers covered hers, strong and sure, flipping the bolt. Greyson yanked the door open. Cold air rushed in, cooling the sweat on her skin. It felt wonderful, but not as good as knowing she could get out. She lifted her foot to take the first step toward freedom, then stopped short when the cold barrel of a gun pressed right between her eyes.

Chapter Fifteen

Time froze while a thumb cocked the gun. It took forever for that movement to complete itself, while Megan's mouth opened to scream. Instinctively she fell back to her knees, knowing it wouldn't help her, it would only delay the inevitable by a few seconds.

She lowered her shields and let her power surge again, fueled by fear and rage and the desperate need to save herself. Simultaneously flames exploded around the gunman. Megan's energy weapon hit the fire, turning it into a conflagration so bright it seared her retinas.

She rolled away, catching glimpses of the gunman as he fell backward, dropping the glowing, melting hunk of metal that had been the gun. The living room windows shattered. Jesus, how many people were shooting at them?

Greyson landed on top of her with a thud. His heart was beating so hard she could feel it through their clothes. "Are you okay?"

Megan didn't realize she was crying until she tried to talk and nothing came out. She could hardly breathe, much less speak, but she managed a tiny nod.

The room fell silent.

"They're waiting for us," he whispered. She nodded again.

Sirens sounded in the distance, growing louder. For a second relief flooded her body, until she realized that if the police and fire trucks were coming, the gunmen needed to finish their work. Now.

Her thoughts were either right in unison with Greyson's and their assailants, or only a split second behind. His fingers curled around her arm and ripped her up from the floor. A barrage of bullets sent chunks flying from the walls and blasted the picture frames on them, glass raining down on their heads like diamonds as they ran for the hall.

Light spilled faintly from beneath the doors. Megan had the sickening feeling they were heading for a dead end as the sirens grew louder and the gunshots started to slow, but Greyson seemed to know what he was doing. He dragged her through a doorway—past a very surprised demon brushing his teeth—and smashed through the small window at the other end of the bathroom, twisting his body so his back took the brunt and dragging Megan after him.

Together they fell onto the icy ground outside.

All she wanted to do was lie there and let the blessed cold seep into her body, but Greyson yanked her from the ground before she even had a chance to take a breath.

"Come on, we have to get out of here before the—"

Another gunshot, and another, but slower this time, as though only one gunman was left. Megan thought she was going to pee herself. The quiet suburban street had become a vast wasteland, with nowhere to hide. Greyson's car was out front and she knew as well as the gunmen did that they had to get back in that car if they were going to escape.

Like mice they scuttled across the lawn. Megan's legs burned and ached. Trying to keep her balance on the frozen ground in her high heels was not easy. Like most petite women she could handle heels just fine, but this wasn't simply trotting across a rainy street. This was balls-out running, while the sweat soaking her previously overheated body started to cool and all she wanted to do was curl up into a ball and hide.

Flashing lights reflected off the front of the houses down the street as the fire engine started to make its turn. Greyson yanked open the passenger door of the car and practically threw her into it, then jumped in himself, shoving her into the driver's seat. He pushed the button on the console to start the engine.

"Go! Go!"

She'd never driven his car before. The seat was way too far back, but there wasn't time to adjust it so she perched on the very edge. He shoved the car into gear for her and she slammed her foot on the gas, glad she knew how to drive a stick.

Only her grip on the wheel kept her from falling backward as the car practically leaped away from the curb. The fire engine bore down on them, but Megan refused to look at it, staring instead at the road in front of her as they raced away from the gunmen, the demons, and the fire.

"Fuck! Fuck! That miserable little—damn it!" Greyson glanced back over his shoulder. "You weren't hit? You're okay?"

She managed a nod, shifted into third.

"Where was that bar?"

"What?"

"The bar, the one you went to last night. We need to go there, immediately."

He was in shock, that's what it was. This was the final straw, he'd finally cracked. "We can send the boys out for something when we get back to the room, let's just—"

"We need an alibi, Meg. I don't doubt for a second Maldon's going to try and pin this on us. We have to go—"

"But Tera and Brian—"

"Tera and Brian aren't from here. Get us to that bar. No, don't slow down!"

"How is that an alibi?" But she was already making the necessary turns, heading for Kelly's Tap. At least it was a plan, and even in her frazzled state she knew he was right about Tera and Brian. Those two could claim they'd been holding a prayer revival at Bev's Holiday Hideaway, complete with choir, and the local police wouldn't give a fuck because they were her friends.

"I'll hypnotize them and you'll help me."

"How can—we don't really look like we've been hanging around in a bar all night." Even in the dim light from the dash she could see his left eye starting to swell from Maldon's earlier blow.

"I'll get in a fight."

"But—"

"I'll be with you, won't I? I'm sure someone will have something to say. They certainly did last night."

The parking lot of Kelly's Tap was about half full when they arrived. Megan recognized a few of the cars from the night before. Great. Bed had never sounded more appealing. Especially now that it started to dawn on her what exactly Greyson meant to do.

"Okay." He took her hand and led her toward the door, then stopped just outside. "Remember how you reached for me at the house? With your power, not anything else?"

She nodded.

"Lower your shields and do it again."

"I don't understand—"

"I'm not sure I do either, but it works in the other direction, so we'll give it a go."

Heads inside the bar were starting to turn. Greyson's hand tensed on the door handle. "Just try it, *bryaela*."

Megan closed her eyes and focused. She'd done it before, she'd felt those things like tentacles inside her body sweep through her veins and break through her skin . . . but nothing happened. She was too cold, she was too scared, she couldn't relax.

He let go of her hand and touched her cheek, tilting her face up. "We'll try it this way then," he murmured, and her eyes fluttered shut again as he kissed her.

Smoothly, calmly, as if they weren't standing outside a crowded bar full of people who hated her while the cops could arrive any moment. After a second or two all of that disappeared, as she leaned into him, clutching him around the waist with both arms while his fingers tightened against her cheek.

She relaxed, no longer cold, no longer worried, and

let him coax her mouth open so his tongue could slip inside.

The familiar rush of his power and heat flooded through her body, turning her sigh into a moan. Alibi, schmalibi. They should go back to the hotel. They should go back right now . . .

Usually he stopped here, holding back to let the pressure build until they both couldn't take any more. Not now. He kept pushing, pressing that glowing energy into her head, into her body.

She started shaking, not able to control it. His hand on the back of her neck forced her not to pull back even when she thought her head might explode in a shower of sparks.

"Give it back," he murmured, his voice rough. "Come on, give it back . . ."

Somewhere in the back of her mind enough sanity lurked to remember what he was talking about, to remember the time he'd put his power behind her abilities and read a roomful of people in seconds.

"Please, Meg, I can't—"

Her abilities . . . she lowered her shield and started to read, but instead of focusing on the people around her she focused on Greyson, and Greyson alone. With all her strength she shoved at him with her mind, pushing into him, and somehow those tentacles sprang again from her head and reached, invisible and intangible but real nonetheless.

For a split second she thought it hadn't worked. For another second she actually caught a glimpse of something, a fuzzy image of an imposing white house set back among flowering trees. Then a flurry of thoughts and pictures, of ugly feelings and happy ones, all smoothed over as Greyson hypnotized the entire bar.

He'd managed to open the door somehow before he pulled away from her. Megan turned, her vision still blurry from passion and the jolting unpleasantness of feeling the crowd's emotions in her head, and saw them all standing calmly, staring at Greyson.

He blinked, and his mouth fell open slightly. She didn't think she'd ever seen him look so surprised. "We've been here since seven. Go back to your seats."

The little crowd nodded and started to turn away. Greyson moved his hand, a gesture almost like pulling a rope back into himself. Megan hadn't realized the air around them was heavy and silent with power until it ceased, as quickly and definitely as a snuffed-out candle.

He took her hand and strode over to the bar. Tension crackled from his body. "Whiskey."

The bartender's heavy features twisted into a scowl. "Haven't you had enough?"

"No." Greyson pulled out his money clip, peeled off a hundred-dollar bill, and tossed it on the bar. "Give me the bottle and two shot glasses."

Silence pressed in on them as the bartender obeyed, silence broken by increasing mumblings from the patrons. Greyson poured out two shots, handed her one, dumped the other down the front of his shirt, and proceeded to drink half the bottle in one long gulp.

"Crazy fucker," someone muttered.

"What d'you expect? He comes in here with *her,* after we tole her—"

Greyson grinned, a singularly unpleasant smile that sent shivers down Megan's spine. He gripped the whiskey bottle by the neck, crossed the room to the mutterer, and smashed it over his head.

Brian picked him up from the police station first thing in the morning. None of them thought it was a good idea for her to go, having barely escaped being arrested herself. She still wasn't sure why he'd allowed himself to be—he'd never even had so much as a speeding ticket and, given the way he drove, it was impossible to believe he'd never been pulled over.

And if she were honest . . . he'd scared her a little bit. Or rather, *she'd* scared her a little bit. Watching the insane glee with which he took on the entire bar, feeling the energy in the air as he fought, smelling the blood and the sweat and the pure ozone-driven violence—it went to her head more than the whiskey. It turned her on, much as she hated to admit it, whether it was because of some demon desire or because there was a heretofore undiscovered violent streak beneath her skin. It had almost been a relief when the police arrived, and now she didn't know what to say to him as he stepped out of the shower.

She should tell him. She should tell him everything. He had to know something was going on. There'd been too many glances, too many suspicious looks. Too many coincidences, and after Maldon's house and the kiss outside the bar . . . There was no way he couldn't have picked up on the fact that something was going wrong with her power, something was changing inside her.

"Anything in the paper?" He wrapped his towel around his waist and kissed her forehead as he walked past.

"Just that there was a fire. Maldon survived with minor injuries."

"More's the pity. It would have been a lot easier for him if he'd died."

"How's that?"

"You know what he did, don't you?"

She nodded. "He tried to kill me. And he set us—you—up. The gunmen . . . he hired them, right?"

"I don't think so. But you're right, he did try to kill you and he did set us up." He finished buttoning his shirt and started fastening his cuffs. "Which means before we leave for the cabin we need to meet with his Gretneg."

"Right." Maldon would be punished, severely. She didn't even want to think about that, especially since she couldn't help feeling he deserved it. He had tried to kill them both.

It was the way things were done in the Meegras, a way she'd been fighting when it came to her own demons. Now she wondered if she was wrong. It was a lot easier to have principles when your life wasn't in danger if you held to them.

"So why did you let them arrest you?"

"Because I wanted to make sure everyone knew where I was, just in case."

"In case what?"

He opened his mouth, but the pounding on the door interrupted whatever he was about to say. "It's Tera, open up!"

"Oh good, she has her voice back," he said, undoing the bolt on the door.

Tera fixed him with a sour look, but her hands twisted together in front of her waist as if she were playing with invisible beads. Her bruises had disappeared almost as cleanly as Greyson's. Only a few faint shadows remained around her throat. "I have some bad news, Grey. Or, well, maybe it's good news for you. I guess it is."

"Tera?" Megan stood up, reaching for her friend. "What's wrong?"

"Templeton Black is dead."

Greyson didn't move. "Dead?"

Tera nodded.

"How?"

"Um . . . they're not sure. He left a note like a suicide, but there weren't any marks on him to say how he did it. They won't know anything for sure until they do the *hynelin*. It's like an autopsy," she added, glancing at Megan.

"No autopsy." Greyson slid his tie around his neck. Megan glanced at him, but he was watching his own reflection in the mirror as he fashioned a knot.

"What? That's not—"

"You can't autopsy him, Tera. Can't remove anything from him, can't disturb the body. It's against our rules."

"He's—he was—in our custody, and we think a crime has been committed."

"Doesn't matter what you think. Vergadering has the authority to jail him and to investigate, but not to do anything against our Trianad. Defacing the body in any form is against Trianad."

"But that means if he drank poison or was murdered, we have no way to find out."

"If he drank poison or was murdered," Greyson said, putting on his jacket, "then you witches better get to work figuring out how you let it happen."

Megan hadn't expected this many people to be at the reading. Her mother and brother, of course—and Dave was with an attractive dark-haired woman Megan assumed was his wife—but the small crowd that greeted her and Greyson when they entered the outer room of the office made her shoulders hunch.

It wasn't just the number of faces—not that many, really, once she got over her shock enough to notice it—but the sheer disapproval on each and every one of them. She half-expected them to pick up torches and come running after her.

"Megan."

Megan jumped. Her mother stood right next to her, as if she'd materialized there. Greyson's fingers tightened around hers.

"Hi, Mother. Am I late?"

"No." Diane's gaze took in every detail of Megan's plain black dress and low pumps, then shifted to Greyson, her expression changing from extreme disapproval to slightly less disapproval as she examined the hand-tailored Savile Row suit, the Italian shoes, the subtle tie.

Greyson just stood impassively under the scrutiny, watching Diane with those dark eyes of his as if she were a piece of dust on the floor. Something for a servant to deal with.

"I'm Diane Chase," she said finally. Her expression wasn't a smile, but it was almost the ghost of one.

Greyson nodded. "So I understand."

"Are you going to tell me your name?"

"No."

Megan pressed her lips together as tightly as she could while Diane's face reddened.

"Greyson! I wondered if you'd be here. Great to see you again."

The crowd turned as one; the inner office door had opened and a tall, heavyset blond man with a ruddy face emerged, his curious expression turning into a smile as he walked toward Megan and Greyson with his hand out.

"You too, Tucker." The men shook hands. Greyson knew her father's lawyer?

That was surely who this man was, because he turned to Diane next and gave her a peck on the cheek. Come to think of it, hadn't she glimpsed him at her father's funeral too? The profile looked vaguely familiar.

"Okay then." Tucker clasped his hands together. "Shall we get started? I've set up the conference room."

Megan and Greyson hung back for a moment while the others trooped past. "You know him?" she whispered.

"He's Caedes Fuiltean. The blood demons."

"But—"

"No, no. I don't think he was involved with anything last night. Tucker's a good guy; we worked together on a project a few years ago. He's a friend."

"He's a friend" meant just that; Greyson never called

anyone his friend unless they'd proved themselves in some way. She relaxed a little.

"My father has a demon lawyer? I mean, obviously he was involved with them, but his lawyer too?"

He nodded. "Part of the exchange for the favors your father did for Orion? This isn't Tucker's office either, or I'd have known."

"So why do this here?"

"Maybe he just needed a bigger space. Maybe he always handles non-Meegra clients outside his own office. A lot of us do that."

"You?"

"I never had a regular practice. I only handled Meegra legal business."

She wanted to ask more about it, but they were late. Everyone else was already seated; a few people leaned against the walls, but two empty chairs beckoned.

As did Tucker. "Greyson, Dr. Chase. Please, sit down."

Christians entering an arena full of lions couldn't have been more exposed than Megan felt as they threaded their way past everyone to sit.

"Okay. Let's get started." Tucker sat at the head of the table and picked up a sheaf of papers. "It's not a very complex will, but David did request a reading, so . . ."

Megan's mind wandered as Tucker read the necessary jargon at the beginning in his slow, calm voice. A few times Greyson tipped his head, as if considering something, but she thought whispering while the will was being read would be akin to giggling at the funeral—which she'd already done—so she didn't ask about it. They'd discuss it later.

". . . with the exception of one tenth interest, which will be given to my daughter Megan Alison Chase. Also bequeathed to Megan Alison Chase is one third interest, my entire holdings, in the lot at 1477 Pike Street, currently occupied by the Trubank Mental Health Center, which is now closed, and all documents pertaining thereto, which are currently housed in the front bedroom at number twelve Hampton Road."

Tucker glanced up, inspecting the stir this bit of news had created. Gasps and murmurs broke out around the room.

"That can't be right," Diane snapped, all decorum apparently forgotten in her fury. "Check that again."

"I wrote this myself, five weeks ago," Tucker replied. "It's all in order."

Her mother continued to argue, with Dave joining in, but Megan barely heard them over the roaring in her ears, the pounding of her heart. Why would he do that? Wasn't it bad enough not to love her, did he have to actively hate her?

He'd left her the land on which the mental hospital sat. The mental hospital where she'd been a patient for nearly six months, sixteen years ago.

Chapter Sixteen

I don't want it," she said, but no one seemed to hear her over the argument. She tried again, louder. "I don't—"

"Meg. Shush."

"I don't want it," she whispered furiously. "I don't want any of it."

"You don't know that." Greyson leaned closer, but didn't look at her, watching the reddening faces of her mother and brother instead.

"I think I do."

"No. You don't. Not until you know why, and what he gave Maldon in exchange for everything he got."

It made sense, just like most of his suggestions, which was probably why it pissed her off so much. She pulled her hand from his and folded her arms across her chest.

"They'll contest the will," he went on, as if she hadn't just distanced herself from both him and the conversation. "And when they do, you can make a decision and I'll handle the legal stuff. But for now don't make any comments on the record."

"There's no record. This is a will reading, not a trial."

"You think that viper and her spawn won't remember everything you say and try to introduce it?"

"That's assuming I change my mind and fight them. I won't."

"You might."

"You! What did you do to him?"

Megan looked up. Diane stood at the end of the table, her red-rimmed eyes blazing. "As if being a disgrace to our family wasn't enough, you—what did you do? Blackmail him? Drug him? We always knew something was wrong with you, always thought—"

"Mrs. Chase!" Tucker's voice cut through the diatribe, hoarse with shock. "Please, sit down! There's no need for—"

"Don't you tell me what there's a need for! That little witch—"

"Mom, Mom." Dave stood up and tried to grasp his mother's arm. "Calm down. We can do this later. We can fight this. Right, Tucker? We can fight this?"

"You can contest the will, yes." Tucker glanced at Megan and Greyson. "But we'll discuss that another time. Please, Mrs. Chase, take your seat."

Megan's mother looked around, seeming to recall for the first time where she was and how many people were watching. Their gazes flipped from her to Megan and back again, as if they expected a slapfight to break out any second.

Diane subsided, then wiped at her eyes with a black-bordered handkerchief. The move, Megan knew, was a calculated one, to remind the rest of the room of her bereavement and bring home the stress she, the loyal wife, was under.

Almost without realizing it, Megan lowered her

shields a tad and reached out. She'd probably never see this woman again after today, at least she hoped she wouldn't. Weren't there things she deserved to know, things she was curious about?

There she was as a child, a pretty little blond girl in a pink dress. Megan remembered that dress. She'd hated it, with its itchy lace trim . . .

"Mommy! Why does Mr. Grubman hate Daddy?"

"Don't be silly, Megan. Mr. Grubman is our friend."

"No, he's not. He thinks Daddy's an idiot and he wants to see you without your pants on."

The slap had been so sharp and unexpected Megan's eyes teared up just seeing it all these years later, but all her mother had felt was rage. Rage and a queasy kind of fear.

More images, more memories. Megan at six predicting her grandmother's death. Grandma . . . she'd liked Grandma, and Grandma had liked her. Funny, Megan didn't realize until now that Grandma had had her abilities too, not as strong as Megan's but there nonetheless. She'd died when Megan was still too young to understand, or to realize what she could do was unusual.

Megan at twelve, wearing the baggy gray sweater she'd thought hid her embarrassing lack of development, while her mother *tsked* and pulled at it and finally gave up, upset Megan couldn't even achieve puberty properly. Megan at fourteen, and Orion Maldon coming to their house to talk to David about something . . .

Oh my God.

She stood up, so fast she almost toppled forward over the table, interrupting again poor friendly Tucker's attempt to finish the reading. "I need to leave."

She didn't care that they were all staring at her. She didn't care what they thought. She knew it now, knew what she'd failed to ask Maldon, knew why all of this had happened to her, and she had to get out of that room before she did something she would really regret. The second heart in her chest pounded, furious, sending heat rushing through her body.

"I want to see those documents," she told Tucker. "Can I see them now?"

"They're in the house, but probate—"

"She's not going into that house by herself," Diane snapped. "I want the police there."

Megan sighed. "Mother, you are such a miserable bitch, do you know that?" It wasn't original or clever, but it was the best her stunned and weary mind could come up with at the moment. "I'm not a thief. I just want to look at what's mine, and I want to do it now so I can get the hell out of this shitty little town."

"Grey, you'll be with her?" Tucker half-whispered in their direction, while the rest of the room stared at Megan in silence. Her mother's eyes narrowed, hatred burning in their icy depths, but she said nothing.

Greyson must have nodded, because Tucker cleared his throat and spoke again. "Mrs. Chase, Mr. Dante is a highly respected attorney. He'll be with Dr. Chase in the house. I trust him—and Megan."

Dave stood up, holding out a set of keys. "Here, Megan."

He didn't look at her, but for some absurd reason tears threatened behind her eyes just the same. "The house is part yours anyway, right?"

*   *   *

Two hours. They figured they had about that long before everyone came back, and Megan had never in her
life wanted anything as badly as she wanted to be out of
the house before they did.

The will reading wouldn't take that long, but the discussion they knew Diane and Dave would have with
Tucker afterward just might.

Megan pulled boxes out from under the desk, lifting
the lids, rifling through loose papers. The documents had
to be in here somewhere. She needed to know who her
father's partners were in that land deal. She had one-third
interest. Who were the other two? She thought she knew.

The blank walls in what used to be her bedroom
stared at her as she worked, while Greyson set another
box on the neatly made bed and started flipping through
its contents. He'd barely said a word since they'd left the
reading, but his silence wasn't cold any more than his
body was.

Her back started to ache from crouching by the
time she found what she sought, by the time the names
leaped out at her from the page. Every letter taunted
her, answering questions she didn't know she had but
leaving more in their wake.

"Greyson. Come look." Her voice sounded stronger
than she thought it would.

He took the sheaf of papers from her and thumbed
through it. "Title deed . . . documents of incorporation . . . here we go. Blah blah blah, board members—"
He looked up.

"Board members, yes."

"David Chase, Orion Maldon, and . . . Templeton Black." He lowered the papers and stared at her. "I didn't know, Meg. I swear I didn't."

So he'd come to the same conclusion she had. The same knowledge. "Look at the date."

"I don't need to." But he glanced just the same. "Temp never told me he—"

"That he'd essentially bought me from my father? That in exchange for me, he and Orion Maldon would give my father part ownership in valuable property, they'd build his practice, they'd—" She stopped, unable to go on. Her hands shook as she raised them to her head.

Sixteen years ago she'd sat in this room and had her first conversation with the Accuser, right before he'd entered her body and changed her life forever.

And that was what David Chase had wanted. In exchange for power and wealth he'd sacrificed his only daughter.

Anger rose in her breast, filling her, making both her hearts beat faster. She wanted to hit someone. She wanted to hit her father. She *should* have laughed at him in that casket yesterday. She should have scratched his dead eyeballs out of his head and stomped them into goo under her feet.

"That bastard, that unbelievable bastard." This time she didn't try to stop her tears. Rage, not sadness, brought them to her eyes, but it didn't matter. She stood next to her childhood bed and cried, and after a second Greyson gathered her in his arms and held her tight, and for once it didn't feel like she was being humored.

It didn't last long. The initial wave passed, and she was left simply raging, wanting to strike out at someone, anyone.

"I hate this room. I hate even being in this house."

"I know."

She turned around to look at the bed, at the window by which the Accuser had rested sixteen years before. Light poured through it, taunting her. "He stood right there," she said. Her palms ached from her fingernails digging into them. "I was in bed and that's where he was. Like . . . like he was my buddy or something. I wondered why no one was home that day. My mother usually was . . ."

She jumped when his warm hands touched her shoulders and rubbed gently. "Maybe it's a good thing," he said. "Now you know."

Her head fell forward as he massaged her, easing some of the tension in her neck but doing nothing for the howling fury gripping the rest of her body. Her muscles ached from trying to still her trembling.

"I always knew. I mean, I didn't *know* know, but it doesn't change anything, does it? I'm still what I am, no matter the reason. They never liked me. They never wanted me around. It must have been like winning the lottery." She couldn't keep the bitterness out of her voice as she uttered the last line. Her blood still raced, her heart pumped furiously. She wanted to go run a mile, she wanted to throw things and attack things and tear them apart. All that excess energy buzzed around in her mind, in her veins, until she thought she might explode from it.

A cold breeze caressed her, like a ghost passing by. "Forget them."

"I can't forget them. I'm too . . . God, Greyson, I'm just so fucking *mad* at them, I can hardly see straight."

The zipper of her dress lowered a bit. His lips tickled between her shoulder blades. "Maybe it's time to let it all go. Exorcise your demons once and for all."

She smiled, surprised it was still possible to do so. "Exorcise or exercise?"

"It's so efficient when you can accomplish two goals with one . . . act, isn't it?" Heat seeped through her dress from his palms as he slid his hands around her, gliding down over her hips and thighs, then back up. His fingers curved around her waist and pulled her back so she could feel his erection.

Her breath caught in her chest. "Do you ever think about anything but sex?"

"Money. Power." His soft laugh warmed her throat as he scraped his teeth over her skin there. "I think about you, *bryaela*."

She refused to say, "You do?" like some innocent heroine in a novel, but the temptation was too much to resist. "Oh?"

"Yes." His right hand sneaked under the neckline of her dress and down into her bra, finding her left nipple and rolling it gently. Her eyelids fluttered shut. The raging demon inside her changed its tune, finding another route to forgetfulness, seeking a different kind of release. "I wonder how your day is going, what you're doing . . . when I'll see you again . . . don't you think about me? Don't you, *sheshissma*?"

"What does that mean?"

He paused, nibbling her earlobe. "It doesn't translate well. My desire."

"I think your desire translates pretty well." It came out as a gasp; he'd started tugging up her skirt with his left hand while his right still played beneath her top, and the feel of his skin on her bare thighs above her stockings sent a violent shiver through her body.

"That's what it means. My desire." His foot nudged hers, punctuating his words, urging her legs apart. His fingers stroked over her panties. "The thing I *want*."

Her head fell back, resting on his shoulder as he rubbed the damp silk against her. All that energy inside her, that fierce need . . . she couldn't seem to catch her breath. Every gasp of air was scented with him, tasted like him.

"So what do you say, *sheshissma*?" The teasing tone didn't fool her; his voice behind it was hoarse. "What do you want? To work off some of that anger?"

He edged the panties aside so he could slide his fingers along the bare, slick folds of her skin. His own rough breath drowned out the moan she couldn't stop. "You want to take it out on me, my *bryaela*? Use me? Hurt me?"

Fear slid down her spine, meeting the heat pooling in her pelvis and sending a shiver through her body. This was dangerous. She should pull away, put a stop to it, because his words were edging her far too close to a chasm she wasn't sure she could emerge safely from.

But oh God, she wanted to jump.

"Do you? Is that what you want? I'm here. Just tell me. Whatever you want, we'll do it."

He unzipped her dress and slid it from her shoulders,

stopping just at the point where the fabric trapped her arms at her waist. Her bra was next; cool air swirled over her aching nipples as the scrap of lace and wire fell from them. She still couldn't bring herself to open her eyes, so she floated weightless in perfect darkness, with only his warmth and hands keeping her in the world.

Those hands sculpted her body from the air, creating every line and curve as they traced them. It should have been as soothing as it was arousing. Normally his touch made her purr like an extremely contented lion. Now . . . like the flames of his energy burning in her chest, between her legs, so her restlessness grew, her need to *do* something, anything, to *move*. Tears of frustration sprang to her eyes. Why was he doing this to her? Why was he forcing her to be still, to not let it go, to not run through the darkness and scream in bloody triumph?

"Jesus, Meg . . . you make me ache. How do you do that . . ." More teeth now, harder, nipping at her shoulders. He filled his hands with her breasts, lifting them, and the heat of his skin radiated out.

Flames appeared, dancing along the top of the window, hovering above them. They were in a different world now, the one where he ruled, and the knowledge of his domination forced the word from her lips.

"Yes . . ."

Megan reached behind her, forcing her hand between them to caress the hard ridge of his cock.

He bit her neck, so hard she felt her skin dent and bruise beneath his teeth, and it was as if he'd flipped a switch, set her free. She spun around and tried to wrap her arms around him, but they were still trapped by her dress. She shoved them forward as far as she could, managing to grip the firm muscles of his ass in her hands before his lips found hers and sent her flying into the burning sun.

His growl rumbled against her lips, into her mouth. Their tongues tangled, fighting a war Megan didn't think could be won, as he shoved her hands away and freed them from her dress, pushing it down over her hips to fall on the floor.

She yanked at his tie, pulling his shirt open, dragging it up from his waistband. Her panties disappeared. She thought she heard them tear, thought she felt the tug against her skin as they did so, but didn't care.

Together they fell onto the bed. Megan thrust his shirt away, desperate to feel his bare skin beneath her palms, beneath her nails. She wanted to bury them in it, to see his blood dark against the tawny flesh.

The thing inside her, the demon or ghoul or simply a part of herself she'd never known before, still raged and ripped at her with sharp, terrible claws, roaring in anticipation when he unfastened his belt with one quick, decisive movement and removed his pants.

He shoved himself inside her with more force than finesse, and Megan screamed his name, her back arching, her legs spreading wider. His answering cry was lost somewhere in the waves of pleasure crashing over her, drowning her. She dug her nails into his skin and felt it break; she smelled his blood in the air. The scream erupting from her mouth didn't even sound like her voice. She was gone, lost, trapped in a body too small for the tumultuous emotions inside it.

His fingers twisted in the hair at her nape and yanked, pulling her head back so far all she could see was the opposite wall. It didn't matter. His face was seared into her brain. She focused on it, seeing him, feeling him burning deep inside with his every rapid, forceful thrust.

"Go on, Meg," he gasped. The pressure on her neck relaxed as he pulled her face closer. His eyes glowed like traffic lights, redder than she'd ever seen them. "Whatever you want. I can take it."

Her hand moved before she even realized it, before she thought of it, striking out at him with the same unreal speed she'd noticed when Maldon had tried to touch her hair.

Not fast enough. Greyson caught it before it hit him, his fingers making the bones in her wrist grind together painfully. Sharp tingles ran up her arm and blossomed into something stronger in her chest.

She tried again, harder, faster, wanting to hurt him, wanting to feel that power, but he caught her again and slammed her wrist down onto the bed. She wanted to cry, but instead of disappointment, instead of anger, she felt relief. She couldn't hurt him. He'd beaten her. He would beat her every time, and for some reason that knowledge made her feel safe. She could let her rage go, let it take over. Permission was granted. Her heartbeat sped up.

As if he sensed this—and he probably did—he let go of her hand and took her lips again, plundering her mouth, not stilling or slowing his movements inside her.

"Just . . . just fuck me," she managed. "Greyson . . ."

She hadn't thought he could go faster, harder, but

he did. He gripped the edge of the mattress, using it as leverage while he reared up over her and slammed into her. The smooth perfection of his chest hovered only inches from her mouth. She lifted her head and sank her teeth into it, twisting her fingers in his hair and pulling as hard as she could while the fingernails of her other hand made fresh gouges in his back.

His voice echoed in the small room, mingling with hers. She couldn't stop herself, couldn't control herself. Flames filled her body, filled her vision, destroying everything else. All the memories of the last few days, all the memories of this house and her childhood, her father's betrayal, eradicated in a second by the voracious fire, mixing with the rage and pain and turning into something so pure she wanted to live on it.

"Greyson!" Her back arched as the first waves of her climax rolled through her. Megan rode it, letting it wash her clean, until nothing was left of her but her bare, stripped soul wrapped around him.

His final thrust almost pushed her off the bed. He swelled inside her, impossibly large, wringing one last scream from her throat to almost cover his, until the walls of her childhood bedroom shook from the force of their release and he collapsed on top of her.

Chapter Seventeen

The room looked as though a lecherous hurricane had blown through it. Papers covered everything, the comforter had somehow ended up bunched on the floor, and the sheets had come away from the corners of the mattress. Droplets and streaks of blood decorated them, visible sins on the snowy white.

It smelled like smoke and sweat and blood and sex, mingling together like a bordello carpet.

All of this Megan observed when she sat up and found the remains of her panties, but she couldn't bring herself to care. The room could be cleaned. Her mind was not so easily erased.

Greyson entered holding a pie plate and a bottle of water, which he handed to her without comment. The icy liquid cleared some of the cobwebs in her head, but when he sat down shock replaced them.

"Oh God . . . did I do that?"

The wounds were already healing, which made them look worse. Deep, angry furrows covered his back from shoulder blades to waist, surrounded by blood dried almost black.

He nodded, sticking his fork into a piece of her

mother's famous apple crisp. His gaze traveled from the top of her head to her feet. "And I did that to you."

She hadn't even looked at herself. Bruises like dark roses blossomed on her wrists, on her upper arms and hips. Her neck was tender enough where he'd bitten her to make her suspect she'd be bruised there too.

She'd never enjoyed or expected pain in the bedroom. He'd never indicated he did either. But God help her if it hadn't been one of the most amazing experiences of her life. Was there nothing about her that was still the same?

"This is pretty good," he said, swallowing a mouthful of crisp. "Do you have this recipe?"

"She wouldn't give it to me."

"Shame." He forked up another mouthful.

"Greyson . . . I'm sorry."

"Why?"

"Look at you."

"I'll heal."

"But—"

"Meg." He turned to her. "At the risk of sounding like some . . . hmm. At the risk of sounding like I do your job, negative emotions affect demons oddly sometimes. It's no big deal. You'll learn to control it."

"I'm not a demon."

He paused. "But you have demon in you, so that's going to change your reactions to things. You haven't noticed anything different about yourself? Anything you find strange?"

Damn it. How much did he know, how much had he been able to feel?

"No," she lied. "Nothing."

He watched her for a minute, while she forced herself to stare calmly into his eyes. Just why it was so important to keep it hidden she didn't know. He could help her, if she told him.

But he would also encourage her to do the Haikken Kra ritual, and she was afraid if he really put his considerable powers of persuasion behind it, she would agree. The prospect of losing a part of herself terrified her. The thought of admitting she wasn't like everyone else—aside from her psychic abilities—made her feel a little sick.

She'd already fed off Gerald's sister in her office. She'd gotten high off the sadness of the mourners at her father's funeral. If she did the ritual . . . she'd become a parasite.

Finally he shrugged. "You should really try to get this recipe. Did your dad have an office here in the house?"

"I doubt she keeps it in there, if he does."

"We need to photocopy those documents. But you should look for this too. We'll copy it. And then you can make it for me."

"I didn't know you liked apples."

"All demons like apples. You're slipping if you didn't get *that* joke."

"What—oh. Right." She couldn't help smiling, whether out of relief that he'd dropped the subject of her unorthodox urges or simply because it was the sort of joke she would make. *Exorcist* jokes about his Georgetown upbringing, Robert Johnson jokes about his CD collection . . . she should have caught the apple thing a mile away.

"Why do we need to copy them?"

"I want to look into it. See if it was a Meegra purchase or a personal one of Temp's. Speaking of which . . ." He picked his watch off the small scratched-up wooden nightstand. "We don't have a lot of time, and we still need to get back to the city for the funeral tonight."

"What—tonight, really?"

"Has to be done as soon as possible. You'll need to come—all the Gretnegs will be there—but the ceremony after is for Sorithell only."

"Ceremony?"

"When I become Gretneg," he said, and before he kissed her forehead she saw the triumph in his eyes.

The policeman held out his hand. Megan shook it, glad they'd gotten dressed and cleaned the room in plenty of time, but uncomfortably aware that she was going commando under her dress.

"Your mother, she asked me to come along—"

"To make sure you didn't steal anything," Diane finished coldly. "Please wait, Officer Dunkirk, while I finish checking the bedrooms."

Officer Dunkirk blushed. Megan didn't. She'd known when she heard the unfamiliar voice downstairs what her mother had done. She didn't care. No matter how long this little burst of euphoria lasted, this new feeling of confidence, she'd at least been able to go back to her indifference to the moods and petty cruelties of her mother. She'd done just fine without the woman for years, and she could keep on doing so.

"Thought you'd want to know," Dunkirk said. "Everything checked out as far as that fire complaint last night. Sorry we troubled you about it."

Because we used supernatural trickery to get it to. But the police didn't need to know that, so she just smiled. "Thank you."

Maldon had indeed given their names to the police—omitting everything but his "idea" that he "might have" seen them on the street right before the fire. Not so brave after they'd escaped and he knew they were meeting with his Gretneg tomorrow.

After which—oh please—they would leave for the cabin and a solid week of relaxation.

They spent a few more uncomfortable minutes standing there. Megan tried not to look around at the walls that had once housed her, the furniture she'd crawled onto as a child, but she couldn't help it. Over there by the kitchen door was where she'd spilled a glass of Kool-Aid and gotten sent to her room for a week. The darkened Christmas tree in front of the window, where it had been every year. She'd broken an ornament when she was eight and hadn't been allowed to help decorate it again for three years.

It had never felt like home, not that she could remember. It had been a prison, as cold and impersonal as any other, as lonely as that damned hospital her father had conspired to put her in. A few years of closeness and happiness, when she was so young the memories existed only in a haze and then . . . nothing.

She would never be in this house again. When her mother died she wouldn't be back, if anyone even bothered to tell her about it. As for Dave . . . she had to admit that made her a little sad. Dave hadn't given up on her as quickly as her parents had.

But he'd given up just the same.

Greyson had been right. She didn't need these people, not for anything. The thought buoyed her despite her worries.

"You stole my apple crisp."

"Excuse me?"

"I made a crisp," Diane said. "It was in the refrigerator. And a bottle of water. You stole them."

Officer Dunkirk looked completely lost. Megan could read his thoughts without even needing to lower her shields. Was he supposed to arrest them over a dessert and a bottle of Evian?

Greyson pulled out his money clip and held out a bill to her mother with the air of a king paying a leper to go away. "Here. To cover your inconvenience."

Diane's eyes narrowed. "I don't think I like you, Mr. Dante."

He shrugged. "Come on, Meg, let's go."

Megan looked at Diane, with her chic silvery bob and her impeccable black dress. Almost like a mirror image of herself, aged and viewed through a lens of ice.

"Good-bye, Mother." Should she offer her hand? She certainly wasn't going to give the viper a hug.

"What did you do to your neck?"

Megan's hand flew to the tender spot on her throat. By the time Greyson put his shirt on, his scratches had started to shrink, but they'd forgotten her bruises. "I . . . I stumbled on the stairs."

Diane watched her for a minute. "You always were clumsy."

She turned and walked back to the kitchen, the conversation clearly over.

"I know this has been a . . . busy week for you," Rocturnus said. "So I haven't wanted to bother you."

Megan lifted her face from her hands to look up at him. This was not the way she wanted to spend the hour she had free between finally arriving home and heading for Greyson's Iureanlier for the funeral. "But you should have. This is something I need to know."

"You haven't been very interested so far." It sounded like a reprimand—she knew it was—but the delivery was obviously calculated to put her at ease.

Too bad it didn't work.

"I don't understand this. I went there not even a week ago and showed them—"

"Being powerful doesn't mean you know how to lead them. You need to *lead* them. I know you don't like it, but . . . this is the way it is."

Shit. Shit shit shit. Megan looked around the little office with its dark wood and comfortable flowered-chintz furniture. Her demons had a taste for the quaint; she assumed it was because they were so small.

She'd assumed a lot of things.

Whatever was happening to her wasn't going to just go away. Roc wanted her to do the ritual. So did Greyson. Because both of them felt she wasn't connected enough, that she wasn't keeping the needs of her demons in mind. And maybe they were right. Her plans for a newer, gentler Meegra weren't going to go very far if she treated them the same way she wanted them to treat their humans.

They wanted her, needed her, to be something different. And she didn't have a choice but to be it.

"Bring him in," she said, steeling herself. John Wayne would know what to do here. Joan Crawford would know how to get those little buggers in line.

So Megan Chase could do it too.

Rocturnus left, returning a few minutes later with Halarvus. She'd seen him before; he was one of the demons who'd grumbled and snickered in the back of the room last time she was here.

His black eyes regarded her coldly. She could feel his indifference. It pissed her off.

"Halarvus, do you know why you're here?"

"No."

"Yes, you do."

"What difference does it make? I don't answer to you. I'm not going to be one of your little demons of light, spreading joy and happiness to all the kiddies. Our mother is offering us a chance to be what we are." His black eyes widened in his dark blue face. "To feed."

"I let you feed." She wanted to smack herself. Why was it so easy for her to take the lead with people, with her clients, but dealing with her demons made her so nervous and unsure of herself? Like a child trying to tell adults what to do.

If she lost them all, she could die. She could lose all of her power and become like a flower with no petals. Nothing.

Come on, Megan . . . you can do this.

"Not the way we want. Not the way we should."

God *damn* it, why was nothing in her life simple anymore?

Her power was always stronger here, always seemed to come more readily to her call. Keeping her face impassive, she lowered her shields and let it go, not all of it, just enough to knock Halarvus across the room.

"You're not going anywhere." She stood up, hating herself, hating the tiny flare of pleasure in her chest. If she did the ritual, would this be easier? Would she be able to accept it? Or would it be worse, putting her more at war with herself than she was already?

Maybe this would be a good test run. See exactly what she could handle.

Halarvus got back to his feet. Dark blood ran from his nose. Megan forced herself to look at it as he wiped it away, making a thin streak across his face.

No desire to taste it came to her, no crazy urge to lick it from his papery skin. Maybe that had ended?

"Just because you're angry—," Halarvus started, but Megan interrupted him.

"I'm not angry." She willed it to be so, knowing he could sense it. "But I'm keeping what's mine."

She turned to Roc. "Take him into the hall."

The others waited for her, the white light from the high ceiling bouncing off their multicolored heads.

Their silence followed her as she stepped up onto the little dais and took the seat that had once belonged to the Accuser. Now it was hers, a heavy, ornate gold thing that looked like Louis XIV had designed it in an opium haze. Knobs and carved leaves dug into her skin when she sat; she'd had the original cushion burned and kept forgetting to get another one.

Another reminder, if she'd needed one, of how far she'd been letting things slip here. She should know better than that. Problems and complications didn't go away simply because one wished they would.

Rocturnus brought Halarvus to stand before her, in the center of the space cleared by the others, and climbed up himself to the chair beside her. She couldn't get out of this one by lashing out at all of them and running away, which was exactly what she'd done the last time no matter how much she didn't want to admit it. She needed to take charge, to really and truly show them she could protect them, could help them, could be to them everything Ktana Leyak was promising to be.

Because if she didn't she probably wouldn't survive.

"Halarvus, you've been working against me?"

"I've been telling the truth," he said. His little eyes gleamed. "That you aren't strong enough. That your human heart isn't in this. You haven't gotten involved with the other Meegras and their businesses. You haven't been looking out for our interests."

Megan snapped her head toward Rocturnus. "What's he talking about?"

"The other Meegra Yezer have been horning in on us," he whispered. "We're small. We don't really have any defenses. When they send some of their bigger demons to force us out . . ." He caught her glare. "What? I told you this before."

"Yes, but . . . " He had told her, and again, she hadn't

really paid attention. That was so unlike her! Had she been so wrapped up in—well, okay, yes, he'd taken up a lot of her time. Plus the radio show, and her practice . . .

Greyson had been right. Maintaining her practice and her demons was too much work. It made the decision to give up the practice sting a little less, like a child giving up a job in the city to go home and take care of an elderly parent. At least she'd made the right decision once in the last few weeks, even if it left her finances awfully tight.

She cleared her throat. "Tonight I attend the funeral of Templeton Black," she announced. It felt a little self-important and ridiculous, but the demons seemed to like the change in her demeanor.

"I want a list of names, if you know them, of demons who've harassed you and what houses they're in. I'll see the other Gretnegs and tell them to leave you alone."

The demons shifted on their feet, looking both slightly mollified and doubtful.

"I'll make sure you stop losing humans. But my rules stand. No child abuse. No murder."

"Not even of criminals? Bad guys?" one of the demons asked hopefully.

She started to say no, then stopped. All the power in the world was no good if she couldn't hold on to them long enough to exert it. "Case-by-case basis," she said, trying not to feel like a monster and failing. "It has to be approved by me."

They waited, their gazes on her, and this time she knew what they expected. Once again that chasm stood in front of her, filled with flames, but this time it was the fire of Hell, of destruction, not of desire.

There was no choice to make. There hadn't been from the moment she'd tied the Yezer to herself. There hadn't been from the moment her father sold her to demons for a piece of land and a successful accountancy practice. Megan took a deep breath. "Rocturnus, Halarvus must be punished."

The Yezer relaxed, their silent pleasure floating through the air. Halarvus's eyes widened as Rocturnus said something in the demon tongue, widened further as he was chained to a frame like the one she'd seen Greyson chained to three months before.

She forced herself not to blink when the whip cracked the air.

This was her life now.

Chapter Eighteen

The white marble floors of Iureanlier Sorithell glowed orange with reflected flames from the torches burning along the walls. The high ceiling, normally white with a dragon mosaic that twisted and shifted, was black. Mystery and power whispered in the dark corners of the entry hall.

Megan stood in her black dress and waited to be noticed, twisting the thin cord of her little silk evening bag between her fingers. Rocturnus perched a few inches above her shoulder, riding weightlessly on the pad of psychic energy all humans had there. He'd been to the mansion only a few times. Normal security kept all demons but family from crossing the threshold, just as it had back at Orion Maldon's place in Grant Falls.

Tonight those barriers had been lifted. Megan recognized a few faces, other Gretnegs, sipping cocktails and talking quietly. All of them wore black. It was like an incredibly formal Halloween party, except she'd never been to a party that glowed and throbbed with so much energy. It bulged around them all, too large even for the cavernous room, and made Megan's heart skip faster in her chest. The atmosphere was charged with possibilities, with savagery. This would not be an ordinary funeral.

The empty air next to her shifted, and Greyson slipped his arm around her waist.

"You're late," he said, handing her a gin and tonic. She meant to take only a sip but somehow ended up drinking down half of it while he greeted Roc. Still not quite settled from her meeting with her own demons, she guessed, or perhaps it was just plain nerves, or maybe even surprise.

"What are you wearing?"

He smiled. She couldn't remember ever seeing him this excited—at least, other than in the biblical sense. He fairly vibrated with it, although outwardly he was as calm as ever. "It's ceremonial."

"It's a cassock."

"Yes, but a demonic one." He leaned over to kiss her, sending a little shock through her body.

Whatever the black outfit was called, it looked great on him. The stiff, straight collar framed his strong chin and emphasized the breadth of his shoulders, while the snug, severely cut fit and long skirt—there was nothing else to call it but a skirt—made him look taller, as if his body was a pillar of black smoke erupting from the floor. He'd never looked as much like a demon as he did in the uniform of Catholicism. The only thing missing was the white square in the collar; the fabric peeking out from the notch was blood red.

"You look beautiful, by the way," he said.

"Funny, I was just thinking the same thing about you."

He smiled and kissed her again, his hand slipping down over her bottom. For a moment she caught a glimpse of how he must have looked fifteen years earlier, when he was apparently cutting a swath a mile wide through the women of the District of Columbia. "We're going to get started in a minute, so I'll need to go take my place. Nick's going to walk with you, okay?"

"I won't be with you?"

"I have to escort Temp's widow behind the cata-falque."

"Oh. Well, look, I'll be fine with Roc."

"I can do it," Roc said.

"I know. But I'd rather you have someone to help. The floors are rather uneven where we're going." He looked pointedly at her heels.

"Grey!" The woman's shiny red lips stretched in a needle-sharp smile as she undulated across the floor, the sequins on her formfitting black gown catching the light and throwing it back so she seemed to glow. She looked like a particularly festive Morticia Addams, with bright red hair flowing down her back.

"Grey," the woman said again, holding out her hand so Greyson had no choice but to kiss it. She totally ignored Megan. "You look splendid in that robe. But then I knew you would, remember? I'm so glad you decided—"

"Thank you, Justine. You remember Megan Chase, right?"

Justine didn't even glance at her. "Of course I do." She stroked her scarlet-tipped hand up Greyson's arm. Her impressive cleavage shifted with the movement. "Have you thought any more about my request?"

"I think of nothing else, my dear."

"Who is *she*?" Roc whispered. "Wow!"

"Go away, Roc."

"But I want to—"

"Go."

Roc obeyed. Justine stroked Greyson's cheek and Megan stood still and resisted the urge to slap her. Justine was head of Meegra Concumbia. Starting a fight with a Gretneg was never a good idea, even if that Gretneg was staring at Greyson as though he was the only glass pipe in the crack den and it had been hours since her last hit.

"You let me know when you decide," she said. "I can be a very powerful ally." The reverse implication hung heavy in the air. Powerful allies could be powerful enemies as well.

"I would never doubt it," Greyson replied. "Now if you'll excuse me, I'm going to get one last drink before the ceremony. Come on, Meg."

Megan forced herself not to look back toward Justine as they walked away, but she felt the woman's eyes on them just the same. "What was that all about?"

He shrugged. "Justine did me a favor."

"And what does she want in return?"

"She's a succubus. What do you think she wants?"

"But—" She snapped her mouth shut. What was she supposed to say? "You can't?" "Please don't?" For all she knew, he was banging half the city on the nights he wasn't with her.

He glanced at her as if waiting for her to continue, but when she didn't he turned away and got drinks for them both. "Here's the plan. After the funeral everyone comes back up here for a drink. Then they leave. You can go if you want, but I'd like you to stay and wait for me. The ceremony doesn't take long. An hour and a half, maybe."

"And what's in it for me?"

He leaned a little closer. "Ever been made love to by the most powerful *vregonis* demon in the country?"

"I thought I had been." She let the sharp pang of desire his words invoked sink into every nerve ending in her body.

"Hmm. I suppose you have, at that. Want to do it again?"

"If you're lucky," she said. "What happens at the ceremony, anyway?"

"No, no. No telling."

"Greyson."

"Yes?"

She put her hand on his arm, drawing his gaze. "This is a big deal for you, isn't it? Not just for the prestige, but for *you*."

He stopped smiling when his eyes met hers. The rest of the room seemed to fade away. "It's what I've worked for all my life."

Even with her heels on, she had to stand on tiptoe to kiss him. Just a quick press of her lips, nothing inappropriate for the somber occasion, but enough to send tingles all the way down her spine. It was like kissing a live wire.

"Congratulations."

"Thank you." His fingertips brushed her cheek. "Now, where is—ah."

Nick Xao-teng's skin glowed in the firelight. He looked like a warrior, like a samurai. Although samurai were Japanese, weren't they? What were warriors called in imperial China? Why was she focusing on dumb trivia in an effort not to meet his eyes?

He looked less uncomfortable than she did, but only slightly. "Hi, Megan. Nice to see you again."

"You too." Even a few feet away from him she could feel the low-level sexual energy emanating from his muscular frame. What was Greyson thinking, sticking her with this man he knew embarrassed her?

"Okay," Greyson said. "I have to go find Lytha. See you guys later."

He squeezed her shoulder and was gone, leaving her to glare after him.

"It's because he trusts me," Nick said. She started; she hadn't realized he'd be able to read her expression so easily. "Everyone in the family has to walk with the body. I'm the only one outside it he'd let near you. Can I get you a drink?"

She lifted her glass. "I'm fine, thanks."

"Look, Megan . . . I really am sorry. About what I did to you the other night. I didn't realize—I mean, I didn't know who you were."

"What did he do?" whispered Roc, slipping back onto her shoulder.

She ignored him. "Would it have been okay if I wasn't who I am?"

She wasn't sure what she expected his response to be, but she knew she didn't anticipate the smile that broke across his face. Nick did not need whatever supersexy mojo he had by virtue of being an incubus. Women would have fallen at his feet without it.

Although it certainly didn't hurt. She would never forget their first meeting.

"No, I guess it wouldn't have been," he said finally. "But most women aren't as susceptible as you are."

She raised her eyebrows.

"Because you're psychic." He shifted on his feet, while she enjoyed watching him sweat. He deserved it, after what he'd done to her. In front of a restaurant full of people. "Can't we just forget it? Greyson's my friend."

The murmuring of the crowd grew louder. They were about to start.

"I promise, I'll never do it again."

He was still smiling, still charming. But Megan knew she'd gotten to him. He wasn't lying when he'd said Greyson was his friend, and that touched her. She decided to let Nick off the hook.

"Okay. Apology accepted."

"Thanks."

"So, which Meegra are you in? Concumbia, or—"

He looked surprised. "I'm not."

"But I thought—"

"Not me, despite Grey's efforts." He shook his head, a ghost of a smile flitting over his handsome face. "There are lots of us who aren't full members—a sizable minority, at least. We go to them for protection or help if we need it, but we don't get involved. Some demons disapprove of them entirely."

"So what do you do?"

The smile became fixed. "All sorts of things. I'm an independent, let's say."

Megan nodded. That ended that line of questioning. She should have known better than to ask.

"How long have you known—" she started, but she was interrupted by the ringing of a bell, a gloomy, mournful deep chime. A funeral bell.

Nick offered his arm. "They're ready."

The torches went out, as if a sudden wind had blown them out en masse. In the perfect blackness of the room Megan heard rustlings, a few footsteps loud on the marble floor, then nothing.

Dead silence.

The bell gonged again. Megan jumped, suddenly glad Nick was there. He put his hand over hers, sending a short but thankfully minor shiver through her. He must be shielding awfully hard. She knew she was.

A voice in the darkness, deep and raw. "Templeton Horatius Black *ga chrino*."

"*Alri neshden* Templeton Black," the crowd responded.

A single light flared in the darkness. A tall, thin man, taller than anyone Megan had ever seen, held his hand high above his head, cupping the tiny flame in his palm. Its faint glow made his face a mask, with nothing but deep shadows for eyes and long grooves down his cheeks that would be wrinkles in ordinary light.

He glared into the crowd. "*Cha krishien.*"

Beside her Nick bowed, the movement of his body pulling her down as well. When they came back up, Megan had the sense that something loomed behind the gaunt man. He was the priest, she supposed, or whatever they called them. The spiritual leader, maybe.

Still holding his hand up, he stalked forward. As he

vacated the spot where he'd been originally, the torches behind him flared.

The light hurt Megan's eyes. She closed them for a long second then opened them again, to see Malleus and Spud through a gap in the crowd. They stood below and on either side of a large platform, its legs gripped in their beefy arms. On top of the platform lay the body of Templeton Black.

Megan couldn't really see him. He was up too high. All she saw was the top of his head, the salt-and-pepper hair thinner than she remembered. For a moment, despite everything he'd done to her, she felt terribly, sharply sorry for him. He'd had everything, been head of this house and this family, and he'd died alone in a witch's prison. In the hands of the enemy.

Would they ever find out what killed him? Or had he realized his pet witches, the ones who'd tried to murder her and Greyson, had been killed, and decided the only thing left to do was die?

The procession inched ahead. Behind Spud, Maleficarum held one of the rear legs of the catafalque. Megan only vaguely recognized the fourth bearer.

Each time the catafalque passed a torch, the flames flared into life. The footsteps of the procession made almost no sound on the marble floor, so it seemed to float, created by black mist. Megan had never seen anything like it. It was beautiful.

Nick edged her closer. Considerate of him. Even with heels she was shorter than almost everyone in the room.

The impression of the catafalque floating didn't

change, although she could now see where the legs ended, could see the feet of the bearers blurry . . . there *was* smoke. Black smoke, sliding silently over the floor, coiling around the legs of the bearers and the priest.

It seemed to take a long time for Templeton's body to pass. Up close she could see the heavy black satin covering the frame. Templeton was wrapped in it like a toga, with a long-sleeved black shirt beneath it to cover his arms. His face and feet were bare. So were the hands clasped neatly together over his stomach. The diamond pinkie ring she remembered seeing on his left hand shot orangeish sparks onto the wall.

Megan held her breath as the body passed, only belatedly realizing a slow drum was beating somewhere in the hall. Like a march it played, while the procession stepped forward with every beat. Her heart started beating in time, and without thinking she knew the same was happening to every demon in the hall. The piece of demon in her chest, the thing she'd started thinking of as a second heart, caught the rhythm too.

Next came Greyson, his expression solemn. Beside him with her hand on his arm walked a woman, her head high, her eyes damp at the corners. She too wore a long black gown, velvet, with a string of pearls around her neck like tiny moons against the darkness. Her dark hair was swept up, exposing a face that Megan instinctively felt drawn to. Motherly, it was kind even in sorrow, but fiercely proud. Templeton Black's widow, so different from the other widow Megan had recently seen that for a moment her mouth flooded with bitterness.

The drum kept beating. Megan wondered if Greyson

would turn to look at her, but he didn't, staring straight ahead as they passed.

Next came the *rubendas,* in dark suits. Some wore shirts of the same blood red as the collar of Greyson's cassock, others white. White, black, and red were the colors of House Sorithell.

"The colors are by rank," Nick whispered. "In case you wondered."

She nodded her thanks.

Almost all of the torches along the walls of the long hall were lit now as the procession passed, on its way to an enormous set of wooden double doors standing open at the end. Megan had never seen those doors open. Beyond them darkness loomed, like the entrance to a cave.

Beat... beat... beat... The drum continued its mournful order as the last of the family passed. Megan turned her head to the left to watch them go, the black smoke still swirling and roiling over the floor, obscuring their feet. Her skin crawled. The energy in the room, the pure, unbridled sense of power, made her hair stand on end.

More than that was the sense she'd somehow stepped back in time. With the torches lit, only the suits of the *rubendas* indicated they hadn't all somehow traveled to the inside of a pyramid, or a Viking longhouse. It was creepy and mournful and exhilarating, all at the same time.

Still creepier were the servants following the *rubendas.* Their faces were smudged with soot and downcast, their hair was tangled and matted. Bare feet peeked out from beneath their shapeless black togas.

She leaned closer to Nick. "Why—"

"It's to show mourning," he murmured. "They absorb

the misery of everyone else, and it destroys their physical appearance. Purely symbolic, of course."

"I've heard of that."

The shadow of his profile bobbed up and down. "A lot of cultures took aspects of our funerals. The Romans copied it almost exactly."

"So every house does their funerals like this?"

The silhouette bobbed again. "With a few minor changes here and there—the colors, the smoke—but basically, as far as I know."

Megan gasped, her hand tightening on Nick's arm. Behind the servants were—demons. Not demons as she'd come to know them, but the demons of legend and nightmare. Red scaly skin peeked out from beneath hooded black capes that dissolved into the smoke. Horns curved into the air over their heads.

Worst of all were the faces, shiny and white, expressionless—masks, she realized. China masks. Some of the features looked familiar.

"Sorry," Nick whispered. "I should have warned you about the masks."

She didn't answer. The blank artificial faces towering over the crowd transfixed her. If they were on stilts—and she imagined they must be—they were obscured by the smoke.

"The masks are ancestors. All the Gretnegs are cast. They attend the funeral, see? To welcome one of their number to death."

Megan didn't bother to hide her shiver.

The last one had a "traditional" demon face, with a hooked nose and cruelly twisted lips. His mask seemed to float above his head, gleaming white and pale. Templeton Black's mask, younger, thinner, but undoubtedly Black.

She glanced at Rocturnus, uncharacteristically silent through this service. His little mouth hung slightly open. "Roc?"

His eyes came back into focus. "Yes?"

"Are you okay?"

"That was beautiful," he said. "We've never done something so elaborate. You don't even have a mask."

"Oh God."

"What? You should have one, I mean, what if—"

"I don't want to talk about this."

Would she have a funeral like this one day? Would her body, old and wrinkled—hopefully—be displayed like this? Who would walk behind her?

"Why? We should—"

She shuddered. "Not now, Roc." Nick was leading her anyway, to join the line of demons following the procession.

"Keep hold of my arm," he said. A few quiet voices rose around them as her feet fell into the rhythm of the drumbeats. Heat flared from the torches to play over her skin as they made their slow way past. "I think the floor's going to get pretty rough."

"Where are we going?"

"Into the catacombs," he said. "Into the dungeon."

Ahead of them the darkness seen through the doorway loomed.

Chapter Nineteen

They walked down the ramp forever, it seemed, until the muscles in Megan's legs started to ache and she had to give up her pride and grip Nick's arm with both hands to keep from stumbling. At least now she understood why Greyson had chosen him as her escort. She might be embarrassed by their last meeting, but at least she wasn't clinging to a stranger.

The uneven stone floor gritted under her feet as they walked, still in time to the drumbeat, the parade winding down the tunnel like a snake dancing to a charmer's flute.

Turn, then turn, then turn again. Down they went, until the torches along the walls no longer put out enough warmth to keep Megan from shivering, until the walls were damp and the air smelled like the inside of a well. She couldn't even estimate how far down they were, and yet they kept walking, the drumbeat moving them forward as inexorably as if they were an army marching to their death.

"We're almost there," Nick murmured. "At least I think we are."

Megan didn't reply. They'd hit a particularly sticky patch; she stumbled, grateful for him beside her but feeling like an idiot just the same.

Finally they reached the end of the path. A room opened before them, cavernous and dark, with greenish bracken decorating the walls and a chill Megan couldn't shake off. From the ceiling dangled the largest chandelier she'd ever seen, its arms stretching like a pale, bony spider twenty feet in each—*oh God*. It *was* a bony spider. Human bones, their white long faded to mellow ivory, like old pearls in the flickering light. The center was formed entirely of skulls, stacked on top of each other. More skulls decorated the ends of the arms, each with a fat, glowing candle stuck in the crown.

The catafalque had been placed near what Megan guessed was the back of the room; an enormous golden urn dominated it, so big she could have lain down and gone to sleep inside it had she wanted to. Even if she'd been tired she wouldn't have.

The rest of the procession stood and watched them enter. Greyson seemed deep in conversation with Templeton's widow. It struck Megan that the woman was losing everything in this moment, her husband and her position, and her heart ached a little bit. To be a Gretneg was to reach the pinnacle of success. To be the wife of a Gretneg must carry its own advantages, especially if her experience at the mall with Mr. Santo was any indication. What would it feel like to lose all of that? Megan had never cared about such things. Did she still not care? Or had the hierarchy of this underworld somehow become as much a part of her as that second heart that still shivered with every drumbeat?

They assembled in rows, still standing, as Greyson

stood expectantly before the giant, gleaming urn. He waited until they were silent to begin speaking.

"Templeton Black *ga chrino*," he said. "*Alri neshden* Templeton Black."

"*Alri neshden* Templeton Black," said the crowd around her.

"Templeton Black is dead, long live Templeton Black," Roc whispered, but Megan shushed him. She didn't need the translation. She wanted to let Greyson's voice wash over her, feeling tears prick behind her eyes when it roughened, letting her lips curve up a little when it lightened. A few times a soft laugh worked its way through the crowd. Even in words she couldn't understand she could see what an effective speaker he was. What a shame the nature of his business kept him out of the courtroom.

Or not such a shame. She had a feeling he would delight in representing the guilty.

He talked for a while, then relinquished the floor to several other Gretnegs. The chill air seeped through Megan's skin and into her bones. She grew bored, as horrible as it was to admit. Her feet hurt. She felt particularly conspicuous in her inability to understand what was being said. She was the outsider, the lesbian at the Southern Baptist church service.

Finally things drew to a close. Greyson escorted Templeton's widow down the center aisle, back to where the body lay. Megan's eyes grew wet when Mrs. Black climbed on a little stool to give her husband a last kiss.

The woman's sniffles were the only sound in the room for a moment. The torches dimmed.

Bluish flames exploded around the body, filling the shadowy dungeon with sun-bright light. Megan squinted as the image seared itself into her corneas.

The demons started singing, a low hum at first, then louder as the fire consumed both Templeton and the platform glowing with heat. Smoke drifted toward the ceiling, trickling at first, then turning into a thick black column. It arced over the body and drifted down, spreading through the room, coating Megan's throat and nostrils with a peculiar acrid, sweet taste. Her second heart sped up. The singing grew louder.

Megan started to feel as if she were floating. Her feet remained firmly on the ground, but her head was full of air, full of that meaty, savory smell. She knew what it was, was a little horrified by the knowledge, but that didn't stop her from having to swallow as her mouth filled with saliva. It wasn't just the smell, it was the sensation behind it, of power floating in the air. It was the chorus of words older than any language Megan had ever known, calling to that part of her that was just as old.

Flames filled her vision. Templeton's soul, or whatever it was he had, was rising now, escaping from the shell it had occupied, and she could rise too if she wanted to—

"Sorry, Megan." Nick's words didn't register in the split second before his shields enclosed her, becoming understandable only when heat flooded through her body. His energy was powered with sex, hardening her nipples, making her back arch slightly. Beneath the sex she felt blood, and anger, something she could connect to and that would bring her back to the real world. Such as it was. His shields protected her, forced her to stay in her body.

Another reason he was her escort. How much did Greyson know about what was happening to her? She wouldn't be able to put off that conversation much longer, and something inside her—something purely emotional, not physical—squirmed at the thought.

They stood there while the body burned, waited and sang until it was reduced to ash on the white-hot metal platform. It took no time at all, and it took forever. Megan's body was so overheated, her mind so fuzzy with sex and power and the thrilling sense of savagery in the cavernous stone room, that she barely noticed when the flames finally died and the torches flared again.

The priest stepped forward and waved his hand. Metal clanged against metal behind Megan. She turned on unsteady feet to see the lid of the enormous gold urn lifted by Malleus and Spud.

Maleficarum and the other pallbearers picked up the catafalque one last time and carried it up the aisle, followed by Greyson and Templeton's widow. The wooden legs were charred black but still solid, the platform already cooling. Iron, she thought it must be, treated somehow to keep it from melting, or magically protected.

A sigh rippled through the crowd as the ashes were poured into the urn. Flames shot from it into the air, so high they almost touched the ceiling. The flickering orange light played across Greyson's face, turning his eyes into sunken sparks, highlighting his sharp bones.

Roc shifted in his position on her shoulder. "You're in love with him, aren't you."

It didn't seem like the time to dissemble, to tell him it was none of his business or shrug it off. So she just sighed. "I suppose so, Roc. I suppose I am."

They all stood and watched the ashes fall into the urn until there were no more, until the fire went out, until Malleus and Spud replaced the lid and the service was over.

"So you're Megan Chase," the man in front of her said. Another familiar face, but then why wouldn't he be? All of the Gretnegs had been there that day three months before, to watch as she struggled to remember the worst moments of her life.

"Yes."

He held out his hand. "Winston Lawden."

"House Caedes Fuiltean," she replied, forcing herself to shake it. It had a familiar hard, tight feel to it. Would Greyson's hands change when he became Gretneg? She sincerely hoped not. Templeton's had been distinctly dry. "Orion Maldon's boss."

Winston's ruddy face darkened. "I hope you know how sorry I am about that. Orion overstepped himself most egregiously."

"Orion tried to kill me."

"I know. And trust me, our meeting tomorrow is only a formality. I am prepared to punish Orion in whatever way you feel is necessary, I assure you."

She nodded, pleasure at his sincerity warring with doubt of the same. Demons prided themselves on keeping their word, but they planted all sorts of loopholes in those words too.

"I'd like to ask you about my demons," she said. Perhaps this wasn't the right time, but she'd promised. "I understand some of your Yezer have been attacking mine."

Lawden's eyebrows disappeared into his hairline. "My Yezer? Oh, dear. My Yezer are very well policed. That's not possible."

"I have a list of names." She pulled it from her little evening bag and handed it to him. "Surely you don't think my demons are lying to me?"

She had to give him credit. He started to read the list, but glanced up sharply after a few seconds. "Two of these Yezer are dead."

"I suppose this was before they—wait, dead? How?"

His blue eyes read the knowledge in her own, and he nodded.

"They exploded," she said. "Didn't they? Greyson said you'd lost two."

Winston folded the paper back up and slipped it into his breast pocket. "They did. What do you know about it?"

The question wasn't a demand, but her skin grew warm anyway, as if he were blaming her. "Not much. But if those who exploded were attacking mine . . ."

"Do you have the lists from other families?"

She nodded and opened her bag again. "Everyone has a few—"

"Megan? What's wrong?"

She forced herself to smile. "Nothing, nothing. What were we saying?"

Every house had lost some. Even Greyson's. Were

some of his Yezer attacking hers, was he actually trying to undermine her, to steal from her?

He'd said he'd lost one, that he didn't know what was happening until one of his had exploded last week.

There had to be some explanation for it, she knew it. But what did it say about their relationship that three months in, her first instinct was to see if she could trick him into telling her what was going on instead of asking him outright?

"You think these explosions are connected somehow to your demons?" Winston shook his head. "Yezer don't have that kind of power."

"It's not Yezer, though. It's—" She stopped herself. If he didn't already know, she wasn't going to tell him now.

"It's the *leyak*?" Winston asked, his blue gaze rooting her to the spot.

She nodded.

"I thought so." Why was he being so nice to her? He was Maldon's boss, and Maldon had been in on the deal with her father and Templeton, and that would be reason enough not to trust him even if he wasn't what and who he was. The head of an opposing demon family was probably not the best sounding board for her fears.

"After I meet with you and Greyson tomorrow, the others will be over to discuss this," he went on. "Will you stay? We all want this problem solved. I think you might be able to help us."

"I—I'll have to check—"

"No, Megan. You'll have to be there. We all know you've been having some difficulty adjusting. Some of us want to let you have whatever time you need. But this is a discussion you must be part of if it centers around your *rubendas*. Failure to participate . . . it may make some of us angry."

She looked up sharply, searching for the threat in his eyes, but finding only kindness. "It's time to take your place, Megan. Ready or not."

She was hungry.

Around her the house was silent, empty, every living being except her back down in the dungeon while Greyson became Gretneg.

Surely it would be okay for her to sneak down to the kitchen and get a snack? She wouldn't go down that long winding hall. She didn't particularly want to, and even if she had, she knew it would definitely not be a good thing to do. It would be violating a trust. She wouldn't be in this house at all if there hadn't been complete confidence in her staying away from the ceremony.

A trust she suddenly wasn't so sure she returned.

"The Gretneg of a Meegra has to do what's best for her family first," Greyson had told her the night she'd connected herself to the personal demons and started this whole thing. Or rather, the night this stage of the whole thing had begun. Apparently it had started even before she thought it had, before the Accuser had shown up in her bedroom and taken over her body.

Greyson was Gretneg now, and nobody knew better than Megan how seriously he took that responsibility. If he thought it served his needs and those of his family best, he would flick her demons out of the way with no more care than he would if a moth landed on his windowsill.

Wouldn't he? Had he done it already?

She knew this was silly. If she asked him he would tell her. He would give her his word, and she trusted that word. But the heavy atmosphere in the house, the sense that the air around her was swirling and shifting, made her skin tingle and butterflies fill her stomach. Something was changing, and she didn't know yet how serious or far-reaching those changes would be.

She got up and started pacing, while the walls and furniture stood as silent observers to her unease. Her stocking feet sank into the soft carpet, whispering at her as she moved.

"This is stupid," she said out loud. She was hungry. There was food downstairs. She'd sneak down and grab something and be back in less than five minutes, long before the ceremony ended. She needed something to do. Her book didn't distract her and nothing on television was of interest. She'd get a snack, she'd bring it back here and try to get some things straight in her head while she waited. Formulate a plan for when Greyson returned.

Her toes grew numb from the freezing marble as she crept down the stairs, and the few oriental carpets in the hall did nothing to warm them. The torches had been put out immediately after the guests left, and only the floodlights from outside provided any illumination. Roc had had to leave too. The complicated process by which demons were permitted into each other's homes still eluded Megan, but there hadn't seemed to be much reason for Roc to stay.

She padded across the shiny white tile floor to the fridge, not turning on the light. Hmmm . . . cheese, the remains of a very rare roast sitting in a pool of blood on its tray—her stomach lurched, but whether from disgust or hunger Megan didn't know and didn't want to contemplate—she grabbed the cheese and slammed the door shut.

There were crackers in the pantry. That was an acceptable snack. A handful of them, a chunk of cheese, and there wouldn't be plates or anything else to dispose of in the bedroom.

She had her hand buried in the cracker box when she became aware of the singing. It had been there since she'd walked into the room, but only then did it register.

A few moments of heart-pounding panic later, she calmed down. They weren't upstairs. The sound didn't grow louder, so they weren't on their way back up the tunnel. It must be an echo, or a thin spot in the walls. Was she directly over the catacombs?

Beside the pantry, almost invisible, a small door cut into the smooth wall. It would be wrong to open it. It would be a violation, even though she hadn't actually promised she wouldn't watch.

Curiosity killed the cat . . .

Her feet moved of their own volition, her fingers found the almost-invisible catch in the door. Probably just a storeroom anyway, or a low dumbwaiter.

But it wasn't. It was a small railed ledge at the top

of a staircase cut into the rough stone of the wall, and directly below it Greyson stood naked on a dais at the end of a long wooden table.

His body was covered from neck to feet in designs, black and red ink on his skin. Greek letters, a few of them looked like, words running down his arms, patterns of twisting vines and flames, triskeles and swirls. Naked he had always looked like a god to her. Now he looked like what he was, a demon, something not of this world, something that perhaps didn't belong in it.

She'd started to turn away, trying in vain to return the privacy she'd stolen, when he burst into flames. His arms raised skyward, like a phoenix, and his voice echoed through the chamber, filling Megan's ears with demon words, words she knew were promises and pledges. She crouched down, afraid to leave, afraid to stay, biting her lip to keep from crying out. It wasn't the fire. It was the power, the sheer heart-pounding energy of it, filling the room, snaking over her skin and trying to gain entry.

The *rubendas* started chanting. A drum beat time in the background, loud and fast. Flames spread from Greyson, touching everyone at the table, crawling across the floor and partway up the walls. The *rubendas* started their own fires, smaller, reaching out to meet his, and the inferno mushroomed and rose toward the ceiling. A thin bead of sweat trickled down Megan's face.

The priest strode forward through the fire, and placed his hand on Greyson's head. The flames died, instantly. An expectant hush filled the room.

"Greyson Plantagenet Dante," the priest said, his voice ringing off the stone. "*Achen* Solomon Plantagenet Dante, *achen* Greyson Plantagenet Dante, *achen* Luchior Plantagenet Dante, *achen* Aradios Plantagenet Dante . . ."

The list of names intoned in that sepulchral voice and the smoky haze in the air, the scent of incense—dragon's blood, if she wasn't mistaken, roundly fruity and spicy—made Megan's head start to pound. She was on the ledge and not there. Only some tiny instinct, like that of a mouse in a wolf's den, kept her from lowering her shields, from trying to fly down to the floor so she could take part. If she opened her fist she knew she could create flames from nothing, could take her part with the rest of them. She was them, she was all of them . . . she shoved her fist against her lips so hard it hurt.

From the right side of the room stepped one of the brothers—she thought it was Maleficarum—holding a covered tray, bright gold and shining in the reflected torchlight.

The *rubendas* started to cheer, to clap, to bang the table. A few called out, "Greyson Dante!"; a few more, "Templeton Black!"

The yells grew louder, more cohesive, until only one word roared off the walls and filled Megan's soul. "Gretneg! Gretneg! Gretneg!"

Maleficarum lifted the lid of the tray. Even at this distance Megan knew what rested there, knew what was going to happen. A ritual older than time . . . a gesture of respect and continuity, a form of communion overwritten by modern organized religions. She'd read about it, studied it, but never thought she would actually witness it. She wanted to close her eyes but the greatest force she possessed would not convince her lids to lower. This was a mistake, this was such a mistake, she shouldn't be here . . .

Greyson scooped the heart of Templeton Black from its pool of blood. The sound of his teeth sinking into it echoed through the cavern, becoming lost only in the sound of Megan's own heart pounding in her ears.

She tried to crawl back toward the door as Greyson extended his arm, tried to scramble to her feet but stumbled as the priest sliced Greyson's forearm with a sharp silver blade. Her hand found the catch again when his blood poured into a golden bowl held by Malleus.

But she did not manage to run away until the *rubendas* came forward with their cups.

Chapter Twenty

She rinsed her mouth again, then once again, spitting into the sink, trying as hard as she could not to see her red face in the mirror. There wasn't time, even if she wanted to. She had no idea how much longer the ceremony would last.

Pushing her sweaty hair back from her forehead, she left the bathroom and grabbed her purse and shoes, then flung the door open and started to run.

The marble stairs had never seemed so slippery, the hall never so threatening. No ghosts lurked in the shadows near the ever-moving ceiling. No demons hid in the corners; they were all down in the dungeon.

The danger came from her, from that place deep inside that had sneaked into a ceremony she had no business witnessing. The part that wanted to see it. The part that recognized it for what it was, the transfer of power, the continuance of a legacy going back millennia, older even than the funeral rite had been, and wanted to participate in it. The part that knew the ritual was not a human one, and he was not human, and she wasn't entirely human either, not anymore.

The part that had watched Templeton Black's blood

spurt from his heart, one last forced beat before all power left it forever, and drip down Greyson's chin.

And had wanted to strip off her clothes and run down the stone steps and go to him, wrap herself around him so the ink on his skin smeared off onto hers. Wanted to lick the blood off and taste it, raw and coppery in his mouth, to feel him force all that power into her body, force himself into her body, to scream in ecstasy while they all watched.

It was a siren's call wending its way to her head, and she had to get out, get back to herself, before she obeyed it.

Her feet slid on the floor at the base of the stairs. She twisted her ankle trying to keep her balance and had to half run, half hop to the doors, across the dim rectangles of light coming through the windows, exposed and vulnerable, like hobbled prey running through sparse foliage.

She twisted the doorknob. It would not budge. She fumbled with the locks, pushing until her fingers hurt, but they would not move.

Nobody entered or left the Iureanlier without permission from the Gretneg. She was trapped.

In her panicked state, when she first heard the pounding she thought she was the one doing it, beating senselessly at the door. It took a moment for her to realize her arms were folded, her fists clenched. Someone was outside, hammering at the wooden gate that separated the house from the street.

She ducked down. The police. It had to be the police,

they'd heard about the ceremony, they knew about everything, they were—

Calm down, for fuck's sake! The police probably didn't even know Templeton Black was dead, much less anything about demon customs or rituals or anything else. The idea that they would be outside, ready to bust everyone for—what? unlawful disposal of demon remains?—was ludicrous.

She curled her fingers around the edge of one of the heavy red velvet curtains and tugged it aside, but the floodlights on the lawn were too bright to see past. She had one brief, heartfelt moment of thanks that she hadn't been able to get out after all before voices flooded into the hall and the lights flashed on.

"M'lady? What's wrong?" Maleficarum stood before her, his stout, powerful hands hovering ineffectually a few inches from her shoulder. "What's 'appened?"

"It's Maldon," Malleus snarled, whipping back the curtain. "What's that Aylesbury think 'e's doing here? Scaring our lady, makin' a scene!"

"You watch yer language, Mal!"

"Yeh," said Spud.

"I presume he's begging for his life."

They turned as one at the sound of Greyson's voice. Megan was afraid to look at him, somehow convinced she'd find him still naked, covered in markings, blood dripping down his chest and pouring—

Don't think about it!

But he looked just as he had before he'd left for the ceremony, save his damp hair and clean, ordinary clothes.

Black pants, a black V-neck. Greyson casual. A sweating bottle of champagne dangled from his left hand.

Some of the choking fear abated. He hadn't turned savage in the last hour. This could have been any night, one of many when he'd greeted her with a cold drink and a warm kiss. If her heart hadn't been pounding in her throat she could almost have imagined it was.

She found her voice. "His life?"

"He knows we're meeting with Winston tomorrow, so yes."

"But his life isn't in danger."

"Isn't it?" The bottle clanked solidly onto the table by the door.

"No. I mean . . . oh."

"He tried to kill you. He tried to kill us both."

"I can't . . . I can't just order someone killed, Greyson. I can't do that."

"I can."

"What if I ask you not to?"

He stepped back and put his hands in his pockets. "If you ask me not to . . . we'll discuss it."

"Now?"

"No. Now he's standing outside on the street, getting ready to make a scene. I don't want him out there any longer than necessary." His glance took in her shoes and purse still clutched in her hands. "Mal, get Miss Chase's coat, please. Better put those shoes on, Meg."

"We're going outside?"

"We should get a look at him before we let him in, don't you think?"

Oh. Ktana Leyak. "He's not a Yezer, though, isn't he safe?"

"I would think so, but I can't guarantee it. Especially not in his—shall we say highly emotional?—state. He's vulnerable, and that's not a safe way to be."

She nodded as Malleus slipped her coat over her shoulders. Her cold, stiff shoes refused to admit her feet. She stooped to shove them on and almost fell over.

Greyson didn't tease her about her clumsiness. Normally he would have. She glanced at him once she'd righted herself and found him watching her. He'd seen her at the door, obviously preparing to flee; was he going to say anything? Did she want him to?

The trouble with keeping secrets was that it became harder and harder to stop as time went on. Tiny discussions, simple questions, grew out of control the more she tried to put them off, until they were no longer simple, but complex and full of mines.

"Open the door," he said.

Cold air blasted into the room, scented with wood smoke and snow. The pale sky hung low and heavy above them. Megan had forgotten it was only a few days until Christmas.

They stepped outside, their shoes scuffing the white stone steps and the sidewalk beyond, until they stood almost at the gate with the boys behind them.

"Greyson, Megan," Orion said. It seemed clichéd somehow for a blood demon to have bloodshot eyes, but the pinkish tinge, like Pepto-Bismol in his eye sockets, was definitely not anger or passion, and the tremulous rasp of his voice made her skin crawl. Greyson was right. Orion had come begging.

"What do you want, Orion?"

"To talk to you. I have information. You came to me for it. I'll give it to you now. Free. A favor you don't have to return."

"No."

She glanced at Greyson, opening her mouth, but his warning look shut it again.

"Megan? Don't you want to know how it happened? What your father did, what he said? Why he left that hospital to you?"

"I'm tired, Orion. And bored with you," she lied, but his words echoed in her head. She did want to know why her father had left it to her, more than almost anything. Was it one last reprimand from beyond the grave?

Or was it an apology he felt he couldn't make in life?

"I can tell you," he continued. "I was there, I know it all. All you have to do is let me live. I'll leave you alone. It wasn't my idea, anyway, at my place. You know that." His horrible pink gaze turned to Greyson. "You know I wasn't behind that, you know it!"

"Just like I know you jumped at the chance to help," Greyson said.

"You fucked my wife! What was—" Orion subsided. His thin fingers curled over the top of the gate. "We've never been friends. But that wasn't personal."

Greyson shrugged. "And neither is this. Come on, Meg, it's cold out here."

He took her hand and started to turn away, but

Orion's next shout stopped them both. "I'll tell you how to stop the *leyak*! I know what she wants!"

For a second Megan thought he'd somehow managed to break the gate and it had exploded with a sound like thunder. Then she heard him scream. She was already throwing herself to the ground when Greyson's hand caught her neck and shoved.

Not an explosion. A ball of something black and shiny, like obsidian or jet, with trails of red sparks in its wake. And not aimed at her, but at Orion, who was now shrieking, "Let me in! *D'sham tergan, chresh! Chresh!*"

The brittle, frozen grass sliced at her palms like razor blades as she clambered out of the way. Greyson caught her around the waist, trying to roll her to the right across the icy lawn, but she didn't want to go. The front of the house was naked, innocent of trees or shrubs, and they would have to climb back up the stairs to find sanctuary. Belatedly she realized he knew that too, and was pulling her toward the break of pines on the side of the house. Together they scuttled toward it.

Another bang. Orion screamed again, and now other voices joined his, harsh muffled voices in English. "He's down! Get him!"

"Greyson, we have to help him," Megan gasped. "We can't just leave him!"

"The fuck we can't. He's going to die tomorrow any-way—"

Maleficarum slammed into them, knocking them into the trees. The scent of pine filled her nose, and for one absurd moment it actually felt like Christmas.

Until a dried pine needle, sharp as a dental instrument, jammed itself into her cheek when she hit the ground. "Ouch, shit!"

"Are you okay?"

Muffled footsteps sounded on the street, some distance away but gaining fast.

"Help me! Chresh!" The hysterical quality of Orion's pleas made her jaw clench. She glanced around and saw another ball hit the fence and erupt into a shower of black sparks like the sequins on Justine's dress.

"We have to help him!"

"This doesn't concern us, those are—"

"Greyson! *Ak vend retchia! Ak vend retchia!*"

Maleficarum said something Megan was fairly certain he wouldn't have said in her presence at any other moment, but the exact phrase was covered by Greyson's much more concise one.

"*Ak vend retchia*—aaaaa!"

"Damn it!" Greyson paused for a moment, then shouted, *"Retchia a capt."* Megan heard the footsteps outside getting closer, heard the front gate squeak then slam shut.

Greyson snatched her hand and yanked her toward a small side door she hadn't seen until then. "Fuck."

"What about—"

His face was hidden by shadows. "Mal and Spud have him. I gave the bastard sanctuary."

"Call Tera."

She actually stumbled. Words she never thought she'd hear Greyson say. "What?"

"Call her, now. Tell her we have Orion and he's been injured, but convince her we're not going to help him escape or anything stupid like that." He paused and glanced at her shoes and purse again, his arms crossed over his chest. "Please, Meg."

The blaze in the fireplace warmed her skin, but the phone was still winter-night cold in her hand. Tera picked up on the first ring.

"Megan, is Orion Maldon in that house? You need to send him out now, out front, unarmed—"

"Wait, wait, Tera, hold on. Yes, he's in here. He's injured. We're not going to help him escape or anything, but we can't—"

"Look, this has nothing to do with you or Greyson. This isn't even me, I didn't order this. This is Vergadering business, and they'll storm that fucking gate if they—"

"Tera, please. Just listen for a minute, okay?"

She didn't know if the silence was her invitation to speak or if Tera was simply too pissed off to continue. Hoping for the former, she plunged ahead. "Maldon has some information I need. About my father, remember I told you about that? About the hospital? He came here to give it to me, and I need it. Please. Don't storm the gates."

Greyson snorted. A chill breeze wafted over her skin, distracting her from the phone call. They were supposed to be celebrating right now. Snuggled up in his big bed with a bottle of champagne or something.

Instead they were here in the study, while someone who'd tried to kill them sobbed and bled just outside the door, a gang of witches waited on the street—presumably with battering rams—and Greyson knew she'd been about to run out on him when he'd come upstairs after the ceremony.

Finally Tera sighed. "Put Greyson on."

Megan did.

"Hi, Tera. No. I *had* to, I didn't want to. He invoked— No. No, I—no. I'm not going to, I give you my word. Yes. I swear it. Hey, I hate the guy, I don't want to help him do—okay. Yes. Here she is."

He handed Megan the phone and leaned toward her, as if to give her a kiss, but stopped himself. Okay, they were definitely going to have to talk about what had happened. Guilt made her duck her head and look away as she raised the phone to her ear.

It wasn't that she didn't still want him. She did, unquestionably. It wasn't that she even thought of him differently—she didn't, not really. It wasn't as though what she'd witnessed was part of his everyday life or anything.

It was herself she saw differently, herself who seemed like some sort of monster, and she had no idea how to admit that to him. To anyone.

"I'm going to make some calls," Tera said. "You should have the night free. But in the morning, you're going to have to hand him over."

Megan's shoulders sagged. She hadn't realized they were tense. "Thanks."

"It's okay. Call me tomorrow."

"Okay. 'Bye." The phone clicked shut. "What's going on? What's all this about sanctuary, and what's Vergadering doing outside?"

He handed her a glass half full of bourbon. "What's going on," he said, "is that we've just interfered in a Vergadering arrest. Sanctuary—the *retchia*—is an ancient demon custom, which essentially has to be granted if requested. And I assume Vergadering is outside because they think Orion killed those witches Temp hired to kill me. Any more questions?"

"Why do they think he did it?" The whiskey burned going down her throat and brought tears to her eyes, but she felt better. Stronger. False confidence, but confidence just the same.

He shrugged. "Probably because some interesting clues to that effect have been planted around the city and the rumor mill is working overtime."

"So you weren't going to have him killed, you were going to have him arrested? Like T-Templeton?" *That bloody heart . . .*

"Oh, no. I definitely planned to have him killed. But this way when his body turns up, Vergadering will consider their case closed." He left *which means we're both off the hook* unsaid, but Megan knew it was there.

Damn it, how did he manage to do this to her? Put her in a position where his way seemed the only sensible and logical way, where it kept coming down to her life or someone else's?

And make himself look magnanimous in the process, as well as right?

"Which reminds me . . ." he said, and picked up his own phone. "I have to call Winston. No point putting off until tomorrow what we can do today."

"No! I mean, can't we . . . you said we'd discuss it."

"And we will. But Win needs to know he's here, so he can come over if he wants. We might as well meet with him now."

She nodded. It wasn't like she'd be going to sleep anytime soon. If she even stayed here.

She was of two minds about that one. Or rather, two hearts and a mind. Both hearts wanted to stay. Her mind thought it might not be a good idea.

It might not be a good idea for her to be involved in any of this anymore. Despite what Winston said to her earlier about it being time for her to take charge, she had a feeling that, as much as the demons might like it, it would be the absolute worst thing she could do for herself. When she started thinking murder wasn't such a bad plan after all, when she started thinking of people—even for a second—as problems to be dealt with and not individuals, that wasn't good.

But hadn't she been training herself for years to think of them that way? To see them in the light of their issues, and to use their lives and the events in them merely as stage settings to help her treat the problem?

Had her career been nothing more than a way to remove herself from people, all along, to let herself feel superior to them? Were these changes in her the result of the awakening of that piece of demon nestled in her chest, or were they simply her true feelings—as black and miserable as they were—finally being allowed to come out?

After all, she hadn't had her own personal demon. Every shitty thing she'd done to other people in the last sixteen years had come purely from the depths of her one human heart.

Greyson looked at her oddly, and she realized she was standing in the middle of the room with her brow furrowed, biting her lip.

"I was just . . . thinking about something."

"I'd never have guessed. Win's on his way over, so let's get Orion in here now. I want to have this done as soon as possible."

"What about—are we going to decide now what to do about him? What to tell Winston, I mean?"

He finished his drink. "Why don't we see what he has to say first. You might change your mind when you hear his story."

Chapter Twenty-one

Orion, shivering and wrapped in a blanket, cata-pulted into the room. The reason for the dramatic vault was soon clear; Malleus stood behind him with an amused look on his face.

"Hello, Orion," Greyson said. The contrast between himself—sharp, clean, well dressed—and Orion in his blanket with blood caked in his hair and along the side of his face could not have been clearer.

She had to hand it to Orion, though. He stood ram-rod straight and nodded with the dignity of a duke. "Greyson. *Cal eptari retchia.*"

"Retchia senshar."

The formalities thus apparently dealt with, Orion started to sink into one of the cushy armchairs behind him.

"I don't recall giving you leave to sit," Greyson said.

Megan glanced at him, then back at Orion, whose face flushed. "I apologize, Gretneg Dante. May I sit?"

Greyson nodded. He'd made his point. Orion was in his house; Orion was in serious trouble.

She'd been so focused on the ritual she hadn't thought about what it meant, hadn't even paid attention to the difference in Greyson. Power curled through the room, the same easy, confident strength Templeton Black and the other Gretnegs she'd met bore. Now Greyson was one of them.

Of course, so was she, but by default. Her power hadn't increased, she didn't live in the Yezer Iureanlier, she hadn't done a ritual and wasn't expected to, save the Haikken Kra. Which she still wasn't sure about.

Maybe it would help her, make it easier to accept and deal with the feral urges. Maybe it would make them harder to resist. She wished she'd asked more about it before everything started going haywire, but it hadn't seemed like such a complex decision then. They'd wanted her to consolidate her demon power, to allow it free reign in her body and become, essentially, demon. She didn't particularly agree. It was that simple—or had been.

"You came to give us information, Orion. Might as well start."

Orion licked his lips. "I'm thirsty."

Greyson flicked his gaze to Spud, who moved to pour a drink. Orion accepted it with both scraped, bloody hands, like a child. Megan's demon heart gave a little leap. She looked away.

"Winston is on his way, Orion. You came to ask Dr. Chase and me to show you mercy. You might want to start convincing us why we should."

The silence beat against Megan's skin. Orion wasn't going to talk after all. He'd come to taunt her with his knowledge, to try and convince her to spare his life in exchange for hints. How could she even be certain he was telling the truth, no matter what he said? She trusted Greyson's word. She didn't trust Orion Maldon's.

"I went to her father," he said finally. "I found her. I moved to Grant Falls and I watched."

"How——," Megan started, but Greyson silenced her with a quick shake of his head.

Orion went on as if he hadn't noticed. "We'd been looking for someone to help the Accuser for a while, me and Temp. You didn't know we were friends, did you? We grew up together—well, he was older than me by a few years, but we knew each other.

"So I started hunting. On my off hours. I wasn't a *lakri* then, I was just a soldier. I had time to look. I visited just about every town and city in three states before I found you." His blue gaze fixed on Megan, and for a second the humbled petitioner disappeared, replaced by the man she'd met the other night. "If you could have seen her then, Greyson, you——"

"Malleus," Greyson said smoothly and, before Megan or Orion had time to react, Malleus stepped forward and smacked Orion across the face with one beefy hand.

It looked casual, as if Malleus was brushing a fly away, but the sound of skin on skin rang through the room and Orion's head snapped to the side. Droplets of blood flew from his nose and mouth. Megan's stomach churned. Somewhere inside her the memory of what she'd seen earlier still lurked, the confused desire still simmered. She did not need to see more violence or smell more blood.

Orion clutched his mouth for a moment, glaring at Greyson, who looked back at him with utter indifference.

Orion looked away first. "I found her," he said, his voice thick. "And contacted her father to make the deal."

Megan saw it in her head, not a psychic vision but

simply the events as Orion told them. He showed up at her father's office one afternoon and presented himself as a man in need of tax advice. His bulging accounts certainly interested her father, and a friendship of sorts had sprung up.

It didn't take long for the two men to get around to the subject of Megan.

"He said you were always in trouble," Orion said. "That you were out of control, neither of your parents knew what to do with you. You started fights with their friends. The kids at school hated you. You—"

"That's enough," Greyson interrupted. Megan looked at him, but his gaze was focused on Maldon. "What was the deal, Maldon?"

The deal was, Megan would be the Accuser's vessel. In return, David Chase, CPA, would find his business prospering, his position in town cemented, and the problems with his children—Dave had already been busted for marijuana possession, which was a surprise to Megan—would be ignored. Maldon had powerful friends who could take care of people's nasty little memories and inconvenient problems like police reports.

"Did . . ." Megan's throat closed up. She shook her head.

"Did the man know what he was doing?" Greyson asked the question for her. "What would happen to her?"

Orion nodded. "She was supposed to live in the hospital. The Accuser could gain strength there, using her body. Then when the time was right . . ." He shrugged. "He would emerge."

"And Megan would die."

"It wouldn't have been much of a life for her anyway. Possessed by the Accuser and trapped in that building."

Her palms hurt. She looked down and saw her own blood seeping between her clenched fingers.

Orion noticed too. His nostrils flared. "I'm awfully weak," he said, staring at her hand. "I don't know if I'll be able to keep talking without a restorative."

"You'll keep talking," Greyson replied.

"*Retchia* says you have to give me whatever I require."

"Malleus," Greyson said again. Malleus stepped forward, pushing up the sleeve of his black sweater. Spud drew his wicked-looking knife.

"No." Orion put up his hand. "Not his. It's not strong enough for me. You know the rules, Greyson. The Gretneg must offer his greatest hospitality to those under his protection."

Greyson stared at him. So did everyone else in the room.

"Otherwise it's a violation of *retchia*," Orion sing-songed.

Oh no.

Greyson sighed and shoved up his own sleeve. The wound made during the ceremony had not yet healed; the angry mark striped his forearm. Megan looked away, but the image stayed in her mind, bringing back every memory of what had happened earlier, every bit of squirming, sickening panic.

"You know, Orion, this really isn't the best way to win my favor."

Orion straightened in his chair, his gaze steady. For the first time he looked like something more than a small, irritating dog who'd been given power he didn't know how to handle. "Let's not play, Greyson. I know as well as you do that you're not going to spare my life. If I hadn't requested sanctuary you would have let those witches kill me, and your only regret would have been that it wasn't by your order."

The two men stared at each other for a long moment. Finally Greyson nodded. "Fair enough," he said. "Fair enough. Spud?"

Spud didn't reopen the old wound. Instead he made a second, smaller cut next to the first, slicing across a vein. Blood spurted into a thick crystal glass, in time with Greyson's slow, steady pulse.

Red spots flared behind Megan's eyes, spots filled with blood and pain and the memory of Templeton's heart, of the flames filling the dungeon and Greyson's naked form, his arms upraised, lord of Hell in his purest, most powerful form. The slash in his skin taunted her and Megan saw his back as it had been in her room, destroyed by their passion.

Her heart pounded. The demon inside her writhed and screamed as blood filled the glass, almost to the rim, before Greyson drew his handkerchief and Spud handed the glass to Orion. He raised it to his mouth, lowered it to show lips stained with red, and Megan couldn't take any more. She wasn't even herself, she was nothing but a desire, a need, something so fierce she could only do one thing to fight it.

She ran.

* * *

Her footsteps echoed on the bare white marble, so it sounded to her as though an army of desperate women raced toward the door, joined almost immediately by one determined man. One man who ran faster than she could ever hope to. She knew he was there but still screamed when his fingers closed over her arm.

She tried to yank it away but succeeded only in losing her balance and almost falling. The floor veered crazily in front of her until his arms closed around her from behind, pulling her to the warm strength of his chest.

"Jesus, Meg," he gasped, his voice hoarse. "Why didn't you tell me it was this bad?"

The words didn't sink in. Nothing seemed able to penetrate the crimson fog in her brain, the choking need in her chest. She fought, struggling against his arms, finally bringing the sharp heel of her shoe down on his toe.

"Ow! Fuck!" His grip loosened, then tightened again before she could take advantage of it.

Dampness seeped through her dress at the waist. Greyson hadn't stopped bleeding. Her stomach lurched. She could smell it, see it, on the sheets earlier, on his back, on Orion's lips . . . she could almost taste it.

She screamed, one short yelp that echoed in the sterile hall, before her body finally gave out and she completed her humiliation by throwing up on the floor.

Her throat hurt, her stomach hurt. She felt like she'd been awake for years, like this day would never end, as she stayed bent over with his arms around her waist.

"God *damn,* that's sexy," he said finally. "I think you actually cut my toe off."

Her stomach twisted again. The only thing worse than vomiting in front of a man was doing it a second time because he'd made a joke. "Don't—"

"Malleus."

Megan turned to see the boys all standing in the doorway, watching them with identical expressions of concern. Spud had his hands clasped in front of his chest like a Victorian lady suffering an attack of the vapors.

Not that she looked any better. Demons in glass houses . . .

"Miss Chase isn't feeling well," Greyson continued unnecessarily. "Will you take her into the den, please, and fix her a drink? Maleficarum, you get her something to put on and a clean washcloth, and tell one of the maids to come take care of this. Spud, go to her house and bring her some fresh clothes of her own. Winston's going to be here any minute and I don't think she wants to greet him wearing one of my shirts. I'll sit with Orion and try to get more information out of him before Win arrives."

It always surprised her how quickly the boys moved. Their stocky figures looked designed for intimidation and brute strength rather than speed, like hippos. But before she could blink Malleus's respectful hands rested on her upper arms, half carrying, half leading her, and the other two disappeared.

The gold-flocked walls of the den welcomed her. This—aside from the bedroom—was where she spent most of her time at the Iureanlier. Not a big room, at least not by the standards of this house, but a comfortable one, with an especially deep and cozy brown suede couch just the right size for two. The TV and stereo sat cold and silent, the only difference between this night and any other.

"Here y'go, m'lady." The tenderness in his rough voice brought fresh tears to her eyes. "Let's just get this undone, you'll feel all better."

She stood like a doll while he unzipped her dress and slipped it off her shoulders, wincing a little as the sticky sleeves slipped over her hands. Blood and vomit . . . her nose wrinkled.

"You hold my shoulders, let's get these shoes off too."

She'd once thought of Malleus, Maleficarum, and Spud as bizarre, criminal grandpas. That thought comforted her now, while her mascara ran down her splotchy cheeks and Malleus removed her shoes and stockings for her, tender as a father with a small child.

Her father was dead, really dead, and long before he'd died he'd sold her to a demon. Given her up, tried to get rid of her, traded her life for whatever success he'd had in some podunk town that nobody else gave a fuck about. His only daughter. The little girl he'd once read bedtime stories to.

She could barely see now. For some reason this helped. It was easier to pretend Malleus couldn't see her, easier to pretend she wasn't really there when Maleficarum entered and started cleaning the blood off her stomach with a warm, damp cloth.

By the time Malleus whispered, "Close your eyes, now," and wiped her face clean, her breath hitched in her chest. She could feel the two demons exchanging worried glances over her head, their uncertainty about what they should be doing. Crying women made most men uncomfortable. Centuries-old guard demons who, as far as she knew, had never even dated were no different.

Together they helped her step into a pair of Greyson's silk pajama bottoms and pulled the drawstring tight around her waist, then slipped a clean white T-shirt over her head and helped her sit down in the corner of the couch. Maleficarum shoved a drink into her hand, cold and smelling of bourbon and Coke, which made sense because that's what it was.

"You need something sweet," he said. "The sugar'll 'elp."

Like she needed convincing. She drank half the glass in one long gulp, took a breath, and got ready to finish it. Drunk had never sounded so good. She wanted to pass out and wake up in the morning unable to remember anything.

Which was impossible. Those images would never, ever leave her head.

"Careful now, m'lady. You don't wanna drink too much on an empty stomach."

Yes, she did. "Yes, I do."

"Naw, naw, now, cuz Lord Lawden's gonna be 'ere, and you don't wanna be all drunk then, right? Ain't ladylike, it ain't."

"Who cares." Nobody did. Nobody cared about her. Okay, it wasn't fair to say that anymore. People cared. But it was more fun at that moment to say nobody did, so she could attribute feeling sorry for herself to loneliness and isolation instead of the reality. She felt sorry for herself because she'd somehow won some kind of misery lottery, and her prize was a parasitic piece of demon wrapped around her heart. Her forehead ached from crying.

How much more of this was she supposed to take? How long would it be before she stopped being able to resist, before she let the demon inside have its way, taking blood, taking energy, feeding on the sorrow of every human she came across?

"Okay, guys." Greyson's voice, smooth and calm. "Orion's having a little trouble remembering he said he'd tell us how to beat the *leyak*. Maybe you could help him with that?"

Maleficarum patted her on the head before he left. The gesture only made her start crying again.

Greyson took away her empty glass. She closed her eyes and leaned forward, resting her forehead on the cool smooth suede, while ice clinked and cracked and soda fizzed.

Light flared against her eyelids. He'd started a fire. A nice gesture, but she doubted she would ever feel warm again.

Finally the cushion shifted with his weight as he sat next to her and closed her fingers back around the glass. His hand found her back, rested there unmoving, warming her chilled skin.

"I know what's going on, Meg," he said quietly. "Are you . . . do you want to talk to—about it?"

"It's not right." Her words were muffled by the thick padded arm of the couch.

"Not right for whom? For you? For me? Maybe not for Brian or Tera or that miserable bunch of hypocrites who raised you. Come on, *bryaela*. You're stronger than this."

"I'm not."

"You are. Now sit up and stop behaving like a child."

"Oh my God." She turned to stare at him. "You are the most insensitive man I've—oh, whatever."

"Part of my charm." His smile didn't reach his eyes, though, and she noticed shadows beneath them that hadn't been there in the study.

She took a deep breath. "I . . . I saw."

"I know you did."

"I'm sorry. I'm so sorry. I didn't do it on purpose. I mean, I did, but I didn't mean to, I was hungry so I went to the kitchen . . ."

"And you found the stairway," he finished.

"I'm sorry." She wasn't sure if she was apologizing to him, or to herself, or . . . to whom, but they were the only words that made sense.

He shrugged. "It's done."

"Wait, you . . . you knew?" *Of course he knew, stupid. You practically hung a sign around your neck.*

"Of course I knew. I felt you in the room. And then you don't normally hang around by the front door with your shoes and purse in your hand, like an inexperienced cat burglar."

"I panicked."

"You're not yourself."

"I'm not sure if that's a compliment or an insult."

"And that's the point."

The urge to slap him felt so good, after the abject misery of the last twenty minutes or so, it took her a minute to realize what it was. None of her problems seemed as bad when he was being this exasperating. "Are you trying to piss me off?"

"Maybe."

Megan watched him for a minute. He watched her right back, his dark eyes serious. It felt a little odd to be having such a—well, such an intimate conversation, that didn't involve any intimate activities to go with it. They talked a lot—even more than they engaged in those activities—but this was different. The subject was open, laying between them. It wouldn't go away no matter how she might want it to, so she might as well have the discussion. Get it over with.

He must have had the same thought. "You didn't really think you could hide it from me, did you?"

"Obviously I did, or I wouldn't have tried."

A quick smile flashed across his face, like a lightning bolt straight into her chest.

"I pay attention, darling," he said. "It wasn't hard to see, even if you hadn't fed off me a few times."

"No, I didn't—did I?"

He nodded.

Why couldn't she get drunk? None of the reasons seemed to be that important. Winston seemed nice enough, and she didn't really need to participate . . .

Unless she wanted to behave like what Orion had accused her of being.

Greyson's chest looked almost as inviting as her

drink. She leaned into him, resting her cheek just below his collarbone. His muscles relaxed and his arm curved around her.

"Why didn't you say something?"

"Come on, Meg."

Right. He wouldn't have invaded her privacy like that, any more than she would have done it to him. "But . . . aside from that, why didn't you?"

"Because it was obvious you didn't know you were doing it. Just like you didn't realize your steak the other night wasn't overdone. Or that earlier today—you didn't see your eyes."

Her hands flew to her face. "Oh God, did they change?"

"Yes. They haven't done that before, at least not that I've seen."

"I don't understand . . ."

"Your demon is growing. It's gaining power, and trying to get more. Maybe because some of your little ones have abandoned ship, like we talked about after your dad's funeral. Or maybe just because. But it's trying to assert itself and your power is too strong to let itself be destroyed. So the demon has to look elsewhere for food."

Your power is too strong to let itself be destroyed . . . "It was feeding off me?"

"At least at first, yes."

"And that's why the stuff Tera taught me stopped working."

She caught his sharp glance. She hadn't told him that. "I would think so."

"So if I . . . if I keep it fed, I can do that stuff again? And I can read people again?"

"You haven't been?"

"No, not really. Not after Gerald's sister came to the office Monday morning. I wanted to comfort her, but . . ." She shook her head. "It went wrong."

"So that's why you quit like that. I wondered."

"No you didn't."

"No, I didn't. For a minute I thought perhaps you'd bowed to my superior wisdom, but that would have been too much to ask. So I assumed it had something to do with the demon."

It all seemed so rational, so sensible, as they sat there sipping bourbon in front of a roaring fire. Megan could have imagined they were talking about dinner plans or what movie to watch, if she didn't still feel so cold and the squirming thing in her chest had stilled itself.

It hadn't. Calmer, yes, but not quiescent.

Spud appeared holding an armful of clothing at the same time the buzzer rang. Winston Lawden had arrived.

Chapter Twenty-two

She started to sweat as she buttoned her jacket. True to form, Spud had selected a skirt she normally wore in the evening—it was shorter than work generally called for—and a summery camisole. Whatever. Given how pale she looked, maybe it was better if no one focused on her face too much. Not that her cleavage was anything to write home about.

"What do I do about it?" she asked, pulling up her stocking.

"Hmm?" His eyes tracked the movements of her hands. "Oh. Just relax. If you don't panic about it, it won't be so bad. It's not like this is some crazy force that's going to overtake you at any moment and force you to do things, especially once you get matters sorted out with your demons. It scared you, right, more than actually bothering you physically?"

Funny. She hadn't thought about it that way before, but he was right. It was the creepy awfulness of wanting to drink blood, more than the actual desire to do so, that had bothered her. She nodded.

"It's just a desire, not a demand. You're not a slave to it. It—you—have specific triggers. You can avoid those or you can learn to accept them and try to find another way to deal with them. It's only a problem because you made it one. Oh, and sex is always a good way to get your mind off it, you know."

She rolled her eyes, but couldn't help smiling. "You're so helpful."

"I try."

She dug her compact out of her purse and smeared a little powder on. Ugh. Blotchy skin, bags under her eyes . . . and so many unanswered questions, still, that she thought her head might explode, although—she hoped—not literally. Of course, if Ktana Leyak got hold of her, it was entirely possible.

Unless Orion Maldon had told the truth and knew how to defeat her.

"We'll talk more later," he said. "Unless you've decided to go home after Winston leaves."

"Talking sounds good." She still hadn't even asked him about whether his demons were picking on hers . . . not that one explosion meant much. Not that the connection was even confirmed. Coincidences did happen, even when it seemed like they shouldn't.

"We'll see if— What the hell?"

Screams of pain tore through the door, mingled with shouts from Malleus and Maleficarum. Greyson started running, Megan right behind him, her heels clicking on the spotless floor.

They burst through the door of the study, where Greyson stopped so abruptly that Megan ran right into him. He hardly noticed. Neither did she.

Orion Maldon glowed like an LED light, sitting in his chair with sweat pouring down his face. Megan could practically see the air above him shimmer as his blood heated, as he got redder and redder until she expected to see his tears boil and sizzle down his tight cheeks. Heat rose from his skin and canceled out the chill of Winston's rage.

Winston leaned against Greyson's desk, his arms folded and his brows drawn. At their abrupt entrance, he glanced up.

"Nice to see you again, Megan," he said, surely the most incongruous greeting Megan had ever received.

"Um . . . you too."

"Winston," Greyson said. "Far be it from me to interfere, but what are you doing?"

"Orion deserves to be punished. You guys do it your way. This is ours."

"Of course. But we still have a lot of questions to ask him. If you wouldn't mind—"

"What questions? He betrayed me. He made a deal with Templeton Black and allowed Templeton to almost bring the Accuser into your House. To defeat our own! I had no idea he was involved in that. The disloyalty . . ." He shook his head. "I know we were going to discuss his punishment, but I hope you'll forgive me if I say I've already made the decision."

Megan glanced at Orion. His eyes weren't bulging anymore. Instead his lids were closing, his head slumping to the side. He was dying, right there beside her, and she couldn't do or say anything to stop it.

"I gave him *retchia*, Win. You can't kill him under my roof, not if I'm aware of it."

"I'll take him outside."

"Vergadering is outside."

"Oh, yes." Winston looked thoughtful. "I did notice them. They're going to want him first thing in the morning, aren't they?"

"I promised them, yes."

"Asterope Green?"

Greyson nodded.

Winston sighed. "Why you let that witch get so close to you I'll never understand. We're not meant to mix with them, you know." His gaze settled on Megan, who had the uncomfortable feeling that both men were in complete agreement but only one was brave enough to say it. Or rather, only one of them was keeping his mouth shut because he wanted to stay in her bed.

"Orion says he knows how to beat the *leyak*," Greyson said.

"He's a liar. What would he know about *leyaks*?"

"If we figured out the connection between the Yezer who exploded and mine," Megan cut in, "maybe he did too."

Greyson shot her a glance. Oops. Well, not exactly oops. She hadn't really had a chance to talk to him about it, what with the vomiting and the cannibalism taking up so much of their time.

Winston sighed. "I'd say you were overestimating Orion's capabilities, but after what he did—what he tried to do—with the Accuser, I don't know I'd believe it myself."

"He was a buddy of Temp's from way back," Greyson said. "Who knows what they talked about?"

They were silent for a moment, then Winston nodded. "I guess it's worth a— What the hell?"

Megan had already started to jump away when Greyson's arm caught her and pushed her back, trying to
put more distance between her and Orion Maldon as
he began seizing.

Pinkish foam oozed from between his tight lips and
ran down his chin. He flopped out of the chair, onto the
floor, a high-pitched sound, a *keening,* coming from his
throat. Megan's demon heart twisted and wiggled; her
fingers dug into Greyson's hand.

"It's her," she whispered. "Greyson it's her, you have
to do something, you have to stop her—"

He didn't argue, or say it was impossible, even though
she knew it should have been. He didn't ask how she
knew. He just crossed the room to the fireplace and
picked up the poker, holding it in front of him like a
baseball bat.

Megan clasped her hands over her face, but couldn't
resist peeking out through her fingers. She didn't want
to watch this, but it was like a gory accident—no. Not
like a gory accident. It *was* a gory accident, about to
happen in the middle of the antique oriental rug on the
floor of Greyson's lovely study, and in her panicked state
she didn't even care. She just wanted the threat gone.
She couldn't face Ktana Leyak again, not in her current
state. Her demon heart might be pumping merrily away
in her chest, but the human one had had just about all
it could take.

Orion started to swell, the thin navy fabric of his shirt
ripping down his spine to reveal flesh mottling blue and

purple. Greyson raised the poker and started to swing it down, but Winston caught it. The sound of the metal hitting his flesh made Megan wince. How had he not just broken every bone in his hand?

"My *rubenda*," Winston said.

"Sorry." Greyson dipped his head and handed over the poker, while sweat trickled down Megan's temple and she clenched her fists to keep from grabbing the fucking poker herself. What was the matter with these two? Didn't they realize how close they were? That they didn't even know if this would work?

Winston brought the poker down in a savage arc. Blood and tissue spattered everywhere as Orion's head exploded like a cockroach under a brick.

Someone shrieked, long and loud, raising the hairs on the back of Megan's neck. For a moment she thought it was her, but it wasn't. This came from elsewhere, circling the room, brushing past all of them before disappearing with a tiny pop.

"*Eshti raika,*" Winston gasped. His casual dove gray trousers and white shirt were spotted with gore. Megan looked down; she and Greyson both resembled extras from the set of a slasher film. "How did that happen?"

"She must have been in there the whole time," Greyson said. Megan thought he looked a bit pale. She was certain she was. Her skin was numb. "She must have called and turned him in to Vergadering, Meg, just like she got you arrested last week."

"She—" Megan stopped. Of course Ktana Leyak had tipped off the police. They'd said it was a female voice.

"And she heard our conversations." Greyson raised

a hand to his head, pinching the bridge of his nose for a second. "Now she knows the story of your father and Orion—if she didn't already. She knows something about the layout of this house. She knows you two figured out why some demons are exploding."

"We're not sure of that," Megan said. "It's just a theory. There's no proof, since every house has lost at least one demon and . . . they can't all have attacked my Yezer. Can they?"

He met her gaze. "Anything's possible. Mine are ordered to leave yours alone, but personal squabbles happen all the time."

A weight she didn't know was still on her shoulders lifted. Not much of a relief, but a relief just the same. She nodded, her lips curving into a slight smile.

Winston cleared his throat. "I haven't ordered any of my *rubendas* to go after your family either, Megan."

"I know. Thanks."

"That doesn't mean the other Gretnegs haven't," Greyson said. "Unless . . . unless she's been possessing them, in order to attack yours, and not the other way around. Who's been attacked, Meg?"

Her evening bag sat on the desk, behind Winston. He followed her pointing finger and handed it to her, with that particular uncomfortable air most men had when touching a woman's purse. Like it was going to explode and spray them with tampons and cooties.

She pulled the lists out and handed them over.

"Okay." His dark eyes scanned the sheets as he shuffled them. "So all of the victims, for lack of a better word, are still with you?"

"You think she was trying to convince them to leave?"

Greyson nodded.

"But I've lost some too."

"Perhaps they agreed to join her, but something went wrong," Winston said. "Perhaps it's their connection to you that drives her out."

"Then how are they managing to leave me?"

"They're doing it themselves." Greyson shrugged. "You're connected to them as a whole, the individual bonds are pretty weak. So she might not be able to undo it, but they can."

"You're probably right," Winston said, "but it doesn't explain how she managed to possess Orion. That shouldn't have happened. He should be too powerful."

"Unless he invited her."

Both men looked at her.

"Well, I don't know," she said, a little defensively. "Orion obviously liked to play with the big boys, right? If he tried to do some sort of deal with the Accuser sixteen years ago, why wouldn't he try something else now?"

"To get her in here," Winston said. His blue eyes— so like Orion's and yet so different—lit up. "To get to you, my dear. Your little Meegra is her goal after all."

"Yes, we already knew that," Megan said, with a businesslike impatience she didn't feel. "But—"

"Your demon is unspecified," Greyson said. "It could become anything, since you haven't done the Haikken Kra. She might not have known that before."

"She had to know it."

"She might not have known what it meant."

Winston snorted. "That's a bit of a stretch, isn't it? The Ancient Ones aren't stupid, Grey."

"But we've never had anyone quite like Megan either. She hasn't tried to possess her, right?" He glanced at Megan. "She hasn't, has she?"

Megan shook her head.

"So she's afraid of you."

"She hasn't tried to possess you either."

Greyson shrugged. "She wouldn't. She's not capable of possessing other demons unless she's somehow connected to them—like the Yezer—or unless she's invited. Orion must not have known what she would do to him when she came out."

"Or maybe she said she wouldn't." Winston glanced around, then picked up his glass from the desk behind him and took a swallow. "If she told him she just wanted to eavesdrop and Orion thought he'd be killed in the morning anyway, why wouldn't he let her in?"

"That would explain why she didn't manage to materialize, too." Greyson sat and pulled Megan down to sit beside him. Her legs ached. She hadn't realized how stiffly she was holding them, her knees locked in an attempt to stop them shaking. "She doesn't get power from other demons. Remember what I told you at Mitchell's, Meg? *Leyaks* are generally dangerous to humans, not other demons. They kill people—sometimes they possess them, but usually they just steal their energy. That's why she hasn't been able to stick around for very long when we've seen her. She's trying to do something she's not meant to do."

"But she did possess a human, at the café."

"An old man," he said. "Elderly and in poor health. He didn't have the energy to power a flashlight, much less a demon."

"So Orion found her," Megan said, understanding. "And he knew my demon was . . . adaptable, because what I felt at his house, that I could use his power if I wanted to, he felt too? He knew it?"

"It's the best explanation I can think of."

"Orion always wanted more," Winston said with a heavy sigh. Megan realized with a start that she'd forgotten all about Orion's body, still and silent on the floor while they talked over him as though he were a needy pet they were ignoring. "That's why he never went further. He was smart enough. But when I made him a *lakri* . . . that's when I realized his ambition wasn't tempered with anything. He wasn't patient. He wasn't willing to put in his time. So he never got closer. He just wasn't . . . good enough to be closer to me."

It was one of the saddest epitaphs Megan had ever heard.

"Feeling better?"

She tied the belt of his bathrobe around her waist and started rolling up the sleeves. "Actually, yes. Does that even make sense?"

The shower and snack helped clear her head, but there was still so much to discuss, so many facts and worries and feelings to slog through. The kind of things she would have advised her patients it was unhealthy to hide from.

But she didn't have any patients anymore. Was she even really a counselor anymore? Her show probably didn't count.

Which meant that as an almost-official-not-counselor, she could engage in whatever unhealthy avoidance she wanted to.

Greyson glanced up from pouring their drinks. By unspoken agreement they'd decided champagne was inappropriate under the circumstances, so he fixed them both Jack and Cokes. "Everybody feels better after eating and taking a shower. It's a scientific fact."

"See? All those years of college wasted, when I could have just charged people for sandwiches and some hot water. I knew it."

He smiled. "Tera said they'd probably want—"

"Can we not talk about it? Right now, I mean. I think I've had enough for one day."

"Of course. We can talk about anything you want. It'll wait until morning."

She sipped her drink, looked around the room. "I can't think of anything to say."

"We don't have to talk at all," he suggested, stroking her back with his left hand and leaning down to kiss her neck. "We could just go to sleep, of course, but . . . I think this might be more fun."

Part of Megan was horrified by the thought. When she closed her eyes, even after the shower and snack, she kept seeing the pool of red spreading from Orion's head and ruining the intricate pattern of the carpet. Or the dungeon, again, the flames almost licking the ceiling, almost finding her hiding place . . .

Too bad other parts of her were intensely interested. What better way to drive the memories of chilling horror away? To replace those images with considerably more pleasant ones?

"Are you going to sleep with Justine?"

He stopped moving but stayed where he was, his face buried in the curve between her shoulder and her neck, and his arm around her waist. "No, *bryaela*, I'm not going to sleep with Justine."

"But if she—"

"She'll accept a substitute. She always did with Temp." His lips resumed their lazy journey.

"But you were the substitute, weren't you?"

"It was part of my job." Strong fingers tilted her chin up, so their eyes met. His were deep, unfathomable; but she realized as she looked into them how shaken he'd been earlier by the presence of Ktana Leyak, saw his need to put it behind him was no less intense than hers. "It's not anymore."

Megan forced her relief not to show. "So what is part of your job now?"

"Ah, that's a secret. If I told you, I'd have to hypnotize you to make you forget."

"I think the line is 'I'd have to kill you.' "

"No. If I killed you I wouldn't be able to do this anymore." He caught her earlobe between his teeth and sucked it softly. She shivered. "And then you wouldn't do that anymore and I do so enjoy it when you do that . . ."

She swallowed. Uncomfortable images and thoughts still played in her mind, but it was hard to concentrate on them while his silver-smooth voice whispered some of John Donne's finer lines in her tingling ear and his hands illustrated them on her heating skin.

What the hell. A little forgetfulness was just what the counselor ordered.

Chapter Twenty-three

H e bashed his own head in? I'm supposed to believe that?"

"No. Your witches did that." Greyson shrugged. "We tried to heal him so you could take him in, but . . . he was beyond saving."

"Our weapons did not do this, Grey. Look at that!" Tera gestured toward her feet, where Orion Maldon's body lay, mostly covered by a white sheet, on a rickety gurney. The damage was obvious. His entire face had sunk when his skull fractured, like a deflating balloon.

"I've seen it, thank you."

"We sent smoke after him, that was all."

"Now hold on, that was *not* all. Have you seen my fence? The gate is practically destroyed."

Megan spoke up for the first time. It was hard to follow the conversation for some reason. Three cups of coffee had failed to perk her up, and she was about to start on a fourth. The week was finally catching up with her. She couldn't remember the last time she'd slept an untroubled night. "They were shooting something else at him, Tera. Something . . . they looked like black rocks, and they exploded."

Tera's brow furrowed as she glanced from Megan to Greyson and back. "Really?"

Megan nodded. "I was there, I saw it." *Please believe me. I'm already having to lie to you, and you're my friend and I hate that.*

"That's . . . well. I don't see that there are any particles of that in his hair. It looks to me like somebody hit him with something."

"The blast knocked free one of the finials," Greyson said. "It flew into the back of his head."

"Shit. This is just what I need," Tera said. "If you'd given him to us last night we could have saved him."

"I couldn't, Tera. You know that. I couldn't ignore his request, especially when I had no idea why you guys were after him."

"Are . . . are you going to get in trouble for this?" Megan bit her lip. If this would cost Tera her job . . . and it was almost Christmas too. Never mind that Tera didn't celebrate. Nobody should lose their job four days before Christmas, it was a crime against humanity—and witches were close enough to human, right?

Tiredness always made her sentimental. Or grumpy. Today it looked like sentimental.

"No. He's right. It doesn't sound like protocol was followed, so the ones in trouble will be the soldiers, not me. This wasn't my affair anyway, I just stepped in because of you. No harm done. Except, of course, that now we can't find out why he killed those witches."

"Killed witches?" Greyson leaned against his desk and crossed his ankles in front of him, clearly ready to enjoy himself.

Tera colored. "Yes. Um, those witches who died, the ones I mentioned at the funeral? It looks like he was the one who did it, so . . . sorry about that. About suspecting you, I mean."

"No problem."

"But you have to admit you were a pretty likely suspect. It wasn't exactly stupid of me to think you were behind it."

"Of course." Not a hint of sarcasm colored his voice.

"Well," Megan said, clapping her hands together, trying to get her blood to circulate. The sleeves of Greyson's shirt flopped from her arms. Her own clothes were being cleaned. "Tera, do you want some coffee or something?"

"I guess I'll have water. Is Winston Lawden coming? He was here last night, right?"

"He'll be here any minute," Greyson said. "He said he was on his way."

And he was. Winston arrived just after they'd settled Tera in a chair with a glass of water.

"Miss Green. What a lovely surprise."

Tera raised her eyebrows. "Mr. Lawden. I have a few questions for you."

He shook his head. "I don't see what sorts of answers I might have. Greyson called me last night to inform me your witches had gravely injured Orion. He was dead by the time I got here."

"Are you sure?"

"Are you implying something, Miss Green?"

"Only that if one of your people killed my witches, you might know something about it."

Megan choked on her drink, but Winston only

smiled indulgently. "Miss Green, I can assure you I did not. I've recently discovered Orion was . . . acting outside his authority, shall we say? This had nothing to do with me."

Greyson must have called him while she was in the shower or when he got up in the morning. Or maybe demons simply had plenty of practice at this sort of thing, which was likely. She knew how quickly Greyson's mind moved. Usually she wasn't too bad herself, but she just couldn't seem to get it together this morning. The coffee actually seemed to be working against her rather than helping; she was starting to feel sick.

Two witches came to collect Orion's body, their faces fixed in disapproving sneers as they pulled the sheet over his ruined head and lifted the gurney with a clang of metal against metal.

"This will still be investigated," Tera said. "Just because we can no longer question Orion Maldon doesn't mean we're done looking into his actions."

"I'm an open book," Winston said. A whisper of cold wafted over Megan's skin. His voice echoed strangely in her head. Was he dragging out his words, or was it just her? He sounded like a record played on too slow a speed. "Feel free to make an appointment to speak with me, if you must."

"How about now?"

"Am I suspected? Are you declaring me so? Because if not, you can make an appointment, and if so, I'm permitted my own witnesses. Uninvolved witnesses."

Megan's cup fell from her hand. The couch was so soft . . . she could just lie down and go to sleep . . .

"Megan? Megan!"

Greyson's hands on her shoulders, shaking her. Maybe a little more roughly than he needed to. She was just tired, is all. Didn't it make sense that she would be, after everything that had happened? And they hadn't ended up going to sleep until almost three. So much to do, so much to discuss . . .

"Le'me 'lone." She brushed feebly at his arm, while Tera's and Winston's voices joined the chorus of concern and she heard pounding in the distance. Someone knocking somewhere . . . why couldn't she open her eyes?

More voices. One sounded like Roc, which didn't make any sense because Roc wouldn't be here. He was with the other Yezer, in his little room that looked like Currier & Ives threw up in it.

"All of them . . . she took . . . destroyed . . . everywhere . . ." The voices sounded like faraway whispers, like television filtered up stairs and under a closet door. She used to like to play in the closet, when she was little . . . it felt so secret and safe in there. Just like now.

"Fuck! Meg, wake up, sit up, come on . . ."

"God, she's so pale." Gentle hands patted her cheeks.

"Is she breathing?"

"Shit, get . . ."

Hands on her shoulders, lifting her from the couch, then sliding up to cup her face. She mumbled feebly and tried to push him away. Just like a man, couldn't he see she was tired?

His lips pressed against hers, forcing her to accept the

kiss. "Go 'way," she started to say, but when she opened her mouth his tongue slipped inside, along with a deep, low rush of burning power. It flew through her body, heating her from the inside, speeding her sluggish blood and making her gasp.

Her eyes opened, then closed again as she leaned forward, raising her hands to his shoulders, trying to pull him closer. Somewhere deep in her mind she remembered there were other people in the room, but it didn't matter. She was waking up, unfurling like a butterfly, going from exhausted to normal to overheated with desire in the space of a few seconds.

Abruptly he pulled away. She reached for him, her eyes widening at the sight of his tense, pale face, but as she did, she caught movement out of the corner of her eye.

Tera's and Winston's backs were politely turned, but she was dimly aware that she'd moaned, or something, and her face grew hot. Or would have, if it wasn't already. Her cheeks stung. How hard had they actually hit her?

Worse than that was the little body next to Tera. It was Roc. And if Roc was here, something was very wrong.

Wreckage.

That's all it was.

Megan blinked back tears as she took in the little doors hanging on their hinges, the broken furniture scattered across the shining floor. At least, it had shone once. Now blood, sticky and dark, slicked the surface and spattered the walls. It formed a clotted sludge in the crevices joining the floors and walls and in the cracks between the floorboards.

Roc righted a chair and slumped into it. "She took everyone," he said for the tenth time, repeating the words over and over as if he could make sense of the event by describing it. "I managed to get away . . . I don't know how."

"She probably let you go," Greyson said. He stood beside Megan, holding her hand, just staring around the room. Megan knew he was imagining his own Iure-anlier, thinking of the destruction that could have been visited there the night before if they hadn't acted quickly enough.

Ktana Leyak had arrived shortly before dawn, some-how managing to remain inside one of Megan's demons long enough to get back here, the one place they should have been safe. Their home.

When the alarm sounded, those Yezer out with their humans had come back, only to face their own destruc-tion. Those who'd remained stalwart to Megan were torn apart. The others acquiesced quickly.

She'd spirited them away, Roc didn't know where. And nobody was alive who did.

Megan reached inside herself, looking for the door, looking for the connection between herself and her de-mons. Her demon heart lay like lead in her chest, cold and unmoving. Dead. The doorknob turned and she braced herself for the truth. No flames hid behind it, no cold breath of power. The demon was gone. She was alone.

Greyson's energy still buzzed through her body, keeping her awake and alert, but for how long?

Roc nodded. "She wanted Megan to know what she'd done. She wants her revenge."

Megan's knees buckled. Greyson held her by the waist and slid a chair beneath her before they gave out, but it was little comfort, especially not since through the handkerchief he'd laid down the cushion was spattered with tacky blood. She'd never thought this much about blood in her entire life and she'd certainly never had to see so much of it.

If the demon inside her was still alive, it would be leaping right now, wouldn't it? Raging at her, clawing at her chest, desperate to feed?

If it was dead, what would happen to her? Sure, Greyson could still shove power into her. Her psychic abilities were still there, her ability to hold his energy intact. But how long could that last? How long would it be before she became an anchor dragging around his neck, something pitiful, a duty?

All that coffee she'd drunk earlier had left a horrible, sour taste in her mouth.

"Isn't this revenge enough?" She didn't bother to hide the bitterness in her voice. "What more is there?"

Her ears rang in the silence. High-pitched, like the whine of Brownian motion only children hear. Must be the shock. Or she was having problems with her ears. Just what she needed on top of everything else. Ear infections.

Maybe she could get diagnosed with Epstein-Barr or something, get some sort of medical help that way . . .

The whine grew louder and broke, then started again.

"What is that?" Greyson asked.

"What? You hear it too?"

"Of course I hear it." He squeezed her hand and let go, picking his way through the panorama of destruction to an overturned sofa and flipping it up.

Another demon huddled beneath it, little eyes impossibly wide. Blood trickled down its forehead and formed a trail down its snoutlike nose. Its mouth opened and closed, trying to form words that would not come.

"Ashtenor!" Roc leaped for it, holding it—him— tight. "Ashtenor, how did you manage to survive?"

"Hid. Pretended . . ." Ashtenor shuddered.

"Do you know where she took them?" Greyson said. Roc glared at him, but he only shrugged. "We don't have a lot of time and there are one or two things we need to figure out."

"Tul azar," Ashtenor whispered. *"Tul azar Akuzi."*

Greyson and Roc exchanged glances.

"Tul azar Akuzi?" Roc asked. *"Tresh tena?"*

Ashtenor nodded. Megan watched a tear trickle down his rough, wrinkled cheek. She'd failed him, God, she'd failed all of them, she hadn't protected them and now . . . now she didn't know if she had enough energy left to protect herself, much less a thousand little demons. Now that her demon heart was dead, she didn't have any way to—

If her demon heart was dead, or at least dormant, could it still stop her from practicing what Tera had taught her?

She couldn't try it here. With her Yezer gone—and she strongly suspected Ktana Leyak was using their connection to Megan to suck her energy away, now that she thought about it—there simply wasn't anywhere to draw power from. Except Greyson himself, and the thought of treating him like her personal battery made her squirm.

But Ashtenor huddled on the floor, staring at her with those damned Keane-painting eyes of his, and the words were out of her mouth before she had a chance to second-guess them.

"Greyson, I need some help."

Bless him—or whatever one would do with demons—he didn't ask why, or even look surprised. He just gave her what she wanted and brought Ashtenor over to her so she could hold him in her lap.

The connection was there, faint but still viable. Megan closed her eyes and reached for it. Greyson's energy had become hers and now she gave it to Ashtenor, sending it sliding along the line connecting them.

His little eyes widened, then closed, as he snuggled into her. She'd never thought of them as her babies before. Well, they weren't babies. Babies were good and innocent. Babies were hope. The Yezer Ha-Ra existed to cause pain.

But they were *her* pain causers. More now than before, when she'd forced herself to watch as Halarvus was punished, she felt the great expanse of what she owed them.

They weren't inherently evil. They were part of life. Isn't that what she'd always counseled her clients? Without the bad feelings, we wouldn't appreciate the good ones?

Being in charge of the Yezer Ha-Ra, even just her small Meegra, was a responsibility not just to them, but to mankind. It was their job to tempt. It was the job of humanity to resist. Without that battle, what was the point of life?

So Megan held Ashtenor close, and breathed her borrowed power into him until his tears stopped and his color—a particularly unpleasant glaring orange— returned. She took care of him.

The way his Gretneg should.

Chapter Twenty-four

B ut we don't know where the Accuser's house was!"
Being back at Greyson's place hadn't really helped
her mood, but realizing she could draw a trickle of energy from the ground outside had a bit. At least she
wouldn't need Greyson to keep kissing her in order to
stay awake. It was a little embarrassing.

Her eyes still itched with tiredness, but she could
handle it.

"That's why Brian is coming over," Greyson said.

"You called Brian?"

"Yes. That's why he's coming over, see. It's very simple."

"But—"

He shook his head. "I think I know where the Accuser's house is. But I'm hoping Brian can confirm it,
because if I'm wrong we'll be wasting important time.
He can read the document. The corporation papers of
your father's? He might get something from those."

"But we only have the photocopy."

"No. That viper who gave you life has the copy. I
took the original."

"You stole it?"

"Does that surprise you?"

She leaned back on the couch. "I guess not."

"The only person besides us who'll need to see it is Tucker, anyway. I'll give him the original next time I see him."

"When will that be?"

"When you decide what you want to do with the property, darling, and we start probate." He sat next to her and handed her a Coke, which she took with the sort of gratitude dogs offer when given table scraps. Her throat felt like sandpaper; her stomach was a hollow, nervous space in her belly.

It tasted like pure, sweet life on her tongue. "So you knew we might need to do this. To get Brian to read it, I mean."

"Of course I did. I certainly didn't plan to have Orion over for a chat before—well. I didn't plan on discussing the situation with him."

And the decision had been taken out of his hands, out of hers too. Orion had needed to be killed. Was Greyson pleased by that? Megan didn't know how she felt. On the one hand she was horrified, absolutely stunned that she had stood and watched Winston Lawden murder a man. On the other hand . . . he would have died anyway, right? The minute he let Ktana Leyak into his body he signed his death warrant, one way or the other. At least this way he hadn't been able to take anyone else with him.

But would Greyson have listened to her, and changed his mind about having Orion killed? He'd said they would discuss it. That didn't mean he would agree with her.

"Greyson, about Orion . . ."

"Brian's here."

"What? How do you know?"

"Nobody enters or leaves the property without the Gretneg knowing, remember? Except witches, unfortunately. They can break our protections."

He got up and shuffled through some files on the desk, finally grabbing one and taking some papers out of it. The documents of incorporation they'd taken from her old bedroom.

Brian came in. He smelled like wintry air when he bent to give her a kiss on the cheek. "Jesus, Megan, what happened to you?"

"My—I'm just tired. I didn't get a lot of sleep last night."

"You should go back to bed."

Ha. He had no idea how good that sounded. All she wanted to do was go back to bed, and stay there with the covers up over her head and the TV on low. "I'll be okay."

"Drink, Brian?"

Brian too took a Coke, then sat down on the opposite end of the couch. "Okay, so what do you need me to look at?"

"This. It's—it's related to Megan's dad. We were hoping you might be able to see him from it, maybe something of his conversation with a couple of demons."

"Demons aren't readable, you know that."

"I know, but Megan's father was, so maybe you could get something through his eyes."

Brian nodded and glanced at his watch. "Okay, sure. But I have an interview scheduled in about forty-five minutes, so—"

"It shouldn't take that long." Greyson handed the papers to Brian, who closed his eyes.

They flew back open as his face turned bright red. "Whoah! Hey, um, I'm not sure you guys want me to see this."

God damn it. She was forever doomed to have Brian watch her have sex, it seemed. He'd managed to catch a glimpse of a college boyfriend the night he'd read her after they met, and now . . . she rubbed her forehead with her hand. This was just perfect.

"Try to go back further," Greyson said, in his just-do-it voice.

"Okay." Brian used his thumb and forefinger to pick the papers up from the floor where he'd dropped them. "I'll try again."

This time he held on. "Okay, your dad—I think that's your dad, he looks younger than in the picture at the funeral—filing these, thinking about what a great deal he'd made . . . um . . . oh, okay. I remember Templeton Black, and that guy from the funeral, Orion? He's there. Blah blah blah, the hospital will be the perfect place to house your daughter, everything she needs is already there and she'll be very comfortable, just sign here . . . they're sort of smirking at each other but he's not paying attention . . ." Brian opened his eyes, and looked up. "Is that it, or do you need more?"

Megan had to force the words from her throat. "No. No, I think we have everything we need."

"The truck," as Greyson called it, was actually a Mercedes SUV, with cushiony leather seats big enough to lie down on and dark-tinted windows. It was about as close to a truck as the *QE2* was to a rowboat, but it certainly did the job.

Trouble was, it wasn't a job she wanted it to do. She'd intended that the next time she rode in this particular vehicle they'd be on their way to the woods for a romantic, relaxing holiday, not headed into the belly of the beast—pretty much literally—back in Grant Falls.

Back to the hospital.

She shifted a little, adjusting her blanket. With her head on Greyson's lap and the soft, heated leather beneath her, she could almost pretend she was back in bed. At least, if not for the murmuring voices of the men and the soft drone of music from the CD player, fading in and out as she dozed.

Nick and the brothers were with them, coming along for moral—well, for support, anyway. But Malleus and Spud in the front seats and Nick and Maleficarum in the back ones did make her feel a little as if she were onstage.

"Just think about it, Nick," Greyson said above her. "I could really use you here."

"I like Miami."

"I know. But I need someone . . ."

Megan drifted back off. They'd been having this discussion on and off all day, and from the way they spoke she had a feeling it had been going on longer than that.

She was back in her own house, on the couch, watching TV, when the doorbell rang. Her feet seemed to sink into the floor as she got up and crossed the room to open it, knowing it wasn't the smartest thing to do but unable to stop herself.

Her partners from work, holding bottles of champagne, come to celebrate her father's death.

Her eyes opened. Only the soft glow of the GPS system in the dash lit the interior of the car; they were well out of the city now, and the moon must have gone behind some clouds. She closed her eyes again, her waking unnoticed. Back to sleep . . . it was so hard to stay awake.

She was back in the house where her demon died, but when the police came this time, they brought flowers.

"She already hinted she'd accept you as a substitute, if you'll do it."

Pause. "You don't have anybody else?"

"Not really, and . . . I can't. I don't want to. I said I wouldn't."

"Yeah, I'll do it for you. But this is why I don't want to get involved, man. I don't get this shit in Miami, nobody bugs me there."

"You know I wouldn't ask if . . ."

Brian Stone took her out to dinner, but there was a huge dog outside the restaurant and they couldn't leave. For some reason they thought this was amusing and laughed so hard Megan fell down on the cold cement, which was soft as a feather bed.

This time when her eyes opened, she smiled. Greyson's hand was warm on her hip. She started to snuggle into him, then stopped when Nick spoke.

"Is she going to do the ritual?"

"I don't know." Greyson sighed. His thigh tensed under her head but he didn't move. "I don't think she knows."

"You're not talking her into it?"

"It's her decision."

"But I thought—"

"It's her decision. I can't interfere with that. Think about it."

Silence. "I guess I see that. But . . . I mean . . ." Nick sounded uncomfortable, as if he'd just offered Greyson oral sex and been turned down.

"Hell, Nick. You know I'd— What the fuck!"

The car crashed into something, skidded, and spun sideways, flinging Megan off the seat onto the floor. For one long, terrifying moment she was certain she was about to die in a crush of metal on a deserted road. Malleus was yelling from the driver's seat.

Then silence. The SUV gave a final rock to the left and stopped. Bright light flooded the interior of the car as the doors opened, and Greyson grabbed her and pulled her out, setting her down on her unsteady feet.

"I'm okay, I'm okay." She wrapped her arms around herself. The night air was freezing and her coat was still in the car. Someone laid the blanket over her shoulders; she didn't turn around to see who. "What happened?"

Greyson pointed behind them.

An oak tree grew by the side of the road, its gnarled arms reaching out as though it could trap the moon between them. From one of those branches dangled a rope, and at the end of that rope hung the body of a man, his eyes black holes in his swollen face. A chair, its legs reduced to splinters by the wheels of the SUV, lay about four feet from the tree.

He'd killed himself. The piece of paper pinned to the front of his shirt testified to that. Suicide, right by the road. It wasn't the highway, as Megan had thought. They'd gone farther than that. The back of the sign welcoming them to Grant Falls gleamed in the darkness beyond the man's swinging feet as the first flakes of snow drifted down.

Sleeping further would have been out of the question, even if she'd wanted to. The specter of that grisly welcome home haunted her.

Aside from a few dents on the right-side doors, the SUV was fine. They piled back in and headed toward the center of town, tooling slowly down the road, all of them on the alert. Greyson gave her his gun, grabbing another one from Maleficarum. It rested in his hand like a cobra about to strike. Nick had a gun too, in addition to, of all things, a sword. She might have laughed at the sight—it wasn't often you saw a man swinging a blade in modern small-town America—if he hadn't handled it with such deadly confidence.

Malleus, Maleficarum, and Spud, of course, looked like they were about to storm Fort Knox. Megan would have prayed they wouldn't be pulled over, but even if Greyson couldn't have handled any police officer who came near the car, she doubted it would be an issue tonight. Something told her the police in Grant Falls would be otherwise occupied.

They rolled past the hotel, silent and dark, and continued on. Through the haze of falling snow Megan saw Christmas lights twinkling still on some of the buildings and in the windows of the shops farther down the road, in town. The clock read 11:00. Surely the stores would be closed, the lights off?

Movement off to the right caught her eye. Emerging from the little forest was a woman, her filthy shirt in tatters. Through the strips of grayish fabric they could see her bra soaked with blood and her bare, ghostly pale skin streaked with it, making her look like a bizarre zebra. Even in the darkness her eyes seemed terribly white, wide with terror or the blank screen of dementia. Something else was wrong too, but Megan couldn't seem to place it and it didn't matter.

"Pull over," she started to say, but Greyson interrupted her.

"No."

"What? Look at her, she must be freezing, she's—"

"Where's the cemetery?"

"What? Malleus, I said pull over!"

"Mr. Dante?" Malleus glanced back. His features, cast in pale green light from the dash, looked somehow leaner, as if his frown was pulling them tight.

"Meg, where's the cemetery?"

Megan glared at him and reached for the handle of the door. They were going slowly enough, and once she opened it Malleus would stop. She knew he would. "I can't believe you're going to let that woman just die like that, I—"

"She's already dead."

"Sure, if you let her . . . oh." Megan subsided. That's what was wrong. Snow was piling on the woman's shoulders and forming an old-fashioned nurse's cap on her head. "Oh."

Somewhere in the back of her mind she'd had this idea—this fantasy—that they'd roll into Grant Falls, pop into the abandoned hospital, take whatever relic of the Accuser still lived there—which in the fantasy was a lock of hair or something similarly inoffensive—thus defeating Ktana Leyak and getting back her demons. Then they'd stop for a piece of pie or something before driving back toward the city singing "Adeste Fidelis."

Nowhere in her fantasy did demon-powered zombies appear. Not once.

So much for fantasies.

Then again, the idea of riding around in an SUV with a bunch of demons singing Christmas carols was rather silly itself, wasn't it? So why should she be surprised that this obviously wasn't going to be the uncomplicated little jaunt she'd hoped for?

"Do you think there will be more of them?" she asked in a small voice. The energy to speak loudly eluded her.

"I think it's a pretty safe bet, yes."

"There are two cemeteries in town," she said. "At least there were when I lived here. There's, um, Holy Innocents, which is that way"—she waved her hand to her left—"and Harbor Lawn, where they buried my—oh God."

The men exchanged glances. "We may not have to see many," Greyson said. "We might manage to get in and out of here before they have a chance to reach us."

Megan just nodded. If she opened her mouth she would start screaming, and if she started screaming she didn't think she would be able to stop.

"Zombies aren't going to be a problem," Nick said finally. "They won't even be able to get close to us, thanks to Grey. It's the people who worry me."

Megan glanced out the window, desperate to look anywhere but at the faces of the men watching her, then wished she hadn't. Behind the picture window of Kelly's Tap bodies lurched and leaped in a brawl of epic proportions. A man flew through the glass, landing on the white-dusted asphalt outside in an ungraceful heap. Blood steamed in the freezing air as the chaos inside the bar became audible, shouts and screams ending finally in gunfire.

The men tensed. Greyson and Nick lifted their weapons, waiting, but they were already passing the bar, leaving the wreckage of it behind them.

More evidence that something was very wrong in Grant Falls awaited them as they rolled past, the low hum of the SUV's engine bouncing off the blank storefronts. A bloody handprint embellished the holiday display in the window of Tommy's Toys. More blood smeared across the wall, ending on the pavement as if the bleeder had fallen, but no body lay there.

Megan pulled the blanket more tightly around her. "The hospital is to the right, closer to the center of town."

They floated down the street, the only warm and moving things in an alien landscape. The blanket didn't help. Even Greyson's warm hand on her leg didn't help.

The *wrongness,* the plain and simple sense that all was not well, soaked into her bones. Even with her shields up she could feel the despair, the misery, the rage.

Especially the rage. She realized that tired as she was her body was still humming, adrenaline making her heart pound and her feet jiggle. Her lips felt raw from where she'd bitten them and stung when a tear rolled down her cheek and touched the shredded skin.

She might be able to draw strength from it. If the Yezer—her Yezer—were causing all of this, it was entirely possible she could, that if she lowered her shields and tried to pull them back she could take all that power and use it.

But doing that would also alert Ktana Leyak to their presence, if she wasn't already aware of it, and that was a bad idea. Yes, Megan would have to fight her sometime, but she would much rather that sometime not be now. Not now and not here.

"Make a left," she said softly. Her voice would crack if she tried to speak much more forcefully.

Malleus did, then stopped abruptly. Four cars blocked the road, their windshields gaping holes with jagged edges of glass protruding like broken teeth. Their dashboards already looked frosted with snow. In the dim light from the pale sky she saw bloody footprints leading away, but there was no other sign of people.

"There another way 'round, m'lady?"

"Um . . . yeah. Go back, we'll head toward the park. We can circle around it and come up from the other direction."

Malleus nodded and executed a three-point turn as

neatly as a driving instructor, while Megan stared out the window at the wreckage.

They made it as far as the edge of the park. Megan was increasingly aware of her skin prickling, of silent watchers from the buildings they passed. Zombies or demons or simply people, twitching their curtains to the side in their apartments above stores, wondering who was out and about on a night this cold, this close to Christmas, in a town that usually bedded down by ten.

Malleus slammed on the brakes. If his reflexes hadn't been quite so fast the truck would have plunged head-first into the gaping hole where the road had once been. The snow fell so thick and fast it was almost impossible to see.

Megan waited in the car with Nick and Greyson while the brothers got out to inspect it. They returned moments later, shaking their heads.

"'S all ice, outside it," Maleficarum said. "That little hill, there, we can't drive up it or nuffin'."

The park itself sat on a rise, not steep but steep enough when frozen. To the left of them sat a row of parked cars, the lead one half-buried in the sinkhole, its rear wheels off the pavement. The SUV could not get through the line, and it could not go up the hill.

Greyson sighed. "I guess we walk."

Why don't we just go home was on the tip of Megan's tongue. She couldn't think of anything she'd ever wanted to do less than leave the warm interior of the car and go traipsing through the park under the watchful gaze of a town driven half mad by Yezer.

Because they were here. She knew it. Nothing else

could account for what was happening. Ktana Leyak was here and so were Megan's *rubendas,* and they were having themselves a merry little Christmas indeed.

"Meg."

"What?" She pulled the blanket more tightly around her, as if trying to save up some extra warmth before they started trekking across the barren park. Not empty, oh no. Things waited in that park that she'd hoped to never see.

Greyson held out his hand. "Come on, *bryaela,* let's go get back what's yours."

Chapter Twenty-five

Malleus took point, while Maleficarum and Spud flanked Greyson and Nick on either side of Megan. Snow stung her bare face and blurred her vision; it trickled down Greyson's cheeks as water when it melted. They could have been the only people in the world, pioneers heading for the old homestead, but they weren't. And they weren't alone.

In all that blinding white she imagined they must stand out like black ants crawling across a wedding cake. It was only a matter of time before someone—or something—found them.

She just hadn't expected them to come from straight ahead. The shapes moving from the snow looked ordinary, or close to it—just people trying to make their way home by taking a shortcut—until they got close enough to realize that these people weren't wearing coats, they weren't bundled up. One woman wore a summery strapless dress that revealed the bones of her left arm showing through holes in her skin. Another woman's evening gown would have glittered if it hadn't been dulled with snow. Two men in identical dark suits completed the little group.

Megan didn't even have a chance to react before

they were aflame, falling to the snow, horrible confused sounds escaping their closed mouths. They rolled, leaving dark marks in the dusty white ground where the snow and ice melted from the heat, their arms waving, like insects on their backs. The fire flared higher, blue-white, and the zombies stopped moving entirely. Megan glanced at Nick, who shrugged. "Told you," he said. "When fire is handy, zombies aren't—shit!"

Whatever sound the beasts made was lost in the wind, so it seemed to Megan that they flew across the snowy grass, great dark shapes with pinpoints of red where their eyes should be. She froze, her mouth open, unable to move as they drew closer.

Maleficarum sidestepped, giving Nick a clear shot. The gun's report was muffled by the blanket of white around them, but one of the dogs jerked sideways, a momentary pause before he headed for them again.

Flames burst around them, haloing them as they ran, but again, the hounds barely paused. Megan could see how shaggy they were, how pinkish saliva dripped from their long, sharp fangs even as the fire went out.

Maleficarum leaped, grabbing one of them by the neck and toppling it into the snow. Its yowl of fury pulled an echoing scream from Megan's throat, a scream that seemed to go on forever. Nick's sword sliced through the air and down, hitting the back of the second hound with a horrible thunk. The beast fell, snarling, its teeth snapping the air only a foot or so from Megan's ankles.

Greyson grabbed her and pulled her back from the squirming thing, while Spud picked up the third dog and lifted it above his head, his squat face set in grim concentration. He heaved the dog back toward the road, where it landed with a yelp on the cracked edge of the hole in the pavement.

Maleficarum still shouted, wrestling with the first dog, but as Spud moved to help him an ugly crack sounded, like a twig breaking at the bottom of a well, and the dog subsided. Maleficarum was bloody, his shirt was torn, but he stood up with a broad smile as if he'd just been on a wonderful amusement-park ride.

"Right, 'oo's next then?"

He and Malleus haw-hawed for a minute over that one, while Megan tried not to scream. This wasn't fun. This wasn't a great night out on the town. This was a precursor to her possible death, and she failed to see the chance to hurt some hellbeasts as an upside to that.

They resumed formation and walked on, trudging through the rapidly deepening snow. Over the whistling of the wind gunshots sounded in the distance, but stopped before Megan had a chance to figure out where they were coming from. All the while her skin crawled, prickled with the power around them, itched with the despair that had taken over the town. She could feel people crying in their houses, could almost hear medicine cabinets opening and bottles of pills and packages of razor blades being removed from shelves.

Red lights, festive in the snow, flashed off the windows of the strip mall nearby as an ambulance passed on a side street at the far side of the square, its siren blaring. It shouldn't have been reassuring, but it was. Somewhere in this place was sanity, somewhere the normal order of life continued.

They'd almost reached the center of the park, where the benches squatted next to a few halfhearted pieces of playground equipment—a wooden swing set, a dented slide, one of those tents made of bars that Megan could never figure out what children were supposed to do with except sit on—when something whispered off to the right.

They all stopped, turning, but it took a moment for Megan's snow-blind eyes to catch on to what she was seeing.

They slithered up the great elm tree by the fence and swarmed over the white earth, their bodies like oozing black stains. Snakes. Serpents, sliding toward them, moving with a speed Megan couldn't fathom. It was so cold, it was too cold for them, too cold . . .

Greyson grabbed her right hand, Nick her left. She saw flames erupt over the spreading mass of snakes but knew it was futile even as they started to run, heading for the far end of the park as fast as they could manage on the icy ground.

Malleus and Spud veered off to one side. Megan started to follow them but Greyson and Nick yanked her back, keeping her moving forward even as something yowled and screeched to her left. She dared a glance and saw the brothers fighting with something, a beast that reminded her vaguely of the Nepalese mountain demon who'd attacked her in a different park months before. That had been a sunny fall afternoon. This night was as if winter had a personal vendetta against them.

It wasn't a *yaksas,* though. She realized it when they reached the far fence and looked back. The snakes were still spreading, moving as inexorably as the tide, getting closer to Malleus and Spud as they struggled with the thing. It was black or green or dark blue, she couldn't tell, but it was huge, and she screamed when it swung a great fist and sent Spud flying. He landed on the grass and stayed there, motionless.

Megan's heart stopped. Beside her Greyson jerked, ready to run to Spud, but another scream rent the air. They turned toward it to see a woman leap from one of the windows on the square. For one sick, dizzy moment Megan thought she was flying, the way her body seemed to hang there, before she plunged to the ground and bounced once, twice, before settling in the middle of the road.

Megan's hands flew to her face, covering her eyes, her mouth. Greyson's coat muffled her cries, his arms like a vice around her shoulders.

She didn't understand when he shifted and gripped her neck hard enough to bruise, when he shoved her violently down to the ground at his feet and stepped sideways. The edge of his overcoat brushed against her face as she scraped her palms on the snow. In the same movement Greyson pulled his gun, aimed, fired, fired again. Off to the side Spud still lay silent. Malleus and Maleficarum were winning their battle with whatever beast had injured Spud.

How she was able to smell the alcohol on the men she didn't know, but she could, just as easily as she could see them heading across the park. She even recognized one or two of them, from Kelly's Tap the night of the fire at Maldon's place.

That they recognized Greyson and her was obvious. That they carried a grudge was even more so, if the shotguns in their hands were any indication. With them came something she hadn't felt in months, the slow malevolence of a person completely overwhelmed by Yezer. If they'd been making themselves visible Megan would have seen dozens of them, she knew.

What the fuck was Roc doing? Everything should have been taken care of by now, he was supposed to be here, trying to sneak some of her *rubendas* back to her, trying to get her as much power as he could. Instead she was looking at three guns, aimed straight at her, her bodyguards were injured or otherwise occupied, and all that stood between her and death were Greyson and Nick. The odds weren't bad, but she would have liked better.

One of the men fell. Blood blossomed like a rose high on the right side of his chest, making his plaid shirt bizarrely effeminate, and poured from his mouth in a dark stream to stain the snow beneath him. Greyson's second shot blew off the top of his head.

Nick twisted his body as she started to rise from the ground, so both of them stood in front of her. That was worse somehow, not being able to see, not knowing if the other men were running or taking aim.

Taking aim, apparently. Nick pivoted again, ducking, and came up with his gun ready. All she could hear were shots, louder than she remembered them from before, and it wasn't until she thought of being in the car with Greyson while the witches attacked that she remembered she had a gun too.

Her cold, stiff fingers slipped on it, fumbled with it, but she managed to edge herself out enough to take aim. Nick stumbled against her so her first shot went wild, but he righted himself immediately before she squeezed the trigger the second time.

Pain exploded in her left arm, so bright and hard she didn't know what it was for a moment. She screamed and dropped the gun as she fell, hitting her right shoulder hard against the wrought-iron fence behind her.

One last shot blared through the park, then screams, then silence. Megan tried to say something but her throat didn't want to work. Nothing wanted to work, not her arms or her legs, or her head. She just wanted to curl up in a ball. It was so cold, if she huddled up she might be warmer.

"M'lady! Mr. Dante!"

Someone lifted her from the ground. She was too tired to help, too cold to care. Her arm felt like it was on fire.

One of the brothers held her, she wasn't sure which one. She managed to look over his arm and saw Maleficarum holding Spud, moving quickly toward the gate just ahead of the sea of snakes.

When she opened her eyes again they were on the sidewalk opposite the park, standing just outside a high chain-link fence. Behind the fence lurked the hospital, gray and silent like a moldering ghost.

Semiopaque plastic bulged and receded in the empty holes where windows had been, moved by the wind. To Megan it looked horrible, the erratic beats of a dying heart.

Automatically she looked for Greyson, but saw the snakes first. They were still advancing, but more slowly now, as if they just wanted to urge her into the hospital. Like they were waiting for her to go in.

Maleficarum set Spud on the pavement against the fence and grabbed the links in his bare hands. They popped like cheap buttons, opening a jagged hole. Metal scratched her cheek as Malleus carried her through, but she couldn't be bothered to even lift her hand to the wound. Where were Greyson and Nick? Where the hell was Roc?

The first question, at least, was answered a moment later. The two demons stumbled through the hole, their arms around each other. She couldn't see them well; even with the white sky above it seemed dark here, on the land she now owned part of. Like all the light was absorbed somehow, all the warmth and joy sucked away by the building looming over them.

She saw them well enough to know something was wrong, though, and when they stepped closer to her she realized what it was. For the second time in a week Greyson had been shot, at least once—in the leg, she thought, from the limp—but as she looked more closely, squinting in an attempt to focus better, she noticed part of his ear seemed to be missing. The bullet must have passed only centimeters from his head. The thought made her knees weak. If she'd been standing she probably would have fallen.

As it was she caught only a glimpse of him before Malleus carried her farther away, stopping on the crumbling steps of the hospital building. Wind swirled and eddied around them, lifting Megan's hair and snapping the heavy corrugated paper of a torn cement bag to their right. She'd been wrong in thinking the hospital was like a ghost. *She* was the ghost, intruding on a world that had nothing to do with her, a world she should have left behind ages ago.

Her legs were steady enough beneath her when Malleus set her down just in front of the empty door frames. Once the doors had been etched glass, with TRUBANK MENTAL HEALTH CENTER printed in block script on each panel. Once the atrium had been painted an institutional pale green and filled with modular furniture and plants to take away the ache of that soulless color, and the light had poured in across terrazzo floors.

Now their feet crunched on litter and broken glass as they picked their way through. It smelled in there, like dead things and mold and rotten food, mixed with the fainter, more lingering fragrance of despair. The misery this building had absorbed! The walls still fairly throbbed with it. She could feel them close around her, like dogs sniffing out which hand held the treat.

But there was no hand to choose. *She* was the treat, and it wasn't just the building that waited for her to feed it but something inside. Maybe more than one thing. Ktana Leyak could very well be here already. The entire room seemed to sigh when she walked farther into it.

Off to her right were the remains of the reception desk, broken and jagged. It had been bolted down, which was probably the only reason it hadn't disappeared completely, along with the other furniture. A few disintegrating boxes littered the floor, along with some animal bones and piles of lint and cardboard that could only be rodent nests. That was another smell in the air, one she hadn't identified until then. Droppings. She sneezed. Just that small movement sent fresh pain shooting down her arm.

A loud sniffle made her turn around. Maleficarum, shaking his head, wiping his eyes.

"Spud," she said, ashamed of herself for not having asked already. "Is he—"

"He'll be all right, m'lady," Maleficarum said. His voice sounded strangled and lost in the empty space around them. "He's tough, he is. But you—you been shot, and Mr. Dante, and Mr. Showtin . . ." He covered his face with his beefy right palm, and after a moment of surprise—Spud was usually the emotional one—Megan went to him and took his left hand. Even now they were separated by rank, but the touch meant more to him for that and she knew it

Greyson cleared his throat. "Meg, we need to get that bullet out of your arm."

To their left rose the wide, sweeping staircase leading to the second floor. Above that were only fire stairs, horrible dark shafts at the corners of the building. But this stairway was for show, this stairway was meant to reassure those leaving family members in the care of medical staff that Trubank was a nice place, a healing place, instead of the bowels of the Accuser.

Greyson slipped her coat off her shoulders and sat down, pulling her carefully to sit on his left thigh with his left arm tight around her waist. His damaged ear wasn't far from her face; she refused to look at it, focusing instead on his eyes, his lips moving, telling her what she didn't want to hear, about holding out her arm and it would only hurt for a minute.

Nick squatted in front of Greyson and took her hand. "Squeeze as tight as you want, Megan, you won't hurt me."

"Hold on a minute, guys, I don't think this is really necessary," she started, but it was too late. Greyson squeezed her so hard she almost couldn't breathe, and Nick pulled her arm taut while Malleus produced a long silver pair of tweezers from somewhere on his person and plunged them into the wound in her arm.

She didn't want to scream but screamed anyway. Her fingers ached from squeezing Nick's hand with her left, Greyson's with her right, while she buried her face in Greyson's chest and cried, and begged him to stop. Deep below the pain was shame, the knowledge that she should be braver than this, should be stronger than this, but somehow the fear of what was to come made it all so much worse. It felt like Malleus was trying to remove her actual bone, like somehow the tweezers could grow and bend and tug out her demon heart as well.

As abruptly as the pain had started, it ended. Fresh blood spilled down her forearm to her hand, still held in Nick's, and covered both of them as though they were being hand-fasted.

Malleus showed her his palm, where three bloodied bits of metal lay among the calluses. No wonder it felt like he was trying to dig out her intestines through her arm. Apparently the bullet had shattered when it hit her bone.

She wanted to laugh. It was the adrenaline, she guessed, buzzing through her body, shooting like champagne straight to her head. Now it was over she felt like she could fly, and while it lasted she wanted to savor it.

Instead she ended up wandering around the ghost town of the lobby while Malleus took care of Greyson and Nick. Both men cursed and gritted their teeth manfully; she felt their eyes on her and tried to pretend she didn't find it amusing, although she suspected they were hamming it up for her. She'd seen Greyson take much worse pain without being quite so noisy, and she had the distinct feeling that Nick was just as tough if not even tougher. But she appreciated it just the same. For a minute—right around the time Greyson moaned, "By the fiery gates of Hell!"—she was even able to forget where they really were and why, and imagine they were on some sort of crazy Halloween dare.

Too bad the jokes, like the adrenaline rush, couldn't last. By the time they were finished her hands were shaking and her fear was flooding back. She needed something hidden in this place, and it wasn't just Ktana Leyak threatening her. It was this building, this place, the memories of the unhappy teenager she'd been, the nightmarish, vague recollections of her time spent here while the Accuser shared her body.

And knowing her father had done that to her. The one man who was supposed to love her more than any other man ever could, who was supposed to teach her how to relate to men and how to expect to be treated by them for the rest of her life, had discarded her without a second thought.

Did that color her relationships? Was she now in love with an emotionally distant demon because her father had never been there for her? It was ridiculous, she knew. It wasn't as though she was an open book emotionally either, or didn't keep secrets, and Greyson was nothing like her father.

And yet . . . he'd gotten where he was today in part by stepping directly on the heads of people who'd helped him. He'd worked his entire life to become Gretneg, and she knew he'd kill to stay there.

Would he discard her, as her father had done, if she became too much of a threat to his position? If dumping her would cement another deal, strengthen an alliance, bring him more power and money?

It wasn't simply the cold that made her shiver. For a moment she just stood there, feeling more lonely than she ever had in her life.

Then he stood in front of her and heat radiated from his skin, and she didn't care anymore what was wrong or right. If the last months had taught her anything, it was that no matter how hard you tried to guard against the unexpected, you couldn't do it. And if her work had taught her anything, it was that feelings and emotions could be coped with but not stopped. She'd deal with whatever fallout happened when it happened. If it happened.

He held her for a minute, then pulled away, stroking her cheek with his fingers. "Ready?"

"My arm still hurts." It did too. He took her hand, and she felt the smooth rush of his power over her skin. The pain lessened a little.

"I don't want to use too much energy," he said. "We'll probably need all we can get. But that should be better."

"It is, thanks." She looked up and caught his eyes with her own.

The others were pretending not to watch them, but Megan knew they were. She cleared her throat and glanced at the floor. "What do we do? I mean, can you feel anything, do you know where it—whatever we're looking for—is?"

"No. This whole place feels like demon."

"Start at the top, work our way down?"

"Probably better the other way around. I'd rather not climb more stairs than I have to."

She'd almost forgotten about his leg. With a concerned little sound she leaned down, but he touched her shoulder to keep her where she was. "It's fine. Listen, Meg . . ."

"What?"

His fingers twined in hers, warm and comforting, while she waited for him to speak. Finally he shook his head. "Never mind. Is this the bottom floor, or what?"

Her heart sank. "There's a basement."

Chapter Twenty-six

Fire filled Greyson's palm as they picked their way down the stairs, throwing shadows on their faces. In its light Greyson looked gaunt, tired; she could only imagine how she must look with her hair frizzing around her head and her eyes wide with fear. Megan didn't think anyone had been down here since the place closed, but she was wrong. Spiders were here and rats and cockroaches, skittering across the mess of strewn papers and dust and bones on the floor when the light hit them. Her skin crawled at the sight. It was bad enough in the lobby, but here, where no light ever came and no workman had been in to even halfheartedly tidy up, it was chaos, a foul-smelling dump where years' worth of waste had settled like silt on the ocean floor.

Cobwebs shrouded the damp, slimy walls, so thick and dusty they were more like curtains. In the center of one lurked the largest spider Megan had ever seen, almost as big as the palm of her hand. Its horrible eyes glittered when the light hit them. She gasped, her fingers twitching in Greyson's. She couldn't go in there, she just couldn't. And she shouldn't have to.

"It's not in here," she said, aware for the first time that her demon heart had moved feebly when they were in the lobby, just when they entered. It lay still in her chest again, even though her own heart—her human heart—pounded like a hammer. "It's not down here, I just . . . I feel it, I know it isn't here."

"Okay." But he paused, and nodded toward the far wall. "Looks like something's down here, though."

"What? I—oh."

Files. The entire wall was lined with filing cabinets, lurking behind the fog of spiderwebs. One of the drawers hung open; Megan could see the files inside.

"Do you want it?" He moved a little closer, still holding her hand. "You don't have to, *bryaela*. You don't have to see it if you don't want to. But if you do . . . it's there."

"I don't." It came out more strongly than she'd intended, her voice echoing off the walls and sending something rustling away through the mess on the floor.

"Okay," he said again. "So let's just head back up the stairs then."

"Wait."

He stopped.

"I . . . I do. I think I do want to see it. Maybe I should see it."

"Malleus?"

The big guard demon pushed past her carefully and headed for the files, sliding his thick index fingers down the faded labels on the drawers, then opening a few and sifting through them. The folders themselves looked surprisingly clean and dry, but that didn't make Megan any more comfortable about actually holding it in her hands after Malleus dug it out.

Which he did, after a minute or so of hunting. He started toward her, holding it out in front of him, but she shrank back. Not yet, not here. She didn't even want to touch it.

But seeing it made something click deep inside her. All these fucking years later, and here she was again in this place. And it was almost Christmas, it was the Friday night before. She was supposed to be home packing right now. Ktana Leyak was ruining the first real Christmas Megan had had in years, and when a wave of rage surged in her chest she realized this was what she'd been missing.

What was wrong with her? It was as though Ktana's stealing her demons had stolen something more than that too. She'd stolen . . . she'd stolen Megan's sense of herself, had picked at it with razor-sharp nails since the first time Megan had seen her. She didn't think she'd had a more difficult week in her entire life and damn it, it was time for this shit to end. Now.

She straightened up, and held out her hand for the file. "Give it to me."

Malleus glanced at Greyson, then obeyed.

"Thanks." She rolled it up—it was surprisingly thick—and stuffed it as best she could into the inner pocket of her coat. She might read it later. She might not. But seeing it, touching it, had reminded her who she was. And who she was would not let some demon bitch steal from her like that.

The triumph of her steely resolve was only faintly lessened when she stumbled and scraped her knee on her way back up the steps. Yes, she was certainly back to her old self.

*   *   *

Another flight of stairs, this one familiar to her. She'd walked up it before, the day she came here—her memory of it was vague and disordered, filtered green—but at that time it had been clean and she'd had an orderly with her. And her parents, faking concern while they checked their watches when they thought no one was looking.

"Each floor has a . . . *had* a . . . rec room, you know, where they did therapy? In the center, with the patients' rooms around it. Maybe we should check—"

"Which one was your room?"

She stared at him, dumbstruck. "Oh my God, of course. It's there, isn't it? Whatever it is?"

Greyson nodded slowly. "It's a good guess, anyway."

"I was on, um, the fifth floor, I think. In the corner. I don't remember the number . . ."

But it would be in her file, the file in her pocket. She reached in and pulled it out, holding it open in unsteady hands.

"Here." Nick held it for her, his eyes averted while she flipped through it by the light from Greyson's hand. Various phrases leaped out at her. "Presented with persecutory delusions . . . No shoelaces or cutting implements permitted . . . refuses to eat . . . fight with another patient . . ." She didn't remember any of that.

"I was in 526."

Greyson thought for a minute. "I still want to at least check the other floors, just in case. But if you can feel it, whatever it is, we'll do it as quickly as possible."

"I think I can. I'll try anyway."

"I can help," Nick said. "I might be able to feel it too. My—my father was part psyche demon."

"Psyche demon?"

"Greyson's a fire demon, the boys are actually *herket* demons—their ancestors performed tortures in Hell. They're physical demons, you know what I mean, with some mental abilities. But psyche demons are like the Yezer, their powers are all mental, with slight physical strengths. I can feel a few things from you without touching you, so it's possible I'll be able to feel the demon here if I focus."

Greyson looked at his friend. Something passed between them, some sort of *moment* Megan didn't understand. "Thanks, Nick."

Nick shrugged. "Let's go, then. Get this over with."

They turned and started back up the stairs. Megan's feet were heavy. She had to force her body to move, to obey her and keep walking toward . . . whatever was up there.

At the top of the staircase the hallway split, leading to the left and the right. The air up here was a little cleaner, but colder too as the wind blew through the empty windows and doorways. Kids had been in the building, teenagers drinking or getting high or just on a dare, and they'd left their calling cards in spray paint on the walls. CP + DK 4-EVER stretched across the wall in blood red paint, the letters dripping like the title of a Hammer horror flick, next to a passable copy of Motorhead's Warpig. Another invited readers to suck his cock. At least Megan assumed the anonymous wit had been male. A swastika—no wall of graffiti seemed complete without some asshole adding that one, especially not in a town like Grant Falls.

The sight of it bothered her, brought memories of the town's hate flooding back even more clearly than they already had been, but she didn't expect Maleficarum to react the way he did. The sound he made could only be called a growl, and he flung his large body at the wall, hammering it with his fists until the plaster gave and nothing was left but a gaping hole. When he turned around his eyes were red, even in the dim light.

There was no time to question it, no time to react, because something moaned at the other end of the hall, something that sent chills rising up Megan's spine. A zombie . . . two zombies . . . the fire flared higher and she saw more, coming around the corner, a small army.

An uneasy moment passed as they stared at each other, demons, human, and zombies facing off in the hallway at the top of the stairs, and then the zombies charged.

She could vaguely remember Greyson telling her that the speed at which zombies moved was related to how strong the zombie maker was. Ktana Leyak must be getting more from the Yezer than Megan ever had.

The hall lit up like a tanning booth as blue-white flames engulfed them, but they kept coming.

"Go! Meg, go!"

Nick was already moving, grabbing her arm, yanking her away from where Greyson stood with his brow furrowed in concentration. Heat roared down the hallway, singeing her eyebrows, and she understood even as Nick and Malleus tugged her around the corner that if she didn't get away she would burn, they would all burn when the zombies fell on them. The last thing she saw was Greyson standing, his body outlined black against the burning bodies advancing on him, his shoulders set as he waited.

They'd almost reached the end of the hall when explosions ripped the air. Megan's hair blew forward, lifted from her shoulders by the force of the blast. To her right the blackness of the empty stairwell beckoned; they all ducked into it and started up the stairs, their feet pounding on the cement.

Another explosion rocked the building and tore a scream from Megan's throat. Blindly she turned, stumbling back down toward the landing. If he was hurt, if he'd died—

"He's fine!" Nick practically pulled her arm out of its socket as he dragged her up the stairs. "He's fine, Megan, come on!"

The edge of a step collided painfully with her shin as she tripped over her own feet, but there was no time to stop, no time even to hear her own cry of pain.

The stained walls were nothing but a jumble in front of her. Something fell with a dull clang on the metal railing. A chunk of the stairs above. The building still shook. Another dull explosion rattled through it.

They reached the third floor and started down the hall, their feet shuffling through dead leaves and refuse. Megan's demon heart gave another leap, bigger than it had been downstairs, and she stopped, almost falling forward.

"Nick? Do you—"

He nodded. "Not here. But closer."

She turned back toward the stairs, but Maleficarum pulled her away. "Down there, m'lady. We don't wanna stay in one place, right?"

Nothing came at them from the empty caves of the rooms they passed, but Megan had the sense of things waiting in there, skulking against the dingy shadowed walls, crouching under windowsills. She ran as fast as she could, hooking her finger into Nick's belt loop and letting him pull her along until he slipped and she crashed down with him.

Her body knew what they'd fallen into before her mind was able to grasp it, to comprehend it. Blood, warm and sticky, spreading in a slow oozing lake across the hall. Her pants and coat were soaked with it, and when her demon heart twitched again she knew it wasn't just blood, it was Yezer blood, her demons were here and they were being hurt, just like in their home. They should have been safe and they weren't and that fucking bitch, she was going to get her—

She didn't think she'd ever felt rage like this before, this bone-deep fury, and it scared her just as much as it elated her, made her feel powerful, more than powerful. *Aroused,* and that's when she realized she had hold of Nick's hand and was taking his energy, sucking it slowly into herself, and if she didn't stop soon she was going to explode. The sex came from him, but it was the anger that shoved its way into her stomach and flooded her limbs. *Jesus, he's so angry, he's so fucking hurt and angry—*

She dropped his hand as if it had turned into a tarantula and backed away, slipping in the blood and falling against the grimy wall. The lake at her feet still spread; she turned, into the gaping mouth of the doorway and saw, in the faint light through the plastic over the empty window, pieces of her demons. Ears, legs, torsos, roughly stacked like Lincoln Logs against the wall, tumbled across the floor. How many of them, she didn't know, but they were there, they were everywhere.

Where was Roc? Was he in there, God was he in there, one of those random limbs making the space look like the back room of a slaughterhouse?

She hadn't realized she'd said it out loud until Malleus took hold of her arms and propelled her away, down the hall, squishing in the blood. "He ain't there, m'lady, don't you fret none, he'll be 'ere soon, you wait an' see . . ."

There were no windows in the far stairwell. It was like stepping into a mouth and being swallowed, feeling their way up the steps, moving slowly enough for Megan to start wondering why she hadn't heard any more explosions in a while, and why Greyson hadn't yet appeared. Her chest hurt.

The pitted metal railing bit into her hands but she was afraid to let go. Why they'd come armed to the teeth but without so much as a cigarette lighter . . . but then, they'd assumed they wouldn't need to make their own fire, hadn't they? It had never even occurred to her that Greyson might not be at her side every step of the way. Dangerous, that. Her vision blurred and she realized she was sobbing as they walked.

Even over the scuffling of their feet on the steps she heard the sound, a low gurgling rumble, like someone with laryngitis trying to yodel. Something waited for them on the fourth floor, and she thought she knew what it was.

Metal clinked and clanged around her as the men drew their weapons. She still had the gun, tucked dangerously in her pocket. Her palms were so slick it was difficult to get a good grip on it, and it wouldn't do much good anyway if she was right.

She was. Her father stood waiting when they left the stairwell.

He hadn't changed since they'd buried him, only two days before—two days, she couldn't believe how much had happened in two days—but the vague emptiness in his eyes, the way he stood as though balancing on two feet was an effort, were things she'd never seen before.

Nick started forward, his sword raised, but Malleus grabbed him by the arm and muttered something. Megan didn't hear it. She'd been expecting this, had known from the minute they saw the zombie coming out of the woods at the edge of town, but now the moment was here, really here, and she didn't know what to do.

She couldn't walk. She couldn't move. She just stood there and stared at him, tears running icy tracks down her face. Was there anything left of him in there, and if there was, would he even care?

The thought had barely gone through her mind when he charged. The men leaped forward, trying to catch him, but he shook them off with amazing speed and agility and reached for her, his freezing fingers clutching her throat.

They crashed backward onto the cement floor of the landing. All the breath left her body; her back arched as she tried desperately to inhale, but his fingers tightened around her throat. This was it, he was going to kill her, just like he'd tried to do before, and she couldn't fight him, she wasn't strong enough . . .

She brought her knee up as hard as she could and smashed it into his groin. He might not be able to think and his nerves might be deteriorating, but she was willing to bet even undead men hurt when solid bone was driven into their balls. He howled, a raspy, animal sound, and curled forward. His fingers loosened. She sucked in a huge, glorious breath and actually *felt* oxygen spread through her entire body.

Too late she realized he was falling sideways, taking her with him to the top of the staircase. Another inch or two and they would tumble back down into the impenetrable blackness.

"Help me!" she screamed, but the words weren't even out of her mouth when the body was lifted away, when Nick's hands found hers and he hauled her up so fast she fell forward into him.

The boys were yelling, struggling with the frantic body of her father. Megan remembered well how strong zombies could be, how terrifyingly focused.

Something cracked. She had no idea what it was, but Malleus's grip loosened for a second, and that second was enough for her father to lunge at her again.

This time she was ready, bracing herself, but at the last second something else happened, something that made her heart—both of her hearts—leap. Roc appeared, and trailing in his wake were four or five of her demons. So few, but enough to get her demon heart moving, to send a jolt of power through her body. It combined with what was left of the energy she'd stolen from Nick in the hall below, and she focused it, focused on it, and put as much of it as she could behind her swinging fist.

Her arm vibrated. All of her knuckles cracked, and she felt two of her fingernails break off at the quick.

Her father—she should start thinking of him as "the zombie," but she couldn't, it was her father, it was his body—barely paused, reaching for her again. Nick's sword came down on his arm, slicing it off, but again, her father didn't stop.

Megan slipped sideways and lifted the gun, but her fingers were too sore and clumsy to fire it. Malleus and Maleficarum dragged the zombie a few feet away and Nick attacked him again with the sword, its blade black and sticky with rancid fluid.

Her father howled, confusion and pain and anger in what was left of his voice, and Megan couldn't take it anymore. It probably wouldn't work, it probably wouldn't even matter, but there was such a cruel, ironic symmetry to it all as she stepped forward and pressed the barrel of the gun to his head, just above his right eyebrow.

It felt like she should say something, but she couldn't think of anything to say; she squeezed the trigger and let the gun speak for her.

Its report echoed so loudly in the stairwell and hall she thought it would never stop. Her father's body slumped forward. The horrible bright light left his eyes, and he became again what he should have been. A corpse. Just a corpse.

The rattles started then, the metal stair railings sounding like a piece of aluminum shaking in the wind. Little snickering sounds, dry scratches and rasps. Her demons were coming, down the stairs from the fifth floor or up from the other floors, alerted to her exact location, and she was crying too hard as she looked at the blurry, messy figure of her father on the ground to care. It wasn't until Roc touched her hand and spoke to her that she was able to look up.

". . . to go, Megan, hurry! Hurry!"

The others stood behind him, terrified. They would die if she didn't beat Ktana Leyak, if Megan didn't manage to get the relic before she did. At that moment exhaustion weighed so heavily on Megan's body that she almost didn't care if she survived or not. It would be so easy to sit down, to rest, to wait for it all to end.

Greyson still hadn't appeared . . .

"Hurry!"

Maleficarum scooped her up from the floor, and they ran down the hall to the other staircase.

Chapter Twenty-seven

Ifinally managed to get Krantus and Rentoran to join up with me and they brought Varigon and Aberas, and we came straight here," Roc managed, panting, as they raced past more empty rooms. The next floor up was the fifth; the next floor up was where the showdown would happen. Megan was trying as hard as she could to care. Roc helped with that. So did Maleficarum's strong arms holding her up. They would want her, *need* her, if Greyson was dead, she knew they would. She couldn't die, she had too many fucking responsibilities.

"I think we can get the others," he continued. "Once they see you're winning they'll come back, and when they bring their power back to you—"

"They won't come back unless I'm winning?"

"Would you really expect them to?"

Right. Stupid question.

They were halfway up the stairs when Megan felt it. Her demon heart leaped, really leaped, and starting dancing in her chest, throbbing.

"I feel it, Megan," Nick said. "It's here, it must be in your room."

They paused at the doorway to the hall. What would

it be this time? More zombies? Blood? Hellhounds? Rabid townies with guns and knives?

But only silence greeted them, silence and the sense of something vibrating, waiting. It seemed to sigh when their feet hit the dirty tile floor.

Maleficarum put Megan down. Her legs jiggled for a minute before steadying, and she took Nick's hand to help her stay that way. If she needed more energy she could have it, especially when Roc clambered up onto her shoulder and the others hovered behind her.

The graffiti on the walls here was worse, more vicious, more plentiful. The entire hospital was a vermin-ridden shambles, but it seemed the particular listless rage of trespassers had been reserved for this floor—or perhaps this floor had attracted the worst of the worst.

She glanced to her left, scanning an absolutely revolting sketch of an eviscerated naked woman, and caught a glimpse of the sky through the window of one of the empty rooms. She'd forgotten it was snowing, forgotten Christmas lights still glowed, forgotten that from this side of the building the town square was visible. It was so beautiful, even with everything she knew, everything that was happening. Her throat closed up and for a moment she just stood there staring.

Then she heard something rustle at the end of the hall and knew Ktana Leyak waited for her in room 526, Ktana Leyak and the last piece of the Accuser that still lived outside Megan's body.

"Let's go," she said, and headed for the door.

Bad as the graffiti was by the elevators, it got worse the farther down the hall she went, hate and pain vomited all over the walls. It was like walking into a museum of misogynistic racism, with some crazy thrown in for spice.

The demon inside her leaped and twitched, a sort of inner Geiger counter, but she didn't need it. The sense of unease, of *wrongness,* coming through her shields would have alerted her without it, just as it had that day at the diner.

The door frame of room 526 had been ripped out, leaving a jagged, gaping hole. Megan stopped in front of it, took a deep breath, and walked in.

A streetlight glowed on the corner, not far from the empty window, making this room the brightest she'd been in since entering the hospital what felt like hours ago, months ago. Even with that light it took her a second to see Ktana Leyak, and that second cost her.

Ktana vaulted away from her hiding spot on the ceiling with her arms outstretched, her face curled into a vicious snarl. Too late, Megan ducked, avoiding having her jugular severed by Ktana's sharp claws but not sparing her left cheek. Her tears ran rivulets down her face and stung in the sharply painful grooves.

Blindly she swung back, using her still-aching right hand. It hurt, oh how it hurt, but she managed to land a solid blow to Ktana's chin as she swung upward.

Malleus and Maleficarum crowded into the room, shoving Ktana, trying to force her down, but Megan already knew it wouldn't do any good. Stuffed with power from Megan's demons and the chaos they'd caused in Grant Falls this night, she was too strong for them. As Nick had said, the boys weren't psyche demons. They had all the physical strength they needed, but they couldn't draw power the way she could.

Still they gave Megan a short respite and for that she was grateful. Somewhere in this room that last relic hid, and she needed to find it immediately if Ktana hadn't already.

Ktana freed herself from the boys and rushed Megan again, this time stopped by Nick, who managed to get in a vicious slash with his sword. Ktana stumbled back, looking up at him with almost comical shock before attacking him, screaming, her arms windmilling while blood pumped slowly from the gaping wound across her chest.

That was Megan's chance, shitty as it was. She dared to close her eyes for a second, trying to feel the exact location of the relic, but with so many demons and so much violence in the room, she couldn't seem to identify it. She hadn't a doubt it was there—and she had some vague sense of why it was there, some half-formed idea that it had stayed here with her, that it was left here the night Harlan Trooper died, waiting for the Accuser to come back and claim it—but where?

The metal bed bolted to the floor looked like a good place to start, even if it did mean making herself completely vulnerable while she looked under it. Why Ktana hadn't checked there already she didn't know, or again, maybe she had, but Megan had to try, didn't she?

She heard Nick's sword ring against something metal, chunk into plaster. Meaty sounds of fists on skin and cries of pain might have horrified her, but they at least told her that Ktana was still being kept busy.

The rodent droppings and filth under this bed were even worse than the basement, piled high. Something with little claws skittered across her arms, and her scream turned into a sneeze. Here were dead things, foul things, and just before her hand closed over it she knew here was the relic of the Accuser as well.

Hard hands grabbed her ankles and yanked, pulling her out from under the bed like a cruel child pulls the legs off a spider. Ktana's foot slammed into the back of Megan's head, driving her face into the hard floor with a terrible crunch and a bolt of white-hot pain. She didn't need to feel it to know blood was pouring from her nose, that it was broken.

She tried to get up, but the foot forced her back down. This time she turned her head at the last second, managing to avoid having her face smashed into the floor again.

She stayed down. She had only seconds to decide what to do next, maybe not even that long before the fatal blow—if there was to be one—fell. Megan took a chance. She opened the door inside her, as wide as she could, praying she was right.

Power flared through her. Her demons, sated on the town's misery, had fed Ktana all she needed; she didn't seem to notice when Megan sent a shivery little feeler down the line connecting her to them and took some of it for herself. Not to mention what Rocturnus and his accomplices had for her. It wasn't perfect, but it was enough to flip her over and send Ktana Leyak flying against the gaping window.

Megan struggled to get up. In her hand she clutched

something soft and revoltingly warm, something that could have been the body of a mouse if it hadn't been slick instead of furry. If she hadn't been so far in the thrall of the demon it would have made her notoriously weak stomach lurch but, as it was, she felt only a terrible, weary resolve. It wasn't what she wanted to do, but she would do it.

Ktana had barely hit the wall when she sprang back again, knocking Megan onto the floor. Megan didn't bother trying to push or fight. Every fiber of her being was focused on getting her hand to her mouth. How did Ktana Leyak not know what Megan held?

No sooner had the thought entered her brain than Ktana's focus changed. She let go of Megan's neck and reached for her hand, making an attempt to grab the relic—*go ahead and say it, it's a heart or a lung or something equally revolting.*

It was a miscalculation. Malleus's boot swung out and clipped Ktana neatly across the face as she moved, snapping it back, and Megan used the opportunity to force herself to bite down on the thing in her hand.

Her first impression was that it tasted almost sweet, not like something foul and rotting for years under a grimy bed in a mental hospital, but that thought, and every other sensation, left her as power swept over her. It washed through her, taking her with it, filling her body with a raging torrent of emotion and fire and strength. She screamed, knowing as she did so that it wasn't just the Accuser, knowing that when she'd taken the bite her demons had rejoined her and the energy they'd built up over this long winter's night would have been enough to send her flying to the moon even without the relic.

For what felt like an eternity she hovered above the floor, riding an enormous rail of gleaming iridescent force, her fists clenched around the useless final bit of the relic and her head thrown back, before somehow falling into place, into her body, to find Ktana Leyak about to shoot her with her own gun.

Megan ducked, feeling as though it was somehow very easy to do all of this now, and swung her arm sideways, realizing her hand no longer hurt. Nor did her face, not really.

Ktana dropped the gun but managed to elbow Megan in the face. In her hyperecstatic state Megan hardly noticed it, but she knew it had happened, just like she knew without the Yezers' power behind her Ktana would be disappearing soon, and this wouldn't be over. It had to end now if Megan was going to have any peace, if she was going to have any real authority over her demons.

She swung again, catching Ktana across the face and knocking her down. *The nose, go for the nose, like she did with you . . .* She had no idea why that seemed right, but it did, so Megan lifted her foot and brought it down as hard as she could on the back of Ktana's neck.

"Kill you! I'll kill you, I'll come back and kill you!" The normally light tones of Ktana Leyak's voice harshened, deepened, turned into something singularly unpleasant. Megan's stomach lurched but she kept going, hitting Ktana on the back of the neck, understanding now that it wasn't the nose, it was the neck, it was something in her neck that needed to be damaged if she was going to win, if she could ever hope to keep her demons safe.

With a scream she stomped, as hard as she could, sending as much of her power as possible along with it, and felt something give beneath her. Ktana Leyak's body went limp, and silent.

Megan backed away, stopping when she hit something warm and solid behind her. Maleficarum, standing against the wall, watching the still body on the floor.

"Is she dead?" Megan whispered.

"Only one way to find out," said a voice in the doorway, and the body on the floor burst into flame.

Megan couldn't speak; there didn't seem to be very much to say anyway. She just flung herself to the side, into his arms, pressing her bloody face against his bare chest. Beneath his sweat-slick skin his heart still beat. She couldn't imagine how or why, but it did, and all she could do was be grateful.

"You sure like to make an entrance," she managed.

"After what I've been through I think I deserve it, don't you?" But his lips cut off her reply, and he held her tight for a long moment while she forgot everything else, and everyone else, in the room.

Finally he pulled away. "I knew you could do it."

"Where were you?"

"Dealing with a zombie horde, a gang of very angry townies with guns and cherry bombs, two cops, and a couple of dogs. Dogs don't like demons. It took me ages to get them off me."

He glanced around the room, surveying the damage, seeing the remains of the relic on the floor. "So you found it. And you got them back."

She nodded, then shivered and leaned against him, becoming aware of the cold for the first time in a while.

"We should go," he said. His lips brushed her hair. "We have to get ourselves packed. And take showers. And eat. And sleep."

Nick laughed. "In that order, right?"

They left the room while the flames from Ktana's body spread through the garbage and papers on the floor. Megan glanced back when they reached the top of the stairs. Orange light pulsed in the doorway, fire crept out along the walls and baseboards. Let it burn, she thought. Let it all burn.

Mercifully they didn't take the stairwell her father's body now rested in. Mercifully nothing else impeded their progress as they finally stumbled back into the lobby and out the front doors. She looked up and saw fire through the empty windows on the fifth floor.

Greyson's arm tightened around her. "That's your investment going up in flames, you know." Now they were outside she could see the bruises on his face and chest, the singed and tattered pants. His shirt was gone—she hadn't made the connection before—it must have burned off.

"I still don't want it."

"I still think you might change your mind. After all, with Temp and Orion both dead . . . the land might belong solely to you. You could sell it, especially once this monstrosity is gone."

For a moment she saw another park, a memorial to Harlan Trooper. A decent rehab center, maybe. It glowed in front of her . . . then disappeared. It would be seen as an admission of guilt here. Just because the hospital was burning and she'd finally managed to put her past behind her for real didn't mean Grant Falls had suddenly turned into Bedford Falls.

"I don't know." She leaned her head to the side, resting it on his chest. "I'll think about it, okay?"

"Think all you want. You've got plenty of time."

The men chatted for a minute while her Yezer started to creep up beside her, some sheepish, some defiant, some frankly supplicant. It didn't really matter if they apologized. Maybe she didn't deserve it. Her resentment of what had happened to her, of being forced to deal with them on their terms, had colored her relationship with them to the point where she couldn't blame those who'd willingly gone with Ktana Leyak. They deserved to feel taken care of, whether she ultimately decided to do the Haikken Kra or not. That was the whole point of a Meegra, to have someone in charge, someone who would take care of you and watch out for you. Someone who would do whatever it took in order to take care of you and watch out for you, like the ritual she'd witnessed. It wasn't just the continuity or the respect, she realized now. It was both of those things, yes, but it was also the physical proof that a Gretneg would do any-thing—*anything*—for the demons in his or her care.

She'd do better from now on, be stronger and more in control. Funny how important that had become to her. Funny how important quite a few things had become to her. She'd have a lot of work to do when they got back from the cabin. It was only the wee hours of Saturday morning; they still had Christmas to celebrate, and the start of a new year. A new beginning.

"It's getting cold out here." Nick rubbed his hands together. "If we're not going to toast marshmallows, can we just get back in the truck and go?"

Greyson turned to her. "What do you think, *bryaela*, you ready?"

She smiled up at him. "I'm ready."